He wanted to survive

Rising to his knees, Bolan leveled the Beretta over the desktop and waited. Excited voices chattered in hushed tones in the hallway. He couldn't make out the words. A second later, a man peered timidly around the doorway.

The Beretta spit again, and when the 9 mm rounds were finished, the face no longer looked like a face at all. Another foolish man stuck his head around the other side of the door to see what had happened.

Bolan blew it off, too.

The Executioner moved to the other end of the desk. He knew he was vastly outnumbered. He had, however, accomplished the first part of his quickly conceived battle plan—none of the men in the hallway appeared too anxious to enter the office after they'd seen what had just happened.

Bolan waited. Finally the babble abruptly halted. Which told the Executioner all he needed to know.

Another attack was about to come.

MACK BOLAN ®
The Executioner

DON PENDLETON'S
THE EXECUTIONER®
TRIPLE REVERSE

A GOLD EAGLE BOOK FROM
WORLDWIDE®

TORONTO • NEW YORK • LONDON
AMSTERDAM • PARIS • SYDNEY • HAMBURG
STOCKHOLM • ATHENS • TOKYO • MILAN
MADRID • WARSAW • BUDAPEST • AUCKLAND

First edition January 2002
ISBN 0-373-64278-4

TRIPLE REVERSE

Special thanks and acknowledgment to
Jerry VanCook for his contribution to this work.

Printed in U.S.A.

No one ever reached the worst of a vice in one leap.
—Juvenal
Satires, II, c.110

There is no vice so completely contrary to nature that it obliterates all trace of nature.
—St. Augustine
The City of God, XIX, 427

Theft, murder, power. At one time or another, all men are tempted to use them to achieve their own ends. Most men overcome the temptation. Others don't. That's how I separate the good guys from the bad.
—Mack Bolan

To R. J. S.

Prologue

The first sputter from the engine hit at the same time as the Antonov An-72 crossed the Nigerian border. Blackie Stevens felt the muscles in his abdomen tighten. The contraction sent a slow burn through his stomach. He squinted, focusing his eyes away from the pain; forcing his attention onto the gauges in the control panel in front of him. Everything looked okay, and Stevens told himself the sound had to have been his imagination. It had been the simple, and not-so-surprising, result of his relative unfamiliarity with the Russian-built transport plane.

But more than that, it had been the result of the risk he'd been talked into taking.

Reaching into the console, Stevens pulled out the half-empty bottle of pink-colored antacid. Holding it to his lips, he swallowed what he guessed was roughly twice the recommended dosage. It went to work immediately. At least partially. The flames in his belly didn't disappear, but they died down to a manageable simmer.

The sputter came again as the city of Kano became visible below. Stevens groaned out loud. Did the sound have something to do with the Coanda effect this plane was supposed to have because of the higher-set engines? He didn't know. He wasn't a damned aircraft mechanic—he just contracted to fly the damn things. What he did know, however, was that this time the sound hadn't been his imagination. And it was louder. That realization produced another, even more intense, contraction between his belt and groin, the muscle cramp seeming to grow in direct proportion to the louder sputter. Another glance to the controls, and a quick swig from the bottle, reassured him once again.

Whatever the noise was, it couldn't be serious, he told himself.

But part of Blackie Stevens wasn't convinced. A small, annoying voice—semihidden in the back of his brain—told him disaster might be just beyond the next cloud formation he saw in front of him. "Son of a bitch," he said out loud to the empty cabin. "When this thing's finished, so am I. If Sally and I didn't need the extra money..." He let that sentence trail off but kept speaking aloud. "Okay, Mr. Blackie Stevens. This is it, the last time I'm headin' for the last roundup." He thought for a second, then jumped to the next logical step. "In fact, when this is over, I'm through with this whole godforsaken continent. Dammit, I'm going home and find a job where every day doesn't start and finish like I just chugged a shot glass of gasoline and chased it with a lit match."

A smile broke across his face as the Antonov continued to glide smoothly through the air just below radar level. Sally had been after him to take her father's offer of a job at the supermarket in Tulsa again, and suddenly the idea of not worrying about anything more dangerous than the frozen food spoiling sounded awfully damn good.

Stevens followed the railroad tracks on the ground below. They led south out of Kano to Zaria, then Kaduna, before finally terminating at the same place he intended to end his flying career—Lagos, Nigeria. There, he was supposed to meet the folks who'd paid him for this job. He'd have an extra fifty grand in his pocket when it was all over, and then he'd take the first commercial flight he could find back to the good old U.S. of A.

Enough of Africa. Enough of the ulcers it brought him. Enough of this trying to fly below radar and still trying to keep from knocking out some damn radio tower or three-story goat barn or whatever the hell those buildings were along the tracks below. Stevens's eyes shot through the side window of the plane at the U.S. Centers for Disease Control emblem on the wing. What a sham. He'd seen the fifty-five-gallon drums of vaccine loaded onto the plane the day before. Then he'd turned his back while the men who had hired him switched the cargo with identical drums. Identical *looking,* anyway. He didn't know what was actually in them and didn't want to know. But he knew that if they were willing to pay him fifty thousand bucks, it wasn't vacuum-sealed Bibles.

His thoughts intensified the fire in his belly once more, and he reached for the bottle again. Yep, he thought as he held it to his lips. This was it. The end. He was going to quit this crap and become the official assistant manager of his father-in-law's grocery store.

"Daddy the green grocer is a-comin' home," Stevens said to the empty plane.

The words were barely out of his mouth when the nose of the aircraft suddenly dipped violently. Behind him, Stevens heard a high, screeching whine, and then something clanked like a frying pan being struck by a ball peen hammer. The aircraft jerked again, then started toward the ground at approximately a forty-five-degree angle.

The pilot didn't have time to pay attention to the inferno in his belly now. The needles on the dials in front of him— which had looked just fine only a few minutes ago—now whirled like kids on a merry-go-round gone mad. Ahead, through the Plexiglas windshield in front of him, he could see nothing but green foliage coming toward him at an alarming speed. Gripping the steering column with both hands, he tried to pull the plane back upward. The nose rose. But not enough. The Antonov was still headed to the ground below, and

Stevens knew he had done nothing more than delay the inevitable. The plane continued toward the jungle.

His eyes darted to the radio mike clipped in front of him, but his hands seemed to have taken on a will of their own. They were frozen to the controls. A radio call now would be useless anyway, he knew. He was going down. Into the jungle. And there wasn't a damn thing he could do about that.

Quick flashes of unorganized thoughts raced through his brain as he tried to pull the plane's nose upward again. He saw his wife, Sally, a bottle of Jack Daniel's bourbon, fifty thousand dollars, frozen food. The fire in his stomach crept to the top of his consciousness again for a moment, then dropped back again as a patch of yellow-brown appeared ahead through the windshield.

Steven's eyes focused on the brown spot. A clearing in the jungle? Large enough to land? He couldn't tell from this distance. And he wouldn't know until he got there. *If* he got there.

It was going to be close.

Sweat broke on his forehead and trickled down his cheeks. He lowered the landing gear and pulled up on the steering column, using his shoulders and arms as if he could somehow keep the plane aloft with manual strength alone. Then tunnel vision set in, and the only thing he could see was the brown spot growing larger in the midst of its green surroundings. As it grew closer, he saw a rough and rugged dirt road running through the clearing. As if from some far distance, he heard the snapping sounds beneath the plane as the landing gear clipped the tops of the foliage below. He closed his eyes.

Steven's ulcer seemed to have moved to his head when he next opened his eyes. He felt the sweat running down his cheeks again. Raising a hand, which felt strangely unattached to his arm, he wiped the moisture away then looked down at his fingers. They were red. And wet.

Gradually, little by little, the pilot's mind began to come back to him. In front of him, he could see the cracked Plexiglas that had once been the windshield. He realized with a start that he was on the ground. Alive. Further exploration of his forehead with his hand told him he had a deep gash just above the left eyebrow. He could move his legs and arms in the confined space behind the controls. The gash would require a few stitches. Otherwise, he wasn't hurt.

As his memory continued to return, Steven's remembered the initial sounds the Antonov had made, then the green jungle, and the yellow-brown spot. He looked through the spiderwebbed windshield and grinned. Directly ahead of him, he could see hanging vines and leaves. Many had been ripped from the jungle growth surrounding him and now rested on the windshield and nose of the plane. Beyond that, he could see yellow-brown grass. The clearing he had seen from the air. He'd made it. He could even see the tracks in the sparse grass and mud where his wheels had slid across it. Even though it hurt even worse than his ulcer, he shook his head to clear it further and looked out again at the ground. The tracks were clear where he'd hit the ground, before speeding across the open space into the dense jungle on the other side. One of the wings had to have hit something hard, causing him to spin 180 degrees, because he wasn't facing the direction from which he'd come.

Stevens turned to the side and saw that one of the wings had been ripped entirely from the aircraft. That confirmed his suspicions. He had rolled across the clearing into the thick foliage on the other side, then spun back. The fact that the worst apparent damage was the missing wing and a gash in his forehead was nothing short of a miracle.

The pilot grinned again, but the smile faded as quickly as it had come. He was alive, yes, but he was in one hell of a fix. He had a call to make. No, he had two calls to make. That had been part of the deal, a—what had the guy called it?—a contingency plan. He looked at the control panel in front of him. None of the dials were functioning. But, ironically, the scratches and screeches from the headset wrapped around his ears told him the radio was still functioning. But the first call he made wouldn't be on the radio.

Unstrapping himself, Stevens rose from his seat and opened the storage compartment behind him. Pulling out a black ballistic nylon bag, he unzipped it and produced a portable global positioning unit. A moment later, he knew where he was on the planet. Another, smaller, black case lay in the same compartment. In it, he found the cellular telephone.

A moment later he had punched in the number he'd been given for emergencies. "It's Stevens," he said into the phone.

The voice on the other end was low and gravelly, and sounded South African. It wasn't the voice of the man who had offered him the fifty thousand dollars. But the voice seemed to know who he was because it said, "You should have been here by now. What the hell's wrong?"

"I went down," Stevens said simply. He gave him the coordinates he had gotten from the global positioning unit, then added, "One of the wings is gone."

There was a short pause, then the voice growled, "Is your radio still working?"

"Yeah."

"Have you radioed in yet?"

"Not yet. But I better. I filed a flight plan and if I don't—"

"I know that," the rugged voice said impatiently. "Give it another half hour. Then radio in and tell them what happened."

"Can you get here that fast?" Stevens asked, frowning.

"Of course not," the voice rumbled, clearly exasperated. "But neither can the rescue workers. And if they don't hear from you soon, they'll start looking anyway." There was a short pause, then the voice said, "Give them bad coordinates. Later, you can say you were in shock. You made a mistake. They can't prove that wasn't true...." The voice trailed off, then asked, "How bad are you hurt?"

The pilot had wondered if the man was ever going to ask

that question. "Just a gash on my forehead," he said. "Nothing too serious."

"Tell them you've sustained head injuries," ordered the voice, "and you don't know how serious they are. That'll help explain the bad directions later, too."

Stevens smiled. Yeah, it would. "Okay," he said. "You got it." He paused, then timidly added, "Uh...is there going to be anything...you know...*extra* in this for me."

The voice didn't hesitate to answer. "Yes. You'll get a bonus. Now, do what I told you. We're on the way."

The conversation terminated, and Stevens set the cellular phone down on the console. He activated the radio and spoke into the transmitter in front of his face. A few minutes later, he had contacted the nearest Nigerian air tower, informed them that he had crashed in the jungle, was alive but seriously injured and had given them coordinates that would lead them at least ten miles from the site of the actual crash.

As soon as he'd ended the transmission, he found the first-aid kit in the storage area and dressed the gash above his eye.

The pilot sat back to wait, suddenly realizing that the fire in his stomach was missing. Blackie Stevens smiled. He was even going to get a bonus, and that almost made the crash worth it.

Two hours later, he heard a rustling in the jungle. Dropping from the plane, he waited next to the ruined aircraft. A moment later, faces he recognized began to emerge from the jungle. Below the faces, the men wore jungle-camo fatigues. All carried rifles and pistols, and either machetes or large knives were strapped to their waists.

Stevens smiled as he waited for them to approach. A short man who looked as if he were no stranger to barbells was in the lead, and he returned the smile as he came to a halt directly in front of Stevens. The muscular man's eyes quickly took in the damage to the plane, then he shook his head in disbelief. "You're one lucky son of a bitch to be alive," he said in the grumbling voice Stevens had heard over the radio.

"Hey, no shit," the pilot answered. "But you said it would get me a bonus."

The sandy-haired man nodded. "It will. And I've brought it with me. Let us get our work done and then you'll get it." He glanced up at the cockpit. "Why don't you get back in the plane and rest. It looks like you've been through hell."

Stevens smiled as he returned to the pilot's seat. He leaned back and the smile widened. In another twenty-four hours, he'd be back in the U.S.A. with fifty thousand dollars, and whatever extra cash the bonus amounted to in his pocket. He closed his eyes as he heard the sound of a truck arriving in the distance.

A moment later, he was asleep.

Death—quick and violent—was gathering fifty yards away on the other side of the pond.

Mack Bolan, also known as the Executioner, pressed the binoculars to his eyes as dusk fell over the Cincinnati suburb. He had come to the neighborhood hours earlier and found it to be laid out just as he'd been advised. Driving down the street in front of the houses, it looked no different than any other upper-middle class housing addition. Brick houses, two-car garages with automatic garage door openers, basketball nets mounted on poles on the double driveways.

Bolan had parked his unmarked, rented paneled van on the street, then walked between two of the houses dressed in the green coveralls of the electrical power company that served the area. With a clipboard in one hand and a canvas equipment bag in the other, he looked no different than a dozen other workmen who routinely made such calls to read meters or make repairs. Few of the neighborhood's residents had been outside their homes, and none of them had given him a glance as he disappeared between the houses.

Once behind the buildings, the soldier saw that his intel had been accurate as to the backyard areas as well. The front doors of the houses might open to the city, but the back doors led to the country. The lawns sloped downward to a four-acre pond. Thick trees ran along the edge of the pond, and through their limbs Bolan could see the land on the other side hadn't yet been fully developed. Part was open prairie. Other areas already had the dirt work leveled, and a even a few concrete foundations had already been laid. But the streets that would eventually lead to the houses were nonexistent. Only a few paths, created by the construction trucks and other vehicles bringing in building materials, led to the construction sites.

The Executioner had quickly secreted himself in the trees next to the pond, then settled in to wait.

Finally, as dusk had begun to fall, the first vehicle—a new Lincoln Town Car—bumped over the rough dirt on the other side of the water. Through the binoculars, the soldier watched four African-American males, all in their late twenties or early thirties, exit the vehicle. They were dressed in orange gang colors, which identified them as members of the 23rd Street Posse. But in the fading sun the bright orange bandannas tied around their throats and foreheads took on more of a soft auburn tint. With a quick glance around them to insure no one was watching, the men opened the trunk of the Lincoln.

Three Uzis and one AK-47 came out. The Posse placed them on the seats of the vehicle and left the Lincoln's doors open. The quartet then took up spots at the front of the car and began their own wait.

Bolan removed his green coveralls to reveal a skintight black combat suit. It contained many pockets, and the soldier had made good use of them as well as the canvas equipment bag. As night continued to fall, he removed all of the gear he knew he would need. And much of what he simply *might* be called upon to use in the mission he was about to undertake.

Among the tools of his trade was an M-21 sniper rifle with bullpup stock, heavy barrel and modified gas system. The scope had been sighted in at a hundred yards. With the men across the pond approximately sixty yards away, the Executioner reminded himself to aim slightly low.

The second car to arrive was a chocolate brown Mercedes, which was almost invisible in the falling shadows of night. From this vehicle emerged four more men. Again, all were African-American, and wore at least one item of orange clothing. They joined the other men at the front bumper of the Town Car, bringing the grand total of gangbangers to eight.

Bolan dropped the field glasses from his face. He let his eyelids drop momentarily, resting his eyes. The 23rd Street Posse was responsible for more illegal drug traffic than any other gang in Cincinnati. They also ran a prostitution ring, a fairly sophisticated protection racket, and many were seasoned arm robbers. A few were even available to take hits, willing to kill anyone and everyone—man, woman, or child—as long as the price was right.

The roar of several motorcycles sounded across the pond. Bolan opened his eyes and raised the binoculars once more. Twilight was almost night now, and he pressed a button on the side of the field glasses to activate the infrared feature. The figures who approached on the motorcycles were white, mostly bearded, with long dirty hair flying behind them in the wind as they made their way over the construction paths. These men, too, wore colors. But their definition of colors bore a different connotation, and had little to do with actual tincture. The term referred more to the biker patches that had been sewn to their filthy denim jeans and sleeveless jacket-vests. Just like the orange bandannas, they announced to all the world who they were: Cincinnati's notorious Outrage Motorcycle Club.

A hard smile set over the Executioner's features. He shook his head. An all-black street gang meeting clandestinely with an all-white motorcycle gang. The irony of the situation didn't escape him. Both groups were confirmed racists, openly professing unbridled hatred for each other and anyone else with a skin color not their own. It was a peculiar meeting.

Bolan watched as the motorcycles—ten of them in all—formed a semicircle around the two cars. Though they made no move toward the assault weapons on the seats of the Lincoln, the hands of the Posse all disappeared under the plaid flannel shirts and basketball jerseys that hung loosely over their khaki pants and slacks. But no weapons came into view. They simply waited.

One of the white men dismounted his motorcycle and lowered the kickstand with a dust-covered black boot. He left on the headlight of his motorcycle, however, as did the rest of the bikers. The front area of the Lincoln was illuminated as brightly as midday, and Bolan switched the off the binoculars' infrared feature again. He could see better without it.

The man who had gotten off his bike had reddish-brown hair, a matching beard and wore a steel helmet with horns jutting from both sides. Along with the dirty denim and other effects, he looked like a modern-day Viking plunderer—an image the Executioner suspected he had carefully cultivated. Had his biker patches, chains and studded leather wrist gauntlets been traded for a sword, shield and breastplate, he would have looked right at home on a longship.

The Viking walked forward, and the Bolan could see the big grips of what looked like a .44 magnum Ruger Redhawk revolver jammed into his belt just above a huge silver-and-turquoise buckle. The man's face was hard, scarred and wrinkled beyond his years by methamphetamine, or crack, or both. Bolan guessed him to be in his early forties.

The Viking stopped five feet from the Posse. There were no handshakes.

As the biker began to speak, Bolan felt a sudden vibration against his hip. His cellular phone—secured in one of the blacksuit's pockets. He had switched the phone from ringer mode to vibrate to insure silence. The steady pulse meant he was getting a call—a call which could come from only one source. And if it wasn't important it wouldn't have been made.

But the fact that the pulse was steady rather than erratic meant the call wasn't an emergency. At least not yet.

Continuing to stare through the binoculars across the pond, the Executioner ignored the vibration until it faded away. Several minutes went by, during which time the biker was joined by two more of his unwashed Caucasian brethren. Bolan watched as the men talked, sometimes calmly, at other times breaking into scowls of anger and moving their hands and arms animatedly. He knew what was happening—the two groups were bartering price. While the Posse had the monopoly on drug sales in the Cincinnati area, it was the Outrage bikers who had cornered the trade in illegal guns, ammunition and explosives. A trade was about to take place; that had been predetermined. What had obviously not yet been decided to the satisfaction of all was the exact value of the guns versus the dope.

Bolan continued to watch the men as the night grew darker and a half-moon rose into the heavens. One of the gang-bangers walked back to the Lincoln's open driver-side door and illuminated the head beams to assist the light from the motorcycles. Bolan noted that he stayed next to the car—and the heavy weaponry on the seats—rather than returning to the council at the front of the vehicle.

Suddenly, the vibration against the Executioner's hip returned as the caller tried once more to reach him. This time, the pulse was a series of jerky staccatos. Whatever the reason for the call, it had now become high priority.

Bolan kept the field glasses in place with his right hand as his left drew the cell phone from his pocket. He pressed it against his ear and thumbed the On button. "Yeah, Hal," he whispered into the instrument.

Hal Brognola, was the high-ranking Department of Justice official who moonlighted as director of the Sensitive Operations Group, based at the secret counterterrorist installation known as Stony Man Farm. "You're speaking awfully quietly. Are you right in the middle of it?" the head Fed asked.

"Yeah," Bolan whispered. "I'm hidden in a grove of trees across the pond watching. The deal's about to go down."

A chuckle came from the other end of the line. "Sounds like all you need is some popcorn and a Coke," Brognola said. Then his voice turned serious. "Okay, listen to me with your ears and watch them with your eyes. The President just called. We've got a problem in Nigeria."

"I'm listening," Bolan said. He watched the conversation across the pond inflame again. One of the Posse drew a nickel-plated Colt Government Model semiautomatic pistol from under his Boston Celtics jersey, and for a moment it looked as if shooting would break out. But another member of the Posse grabbed his arm, said something and the .45 disappeared beneath the jersey again.

"A Centers for Disease Control plane carrying yellow fever and similar disease vaccines went down in the jungle," Brognola continued as the soldier watched the negotiations take up again on the other side of the water.

"Sorry to hear it," Bolan said. "But what's that have to do with us?"

"It wasn't actually carrying vaccines."

"Okay...." The Executioner watched the Viking who was speaking for the bikers, and the gangbanger who had done most of the talking for the Posse, nod their heads at the same time. They shook hands.

"The plane was only marked CDC. It was actually DEA."

"Go on," Bolan said. The Viking turned and gave a thumbs-up to the other men straddling the iron horses. One of them reached into a saddlebag at the rear of his bike, pulled out a walkie-talkie and held it to his lips.

"As you know," Brognola said, "the DEA has been trying to get crop eradication sprays distributed through Africa. Besides the usual ganja, they're now growing poppies faster than bunnies can reproduce. And coca fields are popping up."

Bolan waited. When Brognola didn't continue, he said,

"They've learned a lot from their South American buddies across the ocean."

The biker with the walkie-talkie had replaced it in his saddlebag. Now, twin headlights appeared on the dirt road behind the group assembled near the pond and bounced toward them. As the vehicle reached the illuminated area, Bolan saw it was an old beat-up pickup with a tattered tarp stretched across the bed. Behind it was an equally scarred old trailer. "So what's the problem?" he whispered into the phone. "You said the DEA has been *trying* to get the eradication chemicals in to spray the fields. What's stopping them?" The pickup came to a halt, and two more of the seedy looking Outrage bikers emerged from the cab.

"The two planes that have tried to fly in the chemicals have been shot down," the big Fed stated.

Bolan squinted in concentration, both at what he was hearing and what he was seeing across the pond. "One of the cartels?" he asked. Some of the South and Central American drug cartels, as well as long-established European crime syndicates, had opened new operations in Africa over the past few years. They'd been joined by an enterprising new coalition authorities suspected was native—based in Africa itself. But while the long-established criminal organizations were known to police authorities around the world, these newcomers were still pretty much a mystery. Little was known about this homegrown group of drug dealers and cutthroats, and for lack of a better name the authorities had been dubbed them the Ivory Coast cartel. The Ivory Coast cartel was suspected of having key men in high places in order to have risen to power so quickly. And like all drug cartels, they had more money than King Midas himself. In addition to buying off the government officials they kept in their back pockets, they had equipped themselves with aircraft and weapons that were better than many of the African armies.

So the Executioner's next question was only natural. "Ivory Coast?" he asked.

"We think so," Brognola said.

Across the pond, the bikers began unloading wooden crates from the trailer and bed of the pickup. Bolan watched the Posse haul large cardboard boxes from the trunks of their vehicles. The boxes had been secured with silver duct tape, which glittered in the motorcycle headlights. "Let me see if I've got this straight," Bolan said. "The DEA had two planes shot down by persons unknown—who we assume were with the Ivory Coast cartel. So they marked one of their planes with U.S. Centers for Disease Control insignia, put out the story that it was carrying vaccines and tried to sneak it past the shooters?"

"That's about the size of it."

Bolan continued to watch through the field glasses as the bikers and gangbangers went about their trade. "But the plane got shot down anyway?"

"No," Brognola said. "Not shot down. At least we don't think so. It was an old Soviet jet the DEA had seized on another deal several years ago. It looks like it died of natural causes. Went down in the jungle from some kind of engine trouble. At least that's what the pilot said afterward."

"That sounds like a little more of a coincidence than I'm willing to buy into without further proof," Bolan said.

"I feel the same way. So does the DEA director. And so does our President."

Bolan watched as the men across the pond finished unloading their wares and setting them on the ground. When the task had been completed, the Viking with the red beard walked up to the head of the Posse. The Executioner knew what was coming. A final handshake. But according to the informant he had within the Outrage Motorcycle Club, the handshake would serve as more than the fact that the deal was complete. It was the signal for something else—the Judas kiss.

Bolan reached for the scoped rifle at his side and rolled to a prone position on the ground.

Brognola cleared his throat over the phone. "Maybe it was a

coincidence," he said. "But the President wants to know for sure. He specifically requested that you go to Africa and find out."

As he still grasped the gangbanger's right hand in his own, the Viking drew the big Ruger from his belt with his left. Jerking the man forward by the arm, he jammed the barrel of the gun into his captive's abdomen and pulled the trigger. The gang leader's body muffled the roar but the big .44 Magnum round combined with the gases escaping through the barrel, the shot acting more like a bomb than a bullet.

Flesh, blood and pieces of body organs blew out the man's back. More of the human tissue and body fluids exploded out the front to drench the Viking and those around him.

Now, all of the bikers drew weapons as they dived from the saddles of their motorcycles. Most carried semiautomatic pistols, but from under their cutoff jean jackets several ancient Mac-10 and Mac-11 submachine pistols also emerged. The rapid-fire little automatics hopped in the air as they sent 9 mm and .380 auto rounds pelting into the Posse.

The gangbangers had been caught flatfooted, and three of them fell before the onslaught. Two drew the handguns they had carried beneath their shirts but were mowed down before they could get off a round. The black who had stayed next to the Lincoln reached inside the car as a hail of rounds, which by all rights should have chewed him to pieces, rained down all around him.

Bolan had dropped the binoculars when he reached for the M-21 and now watched the action through the scope. His finger was on the trigger, but he still had the cell phone pressed to his ear with his left hand.

"Sounds like the show just started," Brognola said.

Bolan confirmed it for him. "Yeah, the curtain's up. But my act doesn't go on for a few more minutes." He paused. "If the plane going down wasn't really a coincidence, then it sounds as if whoever shot down the other planes got tipped off about the DEA-CDC ruse. Maybe they just changed tactics—and sabotaged the plane while it was still on the ground." He took time to draw a breath. "All of which makes this more a job for detective than a soldier, Hal. What does the president want with me?"

The gangbanger who had reached inside the Lincoln now pulled out the AK-47. He sprayed the air with a wild stream of autofire. Several 7.62 mm rounds flew from the ejection port of the Russian weapon and gleamed as they arched through the headlights of both the car and motorcycles. The man's firing was frantic and unaimed, but several rounds still found the bikers, copper-jacketed lead penetrating dirty denim. Four of the Outrage gang hit the ground in death. The Viking saw what had happened and swung his Redhawk toward the Lincoln. He ended the AK assault with a well-placed .44 Magnum slug between the eyes of the rifleman.

"The President doesn't know who he can trust on this, Striker," Brognola said. "Like you said, there was obviously a leak. And there's no way of telling where it came from. When you get as much money involved as we have here—not just millions but billions—everyone is suspect." He paused to clear his throat again, then said, "Each dollar they make is more for paying off crooked cops and politicians. And as the payoffs go up, a lot of formerly honest men find that the old adage is true—every man has his price."

The cell phone still pressed against his left ear, Bolan sighted the scope one-handed on the chest of the red-headed Viking. "Not everyone," he said calmly, and pulled the trigger.

"No, not everyone," Brognola agreed. "But most."

The Viking jerked as if struck in the sternum with a baseball bat. He stumbled to his side, then joined the rest of the dead men on the ground.

By now, the Outrage bikers had completed their victory over the Posse. Most of the gang members lay scattered across the prairie grass. A few had run, and taken bullets between the shoulder blades as they tried to cross the construction sites. They lay still, their blood staining the fresh gray concrete dark. The bikers themselves had taken only four casualties—the men who had fallen to the wild "spray and pray" attack of the gangbanger with the AK-47.

"Hang on, Hal," Bolan said. "I need to set the phone down for a second."

"I'll wait."

The Executioner rested the cell phone on the ground beside him, grasped the fore end of the M-21 and squeezed the trigger again. The bullpup stock pressed gently back against his shoulder and through the scope he saw one of the bikers hit the ground. The Executioner had killed their Viking leader before the dust had settled, and the other Outrage bikers hadn't noticed that the shot came from across the pond. But now, with all of the Posse dead, they had thought the engagement over. The bikers suddenly froze. Most looked around them in surprise. A tall, grossly overweight motorcycle outlaw lumbered forward to kneel over the prostrate body of his leader.

The Executioner centered the crosshairs on the bald spot at the back of the man's head, and a second later the fat biker's head exploded like an overripe cantaloupe dropped from a ten-story building. Swinging the M-21 to the side, Bolan put another round into the face of an Outrage biker who still hadn't figured out what was happening. By now the soldier had fired from his spot in the trees enough times that the remaining trio of bikers knew at least the general direction from which the shots were coming. They raised their weapons, firing across the pond.

Three seconds later the Outrage bikers lay dead on the ground while none of their rounds had fallen within twenty feet of the Executioner.

Bolan set the rifle down and picked up the phone again. He held it to his ear as he began gathering his equipment. "Is Jack on his way to get me?" he asked Brognola, referring to Jack Grimaldi, Stony Man Farm's chief pilot.

"He should have landed in Cincinnati by the time you get to the airport," Brognola said.

Without another word, Bolan ended the call, gathered his gear and walked out of the trees.

THE TRUCK BUMPED over the rugged road through the clearing in the jungle, sending Norris Wright bouncing up and down in the passenger's seat. His mood wasn't good, and the bumpy ride wasn't improving it any. But he waited quietly, not speaking until the front wheels finally hit a rut, which smashed the Glock 19 painfully into his spine. "Damn you, Peterssen," he said to the driver. "When was the last time you had these springs replaced on this fucking thing?"

The man behind the wheel had blond hair and matching beard, with a larger-than-average body and head. He was obviously of Scandinavian descent, and just as obviously accustomed to such verbal abuse from the man sitting next to him. Whether he had chosen to simply shrug it off, had grown used to such treatment from all men during his life, or was simply not bright enough that the insults took effect was impossible to tell. Whatever the reason, he simply smiled and said, "I don't remember. But I'll do it when we get back." His accent put the final touch on his ancestry.

Wright turned back to the windshield and let his eyes follow the jungle line along the clearing. This area of the jungle had been cleared several months earlier. The Nigerian government had intended to dig gas lines through it. Wright sneered at how abruptly the work had stopped. Like so many projects started with such zeal by Third World leaders, this one had been forgotten when some other diversion came along and caught their fancies. It was an irritating trait he had noticed in many primitive people. But, Wright had to admit, that same lack of organization, inability to prioritize and basic immaturity had acted to greatly benefit him when he looked at the big picture. Without it, he'd have had to live on the measly salary the U.S. government paid him. Dealing with the Nigerians—and the rest of the black Africans as well as many of the whites—often proved irritating. It really was very much like dealing with children. He had to trick them into doing what he wanted. When the tricks didn't work, he bought them off.

As he steadied himself inside the bouncing truck with his right hand, Wright pulled a cellular phone from the pocket of his khaki bush shirt with his left. He kept his other hand firmly on the door, placing the phone on his lap to tap in the numbers. At that exact moment the truck hit one of the deepest ruts in the road so far. Wright's head banged the ceiling of the cab, and the phone bounced off his legs on the floor. New anger flooded his veins as he scooped it up again and turned to the driver once more. "Peterssen, you son of a bitch, if this thing doesn't have new springs in it by tomorrow morning, I swear I'll blow your fucking head off!"

The big bearded Scandinavian didn't answer. He just smiled and nodded.

Wright tapped the number into the phone. A moment later, Dolph Van der Kirk's harsh South African accent said, "Hello?"

Wright tried to hold the phone steady against his ear as he spoke. "You found it yet?" he asked.

"Yes," Van der Kirk growled. "We mounted a ridge half an hour ago. We could look down and see where the treetops had been clipped off. I would estimate we are no farther than five minutes away from the site now."

The phone fell below Wright's ear as they hit another bump, then rose to strike him in the jaw as the truck's front wheels fell into a dip. Wright kept his curses mental this time, not wanting to have to explain them to the South African already on the ground in the jungle.

"Are you still there?" Van der Kirk asked.

"Yeah," Wright said. "I'm still there. Could you see this road we're on from where you were? On the ridge?"

"Yes. Barely. I would guess you will be able to pull up within fifty yards of where the plane is. Certainly no more than one hundred."

At least that was good news, Wright thought. Even with the phony coordinates Stevens had given the authorities, and the Africans' propensity not to be able to find their asses with both hands, he knew they'd stumble onto the crash site sooner or later. He needed to get his men in and out again, as fast as possible.

"When you reach the crash site," Wright said, "send a man out to the road. I don't want to drive past the spot accidentally."

"Consider it done," Van der Kirk said.

Wright hung up, replaced the phone and stared angrily at the driver as they bounced on.

Ten minutes later, Norris Wright saw a flash of red come out of the jungle ahead. As the truck bounded on, a black face and arms came into view. One of his and Van der Kirk's many lieutenants. He couldn't remember the man's name, but whoever he was, he was waving his arms back and forth over his head to get their attention. The AK-47 slung over his shoulder swayed back and forth in time to the waves.

Peterssen pulled the truck up to where the man stood, and Wright opened the door and jumped to the ground. He walked around to the rear of the cargo area where one of the men riding in back had already slid the curtain open along the rod that held it in place. Inside the truck, a half dozen more men were rising from the floor. All of them had scowls on their faces from the bumpy ride, and Wright knew that while it might have been uncomfortable where he'd been in the cab of the truck, a seat on the floor in the back would have been like riding a stagecoach with a broken wheel over a lava pit.

The men began dropping off the tail of the truck, and behind them Wright could see two dozen fifty-five-gallon drums lashed in place with canvas straps. A half-dozen dollies hung from hooks mounted on the walls of the vehicle. "Get started," Wright ordered the men. "I don't know how much time we've got." He stood back as two of the men slid a ramp out the back of the truck and fastened it into place. A minute or so later, the drums started down toward the ground on the dollies.

Wright turned and looked at the edge of the jungle. His precaution of having Van der Kirk send the man in the red shirt to the clearing had been unnecessary. A strip of foliage had been mowed for thirty yards into the jungle, as if a threshing machine had run over it. But in spite of the vines, limbs and leaves now covering it, the plane itself was visible where it had spun before coming to a halt.

Through the carnage, Wright could see Van der Kirk and the men who had come with him. The short, but powerful South African already had the other men unloading the cargo that was on board. Several black fifty-five-gallon drums—identical to those Wright now had coming off the truck-already stood on the ground next to the Antonov.

Wright hurried forward to where Van der Kirk was not only supervising, but assisting in the operation. No more than five foot six in height, the South African probably pushed the scales at 250. Yet, had his body fat percentage been taken, Wright suspected it might well have scored in the negative range. Van der Kirk was dressed in OD jungle fatigues, leather-and-nylon combat boots and a white T-shirt so tight that the scoop neck and shirtsleeves seemed to disappear into the dark crevices of his chest and arm muscles. In school in Johannesburg, Wright knew Van der Kirk had achieved some degree of fame as a rugby player. He had achieved even more fame later, however, as a power lifter and bodybuilder.

A tan strip of cloth bearing black leopard-pattern spots was tied around Van der Kirk's forehead as a sweatband in the jungle humidity. Yes, Wright thought as he made his way through the ragged foliage toward the plane, Dolph Van der Kirk was one physically powerful man. But his abilities didn't stop there. He was intelligent, organized and goal driven. Best of all, perhaps, he had the ability to be completely ruthless. Of course if that hadn't been the case, Wright would have never agreed to hook up with him.

"Good work," Wright said, as he stepped up to the brawny man.

Van der Kirk set the drum he had lifted single-handedly next to him. Wright couldn't help noticing the similarity between the builds of the man and the container. The South African let a cruel smile trail across his lips. He didn't speak but pulled the leopard bandanna from around his head and mopped his face with it.

"Where's the pilot?" Wright asked.

"I sent him back to wait in the cockpit." Van der Kirk's voice was low and gravelly as seemed to befit his appearance.

"Is he hurt?"

Van der Kirk shrugged. "Small cut on the forehead." He glanced around at the damage to the plane and trees. "Very lucky, actually."

"For now," Wright said.

The South African chuckled. "He has already asked for his bonus."

Wright nodded, glanced at his watch, then said, "Better go give it to him. Even the Nigerians will find this place before long."

Van der Kirk grunted in agreement. "It should look like it happened in the crash, don't you think?" he asked.

"As close as possible," Wright said. "But I wouldn't waste time on details. If there's an autopsy at all, it'll be by one of those clowns half a semester of med school above a witch doctor. And is anything's noticed..." He held out his palm and wiggled his fingers back and forth in the age-old gesture that meant "money."

Van der Kirk nodded. Reaching to a scabbard on his belt, he drew a twenty-inch machete. Holding it by the black of the blade, he shaved a small square of hair off his left forearm.

"That may be taking things a little too lightly," Wright

said. "That isn't going to look like it came from this crash or any crash, ever."

"To use one of your Americanisms," Van der Kirk said, "have a little faith, baby. Have a little faith. You are familiar with the expression?"

"It was about thirty years ago," Wright said. He watched as Van der Kirk jerked the bandanna from his forehead and wrapped it around the machete blade toward the end. He let the inverted machete drop to the end of his arm, then took a half-step in so that Wright's body shielded it from the plane. Then, turning toward the cockpit, he yelled out in his harsh South African accent, "Mr. Stevens, please come down for your reward!"

A moment later, Blackie Stevens dropped down from the cockpit and walked forward. He was rubbing his eyes as if he'd dozed off. Beneath his hands, his lips were smiling.

Van der Kirk took a step to the side of Wright. As soon as Stevens dropped his hands, he swung the machete.

The grip spur at the end of the machete handle struck the pilot squarely between the eyes. Bone crunched as the semi-sharp bump penetrated a half-inch into the skull and sent fresh blood squirting into the air. More blood dripped from beneath the bandage over the man's eyes as the trauma from the blow passed down to it like tremors from an earthquake, reopening the wound.

But Blackie Stevens never felt it. He was dead even before his knees buckled beneath him.

Several drops of blood had flown over Wright, and he looked to Van der Kirk in disgust. "Such finesse you have, Dolphi, such class." He shook his head in disgust as he held his shirt away from his body and tried to shake the still-wet droplets off before they soaked in. "In any case, better get him back behind the controls." He glanced to his watch once more. "I've got to get back."

"Time to put on your other hat?" Van der Kirk grinned as he reached down, grabbing the dead man in a fireman's carry and slinging him over his shoulder as if he were a rag doll.

Wright smiled. Van der Kirk was crude and brutal. But he liked the man. The South African had been a good partner and had helped him build the drug empire the world's cops had dubbed the Ivory Coast cartel. He and Van der Kirk owned poppy and cocoa fields from the Atlantic to the Indian oceans. Scattered in between, they had close to a hundred manufacturing plants that converted the raw crops into heroin and cocaine. They owned transport planes that distributed their products all over the world, and even a few old Soviet fighter jets that had come in handy when the DEA tried to send down eradication sprays to eliminate their crops.

Wright glanced at the big black barrels still rolling through the jungle from the downed plane. And now, they had *this*. What was in the barrels had nothing to do with their other business. It represented the biggest score ever. Good enough, at least, that he and Van der Kirk could live the rest of their lives like sultans wherever they chose to relocate.

Wright glanced back to his muscular partner. "I'm sorry," he said. "What did you ask me?"

Van der Kirk laughed, the dead pilot still over his shoulder and dripping blood onto his jungle fatigues. "I ask you if you had to get back to your other job."

Wright nodded. "They'll send somebody from Washington to check into this one," he said. "I want the bullshit in place when he gets here." He paused, looking down into his partner's eyes. "Besides, I'd hate like hell to miss work, get fired, and lose my pension."

Both men laughed as Wright turned and started back toward the truck. When this was over, he knew it wouldn't be just millions he had in his pockets. It would be billions.

JUST AS HAL BROGNOLA had promised, Jack Grimaldi had been waiting when Bolan arrived at the airport. Being the Executioner's friend as well as his battle companion, the two men had worked together so long they could almost read each other's minds. This was demonstrated almost as soon as they'd cleared Cincinnati airspace when Bolan turned to the pilot.

"In the console," Grimaldi said before the Executioner could even voice his request.

Bolan opened the console between the seats and pulled out a small leather credential case. Opening it, he saw he'd be playing the part of a U.S. Drug Enforcement Administration special agent. The case contained a badge as well as an official DEA identification card. The card even sported a picture of the soldier. But Bolan saw—the sight causing him to squint closer—the picture made him look as if he had been in his midtwenties when it had been taken.

Grimaldi saw him squint, chuckled and read his mind again. "Bear did a little computer work on the photo," he said, referring to Aaron "The Bear" Kurtzman, Stony Man Farm's top computer genius. "You needed to look like you'd been with the dope boys for a while."

Bolan glanced down at the name on the ID card. "Special Agent Kenneth Clarke?" he asked. "Where'd Bear come up with that name? Am I impersonating a real DEA agent?" If he was, he needed to know about it ahead of time in case complications arose.

Grimaldi smiled. "No, it was just Bear's idea of a little inside joke," he said.

Bolan turned toward the pilot and frowned.

The Stony Man pilot continued to smile and pointed to Bolan's pocket. "Call Hal," he said. "And he can tell about the name at the same time he finishes briefing you on the rest of it."

Bolan nodded and dropped the leather credential case into his lap. Pulling out the cellular phone, he double-checked the red light in the corner that insured that the internal scrambler was operating, then dialed Brognola. A moment later, the big Fed answered. "Striker?" he asked, using the name the Executioner employed during missions.

"It's me."

"Okay," Brognola said. "You got your ID?"

"Looking at it now."

"Then listen up." Brognola's voice had changed slightly, and Bolan could tell he had just stuck the stub of one of his never-smoked-but-chewed-until-gone cigars into his mouth. "I've laid the groundwork for your arrival in Lagos. You'll be picked up by agents from the local DEA office and taken to the scene of the crash."

"They've located the plane, then?"

"Affirmative." Brognola answered. "The Nigerian rescue team finally found it about ten miles from the coordinates the pilot had given them."

"Any explanation on the mix-up?"

"No. Not so far. Damaged instruments maybe. Damaged brain on the pilot maybe." He paused. "Or maybe just your average run-of-the-mill screw-up somewhere along the lines of communication."

"Lot of maybes," Bolan said.

"Well, you can check into that, too, when you get there," Brognola said around his cigar. "Your story is you've been sent from the DEA Washington headquarters. This is the third plane to go down in less than a month, and the bean counters are worried about how much it's eating into their budget. They've sent you to find out."

"That's all?" Bolan asked. "In other words, I'm one of the bean counters myself."

"Exactly," Brognola said. "You're a typical bureaucratic paper pusher who wouldn't know a Thai stick from a rock of crack in the field. So play it that way. Paper smart, street stupid. You've got to come off like you don't have much, if any, DEA field experience." Brognola clamped down tighter on the cigar, and his voice sounded almost as if he were talking with his teeth clenched. "There's always the chance the leak is coming from inside the DEA itself. If that's the case, you're likely to meet the traitor face-to-face, you may even be working side by side with him. It may even be him who picks you up when you touch down."

"And if he thinks I'm just a budget man, interested only in the financial end of things, he'll be more likely to let down and make a mistake."

"Exactly," Brognola said. "Let him think he's pulling the wool over your eyes."

"Fair enough. What else can you tell me about whoever's likely to be behind all this, Hal?"

"Not much," the big Fed responded. "But the President's being advised on every new development. And he seems concerned."

The soldier felt his eyebrows lower. "Any particular reason for that?"

"Not that I know of," Brognola said. "But you have to remember our current commander in chief has no clandestine-op experience of any kind. He may just be overreacting to something he doesn't understand."

"It wouldn't be the first time," the Executioner said. He had worked under several presidents since the inception of Stony Man Farm. And to say that the current man behind the desk of the Oval Office was his favorite would have been an outright lie. And to say he was incompetent when it came to orchestrating the type of operations the Farm performed would have been a gross understatement.

"What doesn't make sense," Bolan said, "is that you and I know, and even the president ought to know, that I'm not needed in a role like this. I'm a soldier, Hal. I'm not an undercover operative."

"You've always pulled it off in the past," Brognola countered.

"I'm not saying I *can't* do it. I'm saying that my talents could be put to better use elsewhere. The DEA has some of the best undercover men in the world. They could handle this thing with one hand tied behind their backs and standing on their heads."

"The President doesn't know who can be trusted and who can't down there," Brognola said, but he didn't sound convinced.

"That doesn't wash, either, Hal. If that's the case, they could send a real DEA investigative team down to find out. And if the President thinks there's a possibility that the corruption goes all the way to headquarters, he's always got the FBI, or the CIA, or a half dozen other investigative agencies he could hand this off to." Bolan glanced at the closed credential case in his lap once more. "You could have convinced the Man of that, Hal. But you didn't. That means it's not just the President. *You* want me in Nigeria, too. Why?"

There was a long pause on the other end of the line. But Bolan waited, unconcerned. Like the Executioner and Jack Grimaldi, Bolan and Brognola had been through too many wars together not to trust each other implicitly. The reason the Stony Man director was taking time to answer wasn't due to any reluctance on his part to share information. Bolan guessed he was simply trying to find the correct words.

And he was right. A few moments later, Brognola said, "I can't really put my finger on it, Striker. Call it the hunch of an old cop, I guess. But there's more to this than meets the eye. Much more—I can feel it in my bones. And you're the only one I trust to find out what it is."

Bolan nodded. Considering the trust he returned Brognola's way, that was good enough for him. "Anything else I need to know?"

"I have nothing else. But you'll get it as soon as I do."

"One more thing," the Executioner said.

"Yeah?" The cigar seemed to be gone from Brognola's mouth now.

"Jack seems to think this name on my ID was Bear's idea of a little inside joke. What's that all about."

Brognola's chuckle wasn't forced, but it wasn't jolly, either. "Like I said, you're going in as a pencil-pushing bureaucrat. Meek guy. One of those clowns every agency has who never actually accomplishes anything but looks good on paper. In other words, Kenneth Clarke is about as totally opposite of what you really are as he could possibly be."

"I know it's a long flight to Nigeria, Hal," Bolan said. "But I'd rather spend it doing something constructive than playing word games."

"Kenneth Clarke is your undercover name. Your secret identity, so to speak. Read the name backward, Striker," Brognola said as he hung up.

Bolan ended the call on his end and stuck the phone back in his pocket. He opened the credential case again and looked at the name. Kenneth Clarke. Clarke Kenneth.

Again, Grimaldi appeared to be reading the Executioner's mind, mimicking the voice of the announcer of the old TV show, "Mild-mannered reporter for a daily metropolitan newspaper, fights a never-ending battle for truth, justice and—"

"Enough, Jack," Bolan said. He twisted in his seat and reached into the storage compartment behind him. Inside, he found a world atlas and opened it to Nigeria. "I can spend my time in better ways than listening to your bad impersonations."

Grimaldi nodded, grinning. "Good idea, big guy. You catch up on your reading. And try to get some rest while you're at it. I've got a feeling there might be some speeding bullets in your future, and you'll have to be faster than them. And I don't know how many tall buildings there are in Lagos, but we want you strong enough to leap them in a single bound if necessary."

Bolan didn't answer.

Grimaldi glanced at his old friend out of the corner of his eye. Maybe the Executioner wasn't going to speak to him. But the big guy hadn't been able to keep the trace of a smile off his lips.

2

The cabin of the Lear jet flown by Jack Grimaldi had been totally remodeled. Equipment lockers and other storage compartments lined the walls behind the seats. In the corner, at the rear of the plane, a small shower had even been installed. Hanging his blacksuit in one of the lockers, Bolan hurriedly squeezed his big frame into the small compartment under the showerhead. He lathered himself with soap and water from head to toe and washed away the grime—both physical and spiritual—that had surrounded him during his mission to eliminate both the 23rd Street Posse and the Outrage Motorcycle Club. Five minutes later, he was drying off with a clean towel.

"Hey, Jack!" he called to the front of the plane.

"Yeah?"

"Hal pack any mild-mannered-reporter clothes for me?" Bolan asked as he finished drying his hair and tied the towel around his waist.

"Third locker, left side," Grimaldi shouted back. "You'll love them, Kenneth. They're just your style."

The Executioner opened the door to the green metal locker. Inside, he found a beige suit, paisley tie, a stiffly starched white Oxford shirt and a pair of brown loafers with tassels. They were exactly the kind of Monday-through-Friday wear one might expect from a Washington, D.C., government bureaucrat. And exactly the *wrong* thing to wear in the jungle when the Executioner met the DEA agents after touching down. He would appear to be the "indoor type" who hadn't even thought to bring appropriate outdoor wear.

The Executioner put on the shirt, slacks, socks and shoes, then knotted the tie around his neck. In the right hand jacket pocket, he found a gold tie bar bearing the DEA logo, and anchored his neckwear to his shirt. Turning to the small dressing table where he'd left his weapons, he picked up the shoulder holster bearing his Beretta 93-R and slid his arms inside. The 93-R, a select-fire version of the Beretta Model 92, which had been adopted by the U.S. Army, was capable of normal semiauto fire or 3-round bursts. It also differed from the 92 in that it had a fold-down front grip for use in this mode. Bolan rarely had time to use it. But he didn't need it. He had sent enough gunfire into his enemies over the years that controlling the light 9 mm recoil with one hand was mere child's play. The Beretta had also been fitted with a state-of-the-art sound suppressor.

After snapping the retaining loop over the belt of his slacks to secure the weapon in place, the Executioner shifted the double-magazine carrier under his right arm. The magazines—together, holding an extra thirty rounds—did a good job of balancing the weight of the pistol under his other arm.

But the Beretta was, and always had been the lighter brother to the team of pistols he had chosen years before. Lifting a simple Yaqui belt slide holster from the table next to another gun, Bolan threaded it onto his belt, positioning it on his right hip. Next he lifted the mammoth .44 Magnum Desert Eagle. The 93-R was quiet, but the Eagle roared like a lion. He dropped it into the Yaqui slide, making sure it fit securely inside the carefully molded leather.

The Executioner turned back to the table. The Applegate-Fairbairn fighting knife, with its six inch double-edged dagger blade, took over when even more quietude than the sound suppressed Beretta could provide was called for. An evolution of the Fairbairn-Sykes Commando dagger of World War II fame, it was stronger at both tip and hilt, and could even be put to use as a camp knife if necessary. The A-F was housed in a hard plastic Concealex sheath, and Bolan clipped it to his belt at the small of his back.

Sliding his arms into the jacket of his suit, Bolan returned to the cockpits. "How much longer, Jack?" he asked the pilot.

"Hour, maybe an hour-fifteen," Grimaldi said. "We're over Algeria now. But we're flying straight into one heck of a wind." The pilot glanced to his side, grinned and said, "You look ready for the office Christmas party, Striker. Very nice." After a pause, he added, "Of course I still wouldn't want you dating my daughter."

"You don't have a daughter," Bolan said, as he dropped into the seat next to his old friend.

"Well, not that I know of anyway," Grimaldi said. The pilot was almost as famous for his exploits with the fair sex as he was for his genius flying anything with wings.

Grimaldi looked the Executioner up and down once more, then said, "I forgot to tell you. Couple more things you'll want. You'll find them in the second locker to the right of where you found the suit."

Bolan rose and returned to the rear of the plane. Opening the locker Grimaldi had indicated, he found only three items. The first two were a 9 mm Glock 19 pistol and a black leather thumb-break holster. He nodded to himself. A pencil pusher like Kenneth Clarke would carry what was issued to him by his agency, and the Glock was one of the several pistols from which DEA agents could choose. The Beretta and Desert Eagle were definitely not standard issue, and while he had no intention of leaving them behind, Bolan would keep them hidden while portraying Clarke. The Glock would be the gun he used first if he needed it, reserving his personal weapons for emergencies in which survival meant he had to break cover.

He doubted that would come up, however, during the short period of time he planned to spend as the special agent.

Unbuckling his belt again, Bolan shifted the Desert Eagle farther back behind his hip, and slid the Glock onto his side in front of it.

The third item Bolan found in the locker was a fake leather glasses case, containing a pair of spectacles. He opened the case and held them to his eyes. The glass was clear. But the image was perfect. Gold, with tortoiseshell insets along the side of the frames, they had tan leather molded over the earpieces. They might as well have had Washington Yuppie Bureaucrat stamped on the lenses. The Executioner returned to his seat again.

"I'm rarely speechless, Sarge," Grimaldi said with a grin, "but this is one of those times. If it weren't for all the scars, I'd say you should model for *Gentlemen's Quarterly*."

Bolan strapped himself back into the seat. "I'll give it some hard thought, Jack," he said as he settled in. He had spent most of the flight reading up on Nigeria and the other countries out of which the Ivory Coast cartel was rumored to operate, and he was tired. Not a great way to begin any mission. But a condition in which he frequently found himself. He had roughly an hour left before they touched down, and he took advantage of it to doze.

The Executioner's eyes opened as Grimaldi snatched the radio mike from the dash and requested permission to land. As soon as they was cleared, he replaced the mike and turned to Bolan. "Did Hal tell you the DEA plans to have someone meet you?" he asked.

Bolan nodded.

"You should be cleared to pass customs with no sweat," Grimaldi added. "Just show your badge. Then go to the east door of the terminal, past the taxis."

Bolan nodded. "You're waiting here, aren't you?"

Grimaldi performed the best bow he could in the cramped

seat. "At your service," he said. "And as usual, ready to get back into the air at a moment's notice." He paused, then added, "Even if no one is chasing us."

"Where?"

"I'll rent a hangar. It'll be posted in the private aircraft area if I don't talk to you by phone first."

A few minutes later the Lear's wheels hit the ground. Hal Brognola had indeed worked his long-reaching magic and laid the groundwork, and a Nigerian customs official took one look at Bolan's credentials, glanced at the clipboard in his hand, then waved him through. Bolan carried his bags into the airport terminal, his mind on the quick refresher course on Nigeria he had given himself during the flight.

Nigeria had been inhabited since the Stone Age, and had been part of countless ancient African kingdoms over the centuries. The Portuguese had come to trade for art treasures in the city of Benin in the fifteenth century, and the British had followed three hundred years later when they established a colony in Lagos. At the Berlin Conference of 1885, when the European powers divided up Africa as if it and its people were no more than commodities to be bought and sold, Great Britain was given the entire area. Some small amount of self-government came in 1954, but Nigeria did not officially become an independent member of the British Commonwealth until 1963. Rebellions and military coups—some failing, others succeeding—had been the name of the game since that time. The current government had been elected, but only time would tell if it stayed that way. The citizens of the country came from a wide variety of tribal backgrounds. Nupe, Tiv, Fulani, Kanuri and Hausas were all to be found among the seventy-million people who called Nigeria home. Many did their best to get along with one another. Many others did their best to cause trouble and gain the reins of power.

Bolan found the doors on the east side of the terminal and stepped out into the African sunshine. The air was humid along the Gulf of Guinea, but he estimated the temperature in the low eighties. Two rows of unmarked cabs met his eyes, and black men and a few whites shouted at him in English and a variety of tribal dialects he couldn't understand. Behind the taxis, parked along the curb, he saw a brand-new, dark blue Land Rover. A man wearing a brightly colored batik design sport shirt outside his slacks stood leaning against the driver's door. When he saw Bolan, he waved, then started forward.

"Dirk Woodsen," the man said, extending his hand as he neared. He was in his mid-twenties, roughly five feet ten inches tall, broad across the chest beneath the colorful shirt, and sported pale pink skin that looked as if it might always burn but never tan. "You're Cooper?"

"Clarke," Bolan corrected.

"Yeah, sorry, my mistake," Woodsen said, shaking his head as he grabbed one of Bolan's bags and started back through the taxis toward the Land Rover. "Must be the heat affecting my brain."

The Executioner followed the shorter man to the vehicle. He had taken an instant liking to the young DEA agent, and hoped he wasn't involved in whatever underhanded dealings were going on in, and around, Lagos. He didn't want to have to kill Woodsen if he didn't have to.

Bolan and Woodsen tossed the bags into the back seat of the Land Rover, then the young DEA man slid behind the wheel as Bolan climbed into the shotgun seat. The vehicle was fully equipped, including a state-of-the-art CD player, and even a small television screen mounted in the dash.

"Nice wheels," the Executioner said. "This standard DEA issue?"

Woodsen laughed. "I wish," he said. "No, most of us do have Land Rovers. They say it's for the rough terrain, but my guess is the Administration bean counters got a good deal on them." He turned quickly to his side, his pink face taking on a darker red. "Ah, no offense meant by that."

"None taken. Somebody has to pay the bills."

"Yeah, I know." Woodsen nodded. "But back to the car. This is the boss's ride. The only one fully equipped. Anyway, he gave it to me with orders to pick you up, then drive by the office and get him before we headed out to the crash site."

Bolan nodded. "You have people out there now?'

Woodsen guided the Land Rover into traffic. "Yeah, several of our people are already on the scene. They're with the Nigerian rescue folks. Nigerian air force, mostly. Their version of Special Forces."

Bolan settled in for the ride. They drove past an open market area where hundreds of vendors offered tropical fruits, vegetables, fish, fowl and other eatables. Just past the food market stood more small stalls, which displayed dazzling bolts of cloth, beads, jewelry made of exotic woods and animal horns, and ready-made clothing. Lagos had been built on an island in a large lagoon off the Gulf, and was connected to the nearby island of Iddo by a bridge that spanned a half mile across the lapping blue waters. They passed the bridge and moved through a slum of shacks and dirt streets, then entered an area of modern skyscrapers and paved road. But Woodsen didn't stop there. He drove on, entering a light commercial area a few blocks away from the business section, then turned onto a side street with a few scattered office buildings. Unlike the skyscrapers, none of the office complexes stood more than two stories high.

Woodsen pulled up along the curb in front of one of the one-story buildings. He grabbed the cord connecting the microphone to the radio receiver mounted on the Land Rover's dash, reeled the mike up as if the cord were some curly fishing line and thumbed the red button on the side. "Juma, tell the boss we're outside, will you?"

A feminine voice came back with a quick, "Okay, Dirk," and then Bolan and Woodsen sat back to wait.

"How far to the crash site?" the Executioner asked.

Woodsen squinted in thought and the wrinkles around his eyes made the permanently sunburned pink skin turn white. "Take about an hour, I imagine," he said. "The boss has the directions. So we'll find it."

The Executioner frowned. "He hasn't been out there yet himself?" It seemed to him that with an event of such consequence the local SAC—special agent in charge—would have been the first on the scene.

Woodsen shook his head. "No, he couldn't be reached. Tied up out of the office on some kind of personal business yesterday when it all went down." He snorted, then added, "When the plane went down, I mean. No pun intended."

Bolan nodded. Such things happened. Even DEA supervisors had personal lives.

As they waited, Woodsen turned to face Bolan. "Sir?" he said, and now what had been an openly friendly and straightforward voice took on an edge of uneasiness. "Mind if I ask you a question?"

Bolan turned in the seat to face him. "Of course not," he said.

"What do you do back in Washington?"

The soldier tightened his abdominal muscles, forcing blood to his face as if embarrassed. He wanted to appear to be a man somewhat uneasy with his lack of field experience, and somewhat intimidated by those who were regulars in the dangerous back streets and alleys of the drug world. "Well, my primary assignment is the distribution of finances to the field offices," he said. He paused, as if thinking hard for more to say. "One of the bean counters, like you said."

"I didn't mean—"

Bolan smiled. "Like I said, forget it. But don't think for a moment that's *all* I've done. I worked undercover last year for a day and a half. We had a deal going down in one of the local Holiday Inns. *Big* deal. Cocaine."

Woodsen nodded. "No kidding. You make the buy yourself?"

Bolan forced the flush to his face again. "Well, no, not actually. It was important to get the motel staff evacuated in case shooting broke out. These were extremely violent people we were dealing with, you understand. Colombians. Anyway, I was in charge of sequestering the maids and other staff, and getting them on the bus that took them safely out of the area." Now, he let his chest puff up slightly in pride. "But then I played the part of one of the desk clerks. In fact, it was me who checked the Colombians into their room." Bolan beamed with pride.

Woodsen smiled. "Bust 'em?"

"You bet we did."

The young DEA agent's smile grew wider. "Great," he said. The smile was meant to convey that Clarke had done a good job, but Bolan knew what it really meant was that Woodsen was pleased to have found out what he wanted to know— Clarke was indeed a desk jockey. A number-crunching nerd with a capital *N*. He had probably bugged the real undercover guys so long that they'd finally agreed to let him go along on a deal. Then they'd run him in as a desk clerk to keep him far away from the action where he couldn't screw things up.

Bolan turned back to face the windshield as they continued to wait. He liked Woodsen, and it was only normal that the man would want to know what kind of agent he was dealing with from the home office. But the Executioner hoped undercover work wasn't any bigger part of Woodsen's job description than it was of the fictitious Kenneth Clarke. The very tenor of the man's voice had told Bolan he was fishing, and turning the ploy around on him had been like taking candy from a newborn.

"Care if I ask you another question while we wait?" Woodsen asked.

The Executioner stared straight ahead but focused his attention on Woodsen, glancing around the corner of his clear-lensed spectacles. Still playing the part of the office nerd, Bolan said, "Shoot. Not literally, of course."

The young agent laughed politely at the inane joke. "Why, exactly, did they send you down here, sir?"

Bolan waited a moment before answering, knowing it would appear that he was trying to decide if Woodsen was to be trusted or not. Finally, he said, "Two of our planes have been shot down. This third one may have been, too, for all we know. The big boys at home want to know what's going on. The bills are mounting up, and we're going to have to answer to Congress for it."

It looked like a light bulb had just flickered on over Woodsen's head. "I imagine it *is* costing a lot," he said. Some of the tension had faded from his voice. Combined with what Bolan had just told him about his duties dispersing funds, the young agent had obviously jumped to the conclusion that Clarke had been sent to find out just how much money the Drug Enforcement Administration was out. "So, you'll need help putting together a financial report that includes not only the loss of the planes themselves but man-hours, equipment, and other expenditures?"

Bolan nodded. "Yes. All the help I can get. Are you volunteering?"

Woodsen had painted himself into a corner, and he knew it. "Well …sure, if I can help," he said. "But I've never been that good with the paperwork."

Bolan's eyebrows lowered. "You might want to consider working on a business degree in accounting like I have," he said seriously. "It's a fast track up the pay scale. And the hours are more regular."

A business degree in accounting, and regular boring hours in an office where clearly the last thing Woodsen's envisioned for his future. But the young man nodded anyway. Then, he asked, "Are they sending anyone down for a general investigation? To find out who, exactly, is behind all this?"

The soldier shrugged nonchalantly and faked a yawn. "Not that I've heard of," he said. "I imagine they'll be leaving that up to you guys."

Woodsen didn't answer verbally but his face, and entire body, visibly relaxed. Again, Bolan had to wonder of the man's obvious distress was the byproduct of the normal resistance of field operatives to deal with the headquarters crew, or if something more sinister was behind his concern. If he had to guess, he'd have picked the former. His take on Woodsen was that he was a young, energetic, adventuresome man who just didn't want to have to deal with any more home-office people than necessary. Not a crooked cop.

As Bolan was considering all this, a tall slender man wearing a lightweight cotton suit came out of the building and walked toward the Land Rover.

Woodsen hit the power button, rolling down the window. "You still want me to drive, boss?" he called out as the man approached. The man's only answer was to open the back door and get into the SUV behind Bolan.

"Let me introduce you two," Woodsen said. "Special Agent Clarke, meet Special Agent in Charge Wright."

A hand reached over the seat and Bolan shook it. The grip was firm.

"We don't stand on formalities too much this far from D.C.," said the man in the back seat. "Call me Norris. Can I call you Ken?"

"Yes."

"Okay, then," Norris Wright said.

His attention turned to Woodsen. "Well, Dirk, what are we waiting for? Christmas? Let's get Ken here out where he can do his job, then get back to doing ours."

"Yes, sir," Woodsen said, throwing the Land Rover in gear.

A moment later, they were heading for the jungles of Nigeria.

IT DIDN'T TAKE a Daniel Boone or Davy Crockett to tell where the plane had gone down.

Bolan watched through the clear lenses of his glasses as

the Land Rover neared the spot where the treetops had been clipped as the plane made its decent to earth. Norris Wright had explained that the clearing along which the vehicle now rolled had originally been cut through the jungle in order to lay a gas pipeline. Whatever the reason, the spot had obviously been visible to the pilot from the air. And he had zeroed in on it as the only possible place to land for miles around.

The Executioner had listened to Wright speak almost constantly during the drive out to the site. The man seemed to love the sound of his own voice. First, Bolan had gotten what a man in the Kenneth Clarke role—now shortened to Ken and sometimes even Kenny by the overly familiar Wright—might have expected: a rundown on the local illegal drug trade within the area of Africa for which his DEA office was responsible. But then Wright had gone on to talk about sports, movies and finally women. He had even subtly hinted that he could furnish the Washington, D.C., agent with female companionship during his stay in Lagos if that was his desire.

Such offers were hardly uncommon. Any "hammer" field agents could get, then lower or at least threaten to lower on a home-office boy might come in handy at some time in the future. Bolan had played dumb, acting as if he hadn't caught onto the intimation. Finally, Wright had gotten around to the two aircraft that had been shot down, then this third plane—the cause of which it had crashed still being anybody's guess.

"It's one of the cartels, no question about that," Wright said. "The question is, which one? And what do we do about it if and when we find out? You realize some of those guys have Soviet surplus fighter jets? Fucking *tanks?*"

"So I've heard," Bolan said.

"If I had to guess at this point, I'd lay it on one of the South American groups," Wright said.

"Not this Ivory Coast cartel we keep hearing about?"

Wright chuckled politely. "Ken, I'm going to let you in on

something. There probably is an Ivory Coast cartel. But whoever they are, they aren't as big as you home-office boys insist on thinking. If they were, we'd know more about them down here." He ran his fingers through his hair, smoothing it, then went on. "No, I'd say Mexicans or Colombians. They're better equipped than most of the armies on this continent." His prattle continued, and gradually proved that his real purpose was little different than what Woodsen's had been—he was pumping the agent from Washington for information on why he was in Nigeria. But there were several differences in the styles of the two men as well as similarities. First, Wright was far more subtle and skillful at what he was doing than his subordinate had been. And along with trying to get a read on Bolan, he was also very delicately attempting to take the Washington man's mind off the Ivory Coast cartel and put it onto the South Americans.

"Well," Wright finally said as he appeared to run out of air, "we'll find out who the hell is behind this. Sooner or later, we'll find out. I've got my men working on it. When we do, we'll notify you guys and bring in the fuckin' U.S. Marine Corps if we have to."

As the Land Rover neared the spot ahead where the plane had gone down, the Executioner looked out the window to his side. Earlier, he had noticed other tire tracks in the soft earth over which they were traveling. That only made sense—the Nigerian rescue teams and the DEA agents already on the scene would have followed the same path. But now, farther away, he saw two sets of tire tracks that had sunk much deeper into the ground. One set looked as if it led toward the same spot they were heading. The other set of tracks appeared to have been made by the same vehicle—some type of multiple-wheel heavy-duty truck—but they led *away* from the crash site.

Bolan frowned. He knew they weren't the first to visit the scene since the crash. The Nigerian rescue team had finally found the site after being given faulty coordinates by the pilot.

And DEA men were now on the scene. But the agents would have come in their all-terrain vehicles, like the one he was in now. And he suspected that the Nigerians would have used military-style jeeps, or similar vehicles.

Why would a heavy, cumbersome transport truck come to the crash site? To haul away the wreckage? Sure. But not yet. Not until the investigation at the scene had been completed, and that hadn't been done. So why was he seeing fresh tracks through the soft earth that indicated that a truck had already come and gone?

Bolan glanced up at the rearview mirror. From where sat, he could just see the corner of Wright's face. While the Executioner had immediately liked Woodsen, he had immediately taken the opposite view of the local special agent in charge. There were two possible reasons for this instinctive reaction. It could be that Wright was an honest agent, and simply a loudmouthed blowhard braggart. Every agency had their share of such men. The other possibility was that there was something more sinister behind Wright's questions, and the fact that the Executioner simply didn't like him.

There was one other thing bothering the soldier about the SAC. His name. Bolan didn't know when, or where, but he had heard it before. Wright, he knew, was almost as common as Smith or Jones. And Norris—while it might not be like Joe or John—was certainly not unheard-of as a first name. Norris Wright. Where had he heard that name before?

Ahead, a number of other four-wheel-drive vehicles appeared. They had been parked near where the plane had skidded across the clearing before entering the jungle again on the other side. Woodsen pulled to a halt between two vehicles and twisted the key, killing the engine.

Forty yards or so inside the jungle, the soldier could see men still working to clear the trash away from the aircraft. His guess was they planned to pull the wrecked aircraft into the clearing with a tow truck, then load it onto a transport vehicle to take into Lagos. A preliminary team of crash investigators was probably already been on the scene. But there was a limit as to what they could do there in the jungle. And eventually, every square inch of the airplane would be thoroughly gone over to determine what had caused the malfunction.

Bolan, Wright and Woodsen got out of the Land Rover. The Executioner let his eyes skirt quickly across the ground. Partially hidden by the other parked vehicles, but still clearly visible between them, the deeper tire tracks he had seen earlier were more obvious now. It looked as if the heavy truck had been there earlier before making its return trip through the clearing. Around the site, the Executioner could also see the footprints of many men who had approached the truck while parked. In addition to them, the more slender furrows made by small wheels were visible. What were they? Wheelbarrows? Maybe. Or loading dollies?

"Should have dressed a little differently today, Ken," Wright said, as he led the way into the jungle. The soldier glanced at Wright's suit. He didn't know if the man meant himself, Bolan, or both of them.

Bolan walked carefully, as if overly concerned that he might dirty or scratch his tasseled loafers. He carried a clipboard and gold fountain pen he had taken from the briefcase he'd left in the SUV. They reached the plane, and Wright stopped to shake hands with a tall middle-aged man with reddish brown hair and a light sprinkling of freckles across his face. "Ken Clarke," he said, "Meet Ryan Charles, U.S. Federal Aviation Administration. Ryan had to come all the way over from Marrakech to check this out for us."

Charles extended his hand, which was muddy from helping clear the downed foliage off the plane. He noticed the mud a second before Bolan lifted his own hand to take it, laughed and wiped it on the already dirt-caked T-shirt he wore beneath a light nylon safari-type vest. "Good to meet you, Clarke," he said. "But maybe we better skip the handshake. You look like you just took a shower, and you never know when another one's coming when you're in the jungle."

Bolan chuckled politely and nodded. "Has the pilot been evacuated yet?" he asked.

Charles looked at him quizzically. "Well, no...."

"Good," Bolan said. "I'd like to talk to him. I need to check whatever paperwork he has on the eradication chemicals he was flying. Get the cost for my report."

Charles's expression had changed to one of understanding. "It sounds like you haven't gotten the whole story, Clarke," he said.

Bolan frowned.

"The pilot is dead."

The Executioner turned to Wright with a questioning look. But Wright looked as surprised as he did. Maybe even more so.

"Wait a minute, Ryan," Wright said. "The pilot radioed in after he made it to the ground. He said he was injured but—"

"Evidently he was injured worse than he thought," Ryan said. "He was dead by the time we got here." He paused, then said, "Come on. I'll show you."

He glanced at Bolan. "I should warn you, though. It's not for the faint at heart." Turning his back on the two men, he led the way along the side of the aircraft to the cockpit.

The door to the plane had been left open, and Bolan could clearly see the pilot still sitting behind the controls. His eyes were wide open, with a look of horror frozen for all eternity on his face. Two abrasions were visible on his face. The smaller of the two was just over one eye, and looked much like the cut along the eyebrow a prizefighter might sustain from his opponent. It wasn't deep enough to kill him—knock him out, maybe, but not bring on death.

The second blow was what had ended his life. Deep and wide, the wound was centered between the man's eyes. The skin around it had been violently broken and curled back away from the wound. Blood had soaked these peelings, then dried to leave them stiff and flaky. Through the middle of the wound, the Executioner could see white fragments of shattered skull.

Bolan glanced to the control panel in front of the man. There were any number of things the dead pilot's head could have struck that might have made the shallow wound above his eye. But the blow that had killed him was deep. And far more pointed. The Executioner saw nothing in front of the seat that looked as if it could have penetrated the skull in that way.

The soldier didn't know what had caused the second wound, but it hadn't come during the crash.

"Poor bastard," Wright said. "Must have radioed in, then died before anybody could reach him." His thoughts had been directed at both Bolan and Charles, but now he reached out and took Charles by the arm. "Who got here first?" he asked.

"The Nigerians," Charles said. "They radioed us. It took them a while to find him. Seems like the coordinates the man gave were off."

Wright snorted. "Heard about that part already. With head injuries like that, I'm not surprised." He shook his head sadly, then said, "But it's too late to worry about him now. Did you find the paperwork on the chemicals? Like he said, Special Agent Clarke here is going to need it for his report."

Charles nodded. "Got the paperwork all right. But it won't need to be entered into the damage report. We recovered all the chemicals. No damage to the containers."

Bolan glanced at the wreckage of the plane. The crop killers arriving safely through the carnage the aircraft had experienced—which they were claiming also killed the pilot—seemed somewhat unlikely but hardly impossible. He'd seen far stranger things during his lifetime. Through the trashed doorway to the cargo area, he could see the black fifty-five-gallon drums still neatly stacked on the floor and secured with canvas straps.

As he glanced into the cargo area, something else caught his eye, on the fuselage to the doorway. Large brown spots.

And they didn't match the mud splattered along the rest of the plane. He instinctively started to move closer, then stopped. If he showed too much interest in anything that didn't directly apply to the financial losses of this fiasco, he risked blowing his cover. But what he had seen bore further inspection. Later.

Because what he saw looked very much like dried blood.

"Is any of the aircraft going to be salvageable?" Bolan asked.

"I doubt it," Charles said. "We'll haul it into town. Go over it with a fine-tooth comb to find out what happened. But I'm afraid you'll probably have to write the plane off as a total loss."

He glanced at Wright. "Norris, do you know a place we can rent to store it temporarily until we can check it out?"

Wright shook his head. "No, but I can find one for you. Let me handle it. I'll get on it as soon as I get back."

"Thanks. Sorry, but you'll have to leave the chemicals where they are until we get done."

Wright shrugged. "A few more days won't make any difference," he said.

"I'd like to take a look at that cargo if you don't mind," Bolan said. "I need to ascertain for certainty that the chemicals are undamaged."

Charles nodded toward the open doorway. "Be my guest," he said.

Bolan climbed into the cargo area with a feigned awkwardness that befit the image he was trying to maintain. He set his clipboard and pen on top of one of the drums and began looking at the markings on the lids. Behind him, he heard Wright and Charles climb into the plane.

After inspecting the labels on several of the huge black containers, Bolan said, "Perhaps we'd better open them to make sure." He got the reaction he knew he'd get.

"Not with me here," Wright said.

"Or me, either," added Charles. He frowned at the Executioner. "Don't you know what's in those things?" he asked.

"Eradication sprays."

"The chemicals aren't in spray form yet," Wright said. "That's a concentrate inside there. It hasn't been mixed. One whiff of that stuff and you'll look worse than the pilot."

Charles was more patient and understanding with the office boy from Washington. "I don't think Ken fully understands what we're dealing with here," he told Wright. "You mix this stuff with water before you spray it on poppy and coca fields. Or marijuana. It kills the plants. But it doesn't really know the difference between plants and animals sometimes, and even after it's diluted you have to wear protective gear around it. In this concentrated form..." He let his voice trail off. "Well, I think you get the picture."

Wright patted Bolan on the shoulder as if he and Charles were dealing with a slow-learning child. "Even breathing in the vapors could kill us all, Ken," he said.

The Executioner feigned embarrassment at his own ignorance once more.

"Need to see anything else?" Charles asked.

Bolan shook his head. "No, I guess not. In fact, I'd probably better be getting back to town and find a room for the night. I've got a long evening of report writing ahead, and I'd like to get started." He stepped carefully down out of the cargo area, again looking as if he might be afraid to get his shoes dirty. Then, off-handedly, he said, "When do you suppose you'll have the plane out of the jungle and into Lagos?"

"Before the day is out," Charles said. "We've got a transport truck on the way now."

The Executioner nodded and looked at Wright. "You ready, or do you need to stay?" he asked. His voice made it clear he had experienced more of the rugged jungle than he, or any other bureaucrat more comfortable behind a desk, could ever want.

"No, I'm ready," Wright said. He turned to Woodsen, who had followed his boss around like a silent puppy dog since they'd arrived. "Dirk, why don't you stay here and see what you can do to help out?" the DEA supervisor said. "I'll drive Ken back to town, and you can catch a lift in one of the other vehicles."

"Yes sir," Woodsen said. He moved quickly away.

Bolan led the way back toward the Land Rover, again portraying a man who couldn't wait to get back into an environment he better understood. He still needed the answer to two questions, and he needed them without alerting Wright to the fact that he was even interested. First, while he already knew in his heart what the dried brown spots were, he wanted to inspect them closer to make sure. His first thought had been to return to the scene that night. But now it looked as if the plane would be gone by then. He'd have to find out where Wright planned to store it, then infiltrate the new site later.

The plane was going to be taken back into Lagos by truck, and that linked him to the second question. Why had another truck already been there? What had it done, and why hadn't anyone mentioned it? And what did the smaller wheel tracks around the parked vehicles—the ones that looked as if they'd been made by wheelbarrows—mean? Again, he had first thought to return clandestinely that night for a closer inspection. A vehicle large enough to load and transport the plane would most certainly by large enough to completely obliterate the tracks.

Bolan stepped out of the jungle into the clearing. He'd have a second shot at the blood on the plane when he found it where it was stored. But if he was going to learn anything more about the mysterious tire tracks leading to and from the crash site, it would have to be now. Exactly how to get that done suddenly hit him, and the facade he had built up as the incompetent city agent was the key.

Bolan started toward Wright's Land Rover, his eyes skirting across the ground for a place where the deeper treads were visible along his path. He saw the spot he wanted just in front of a black Ford Bronco, and angled slightly toward it. When he was two steps away from the where the deep tire track emerged from under the Bronco, he turned as if to speak to Wright but kept walking.

"Do you suppose you could help me find me a hotel roo—" the Executioner said, as he felt his foot hit the depression in the ground.

He hit the ground on his right side, the clipboard and pen flying out of his hands and into the air.

Bolan rolled to his back with a low moan. He came up in a sitting position, reached down with both hands and grasped his ankle.

Wright hurried forward and squatted in front of him. "You okay?" he asked.

"I think I've sprained my ankle."

Wright stared down at the Executioner's foot. "Can you move it?" he asked.

"I don't know. Give me a second to catch my breath."

Bolan took several deep breaths, then moved his foot timidly up and down. The movement was accompanied by another false moan of pain from his lips.

"Let me see," Wright said. He grabbed the soldier's foot with one hand and moved it gently back and forth. Bolan groaned again.

"Well, at least it's not broken," Wright said. "You're probably right. Sprained." He stood and extended a hand to help Bolan to his feet.

The Executioner took the DEA man's hand and pulled himself upward. With all his weight on one leg, he looked down at the ground. "What did I trip on?" he asked. When Wright simply shrugged, the Executioner looked down at the ground again. "That ditch. Wait. That's a tire track."

Wright shrugged again. "Let me help you to the car," he said.

Bolan didn't take the offered arm. "That track," he said. "Why is it so much deeper than the rest?" He continued to stare at the ground but watched Wright out of the top of his eye.

The SAC hesitated. Then his face told Bolan he had decided a quick cover story was needed. "I guess those tracks are from the truck, Ken," he said.

Bolan looked up inquisitively. "Truck?"

"The transport truck," Wright said quickly. His face was blank. But something in his eyes told the Executioner he was making up this story as he went. "I sent a truckload of agents out to secure the scene as soon as we heard about the crash."

Bolan continued his puzzled expression. "Where are they now?" he asked.

Wright smiled. "That was yesterday, Ken," he said patiently. "They've gone back since the rest of these guys relieved them." He waved a hand toward the jungle. "You don't expect anyone to work twenty-four hours a day, do you?" he added with a slick chuckle. "But that's not the important thing, now. We need to get you into town and get some ice on that ankle."

This time, when the DEA man stuck out his arm, Bolan took it. He limped along beside the man the rest of the way to their vehicle.

Wright opened the passenger's door for him and helped him up and into the dark blue Land Rover. The SAC circled the vehicle and got in behind the wheel. "Let's get back and find you a room." he said. "That was what you were asking me about right before you took your fall, wasn't it?"

The Executioner nodded.

Wright stuck the keys into the ignition and the Land Rover's engine sparked to life. He backed away from the jungle, twisted the steering wheel and started along the clearing in the direction from which they'd come.

Bolan grimaced in more fake pain as he settled onto the seat. He wanted Wright to think his mind had now moved far away from the truck tire tracks now. He'd have to keep up the injury act until Wright was gone. But that wouldn't be hard. And he had found out at least two of the things he had needed to know.

First, there *had* been a truck at the site earlier. Why it had been there remained to be discovered because the story about hauling out DEA agents to secure the scene simply didn't hold water.

The second thing Bolan was now sure of was that his instinctive dislike of Norris Wright wasn't simply due to the man being a loud boisterous braggart.

Norris Wright was also a liar.

3

The Bristol Hotel, near Tinubu Square, was located on Martins Street at the west end of Lagos Island. Once a respectable inn, it had gone down considerably over time. Wright helped the limping Bolan into the lobby and up to the desk to check in. A bellhop wearing a worn-out jacket with frazzled cuffs accompanied them up the steps to the second floor, carrying the Executioner's bags. He opened the door, and Wright lowered Bolan to a sitting position on the bed, then turned to the bellhop and handed him a generous tip.

"Get this man some ice for his ankle," he said.

The bellhop's eyes widened when he saw how much money was in his hand. "Yes sir!" he said, and hurried out of the room.

Wright turned back to Bolan. "I can't tell you how sorry I am this happened," he said, looking down at the soldier's ankle.

Bolan simply nodded, as if the events of the day had been too much for him.

"Is there anything I can get you?" Wright asked.

Still playing the part of Kenneth Clarke, the Executioner shook his head, then lay back on the bed and closed his eyes.

Wright took that as his cue to leave. "Then I'd better get back to the office," he said. "It's going to be busy as hell around there for the next few days. You've got the number. Call me if you need anything."

His eyes still closed, Bolan nodded.

The local DEA man was no sooner out the door than the Executioner sprang to his feet. He glanced at his watch. It would be dark in a few hours, and he had work to do before then. The room was swelteringly hot, and he took off his jacket and dropped it on the bed. He moved quickly to the air-conditioner unit beneath the window. It was broken, so he raised the glass above it to allow what little breeze was available into the room.

A quick check around the room proved that little else functioned the way it was supposed to, either. The television clicked on but showed a blank black screen. The telephone was dead when he held it to his ear. And when it came to cleaning, the maids appeared to have taken the last week—or decade—off. The carpet looked as if it hadn't been vacuumed in months.

The Executioner doffed his shoulder rig and shirt, took a seat on the bed and pulled the cellular phone out of his jacket. After quickly checking the scrambler—a task he had done so many times it was now as natural as breathing—he tapped in the number to Stony Man Farm.

Barbara Price, the mission controller, eventually took the call. "Hello, Striker."

"Hi, Barbara. Patch me into the Bear, will you?"

A moment later, Stony Man Farm's computer genius was on the line. "What's up, big guy?" he asked.

Bolan pictured the burly paraplegic seated in his wheelchair in front of the long row of monitors, keyboards and hard drives. "I need you to check on somebody," he said.

"Just give me the name."

"Norris Wright," Bolan said. "The DEA SAC at the Lagos office."

"Hang on a second," Kurtzman said.

Less than thirty seconds had elapsed when the man was back on the line. "Okay," he said. "Tapped into the DEA personnel files. What do you want to know?"

"First of all, he's for real?" Although it was unlikely, it wouldn't have been the first time the Executioner had come upon a situation in which a savvy criminal had impersonated a legitimate law-enforcement officer and gone to the trouble of setting up enough trappings to pull it off right under the noses of the real authorities.

"Yeah, he's for real. At least the DEA thinks so."

"Then what else can you tell me about him?"

"Well..." Kurtzman said. "Let's see. Been with the administration about eight years. Started off in the New York office, then worked the Mexican border, out of El Paso. On loan to the Border Patrol down there for eighteen months." The computer man hesitated, then continued. "Did a stint in South America. Promoted to SAC two years ago and sent to Africa." Kurtzman's voice stopped again, then said, "Anything else?"

"Anything suspicious?" Bolan asked.

"Let me check for letters in his file." Another ten seconds went by, then Kurtzman said, "Nothing but good stuff. Unless you want to count a couple of citizen complaints, which are to be expected."

Bolan nodded. There was even an old police adage on the subject: Any cop who didn't get a complaint once in a while wasn't doing his job. The Executioner raised his free hand to his head and rubbed it. Norris Wright. The name rang a bell someplace. But he still couldn't remember where. Maybe Kurtzman could. "Bear," he said into the phone, "you ever hear that name before?"

"Norris Wright? Not that I can remember."

"I have. I just can't place it." Bolan continued to massage his temple. "You said Wright's been with DEA for eight years. That's not all that long. And it's fast for the promotions he's had."

"Yes, it is," Kurtzman said. "Maybe he was one of those little golden boys. Or had connections inside the political arena."

"Yeah, but he's in his late thirties."

"Thirty-seven, to be exact," Kurtzman said.

"That means he didn't start work with the DEA until he was thirty-one. What was he doing before that?"

"Let me check." A second later, Kurtzman said, "Well, it's marked classified."

"How long will it take you to break in?" Bolan asked.

"Already did."

There was simply no one better in the world with computers than Kurtzman. Had he taken another track in life, and become a computer hacker by profession, he'd have been a multimillionaire who probably never spent a day in jail. "So what else have you found?"

"Hang on a second," the computer genius said. A few seconds drifted by, then Bolan heard, "Well, well, well. Our little friend did indeed have another job before DEA. He was Company."

Bolan stopped rubbing his head. CIA. He should have known. "Does it give any reason for why he transferred?"

"Give me another second."

Bolan waited, listening to Kurtzman's fingers tap the keyboard on the other end of the line. When he came back, he said, "Nothing. But you want my two-cents'-worth guess on the matter?"

"Sure."

Kurtzman cleared his throat. "From what I see in front of me here, it looks like Wright pretty much worked all over the world when he was with the CIA. And according to the files, a good portion of that time he he as assigned as a liaison to DEA. So he got used to working dope, and he'd have developed connections inside the DEA. Off the top of my head—and don't take this as the gospel, remember—I'd surmise that what he saw as a faster track up the pay scale ladder opened up with the Administration. Quicker career promotions, and therefore more money, than he saw available with the spooks." Kurtzman cleared his throat again. "Situations like that aren't all that uncommon. Especially when they can swing a lateral transfer—keep the same G-rating and pay scale instead of starting over at the bottom again."

The Executioner was silent for a few seconds. Everything looked to be on the up-and-up as far as Wright being who he said he was. But that wasn't surprising—Bolan had expected that to be the case. The problem was that he knew Wright had lied to him about the truck tracks. He just didn't know why. Even more important than that, the Executioner's instincts told him that there was something was wrong with Wright. And those instincts had been honed over the years to a razor's edge, and rarely failed him in the past.

When Bolan didn't say anything, Kurtzman came back with, "You need anything else from me, Striker?"

"How busy are you?"

"Well, I'm not sitting here playing computer solitaire, if that's what you're asking." Kurtzman didn't give Bolan a chance to respond before adding, "Just trying to work out a pattern for a serial killer operating in California and Oregon. Nothing I can't put aside for a little while if you need something."

"Run the name Norris Wright then, Bear," Bolan said.

"In what respect?"

"I don't know. Every respect, I guess. I just can't get it out of my system that I've heard it before and there's something more to it than I realize."

"That could take a while."

"Guess you better get started then, huh?"

Kurtzman laughed out loud. "Aye, aye, Captain," he said. "You're lucky I'm in this chair or I'd kick your ass for trying to order me around like that."

"Thanks, Bear. I appreciate it."

"Over and out, Captain," Kurtzman said, then hung up.

Bolan glanced at his watch once more. He needed to find out where the downed Antonov was being taken, and like all of the rest of the information he's needed since landing in Lagos, he needed to do it without playing his hand and tipping Wright off that he was interested in more than how much the downed planes were costing the DEA. He picked up his phone again and dialed the number to Wright's office.

A female voice with a local accent answered.

"This is Special Agent Clarke," he said. "I need to speak with SAC Wright."

"I'm sorry, Agent Clarke," the woman said. "But Agent in Charge Wright is out of the office right now."

Bolan nodded to himself. That was good. Chances were he could get what he needed from this secretary. And if he questioned her subtly enough, she might not even think enough of it to remember to even mention it to Wright later. "I'm the agent they sent down from Washington," the soldier said. "The one doing the financial investigation concerning the downed aircraft?"

"Yes, Agent Clarke," the woman said. "I know who you are. How is your ankle?"

The question threw the Executioner off guard for a moment. She not only knew who he was, she knew he'd sprained his ankle. That meant Wright had either returned to the office or at least called in. And a sprained ankle didn't seem like something he'd bring up in a quick phone call.

What that meant was that there was every likelihood that Wright was in the office that very second, and had simply given his secretary instructions to tell Bolan he was out. If that was the case, there was also every likelihood that the man was listening to their conversation right now.

"It's painful but I'll live," Bolan said. "One of the bellhops found me an ice pack."

"I'm so very glad to hear it," came the voice on the other end of the line.

"Since I'm temporarily immobile, I'm trying to get my reports started. And I need to know where the wreckage from the airplane is being taken. Do you happen to know?"

The secretary hesitated, and Bolan could have sworn he heard some kind of scratching sound on the other end of the line. A few seconds later, the woman said, "There's a warehouse at the east end of the island. Not far from the racetrack. Do you need the address?"

"Yes, please," Bolan said. "I'm in no condition to go out there myself, but the big wigs in Washington are sticklers for such things."

"It's on Strachan Street, which is just off Tafawa Balewa Square." She gave him a street number, then said, "Do you know how to find it?"

He had already told the woman he had no plans to go to the site, so she had clearly asked the question in the hopes of tripping him up if he'd been lying. And Bolan's guess was that Norris Wright had just prompted her to ask.

Bolan decided that a low-key response would be best. "No, I don't know how to find it," he said. "But I'm in no shape to go anywhere and wouldn't really need to see the site even if I was. I just need to be able to include the address in my report."

"All right. May I help you with anything else, Agent Clarke?"

"Not right now," Bolan said. "But I thank you, and I'll call you again if I need to."

"Please feel free to do so. Good day, Agent Clarke."

Bolan hung up, set the phone on the bed and leaned back in thought. He couldn't be sure, but he was ninety-nine-percent positive that Wright had been standing next to the woman, cuing her in on what to say and what questions to ask. He obviously wanted to know if Bolan was going out to check on the plane himself. Which meant either the Executioner's act of being nothing more than the mild-mannered bean counter hadn't entirely fooled Wright, or the man was simply borderline paranoid and double-checking every angle. But either way, it also confirmed Bolan's suspicions that Wright was hiding something.

The Executioner stood and removed the rest of his clothes. He walked into the bathroom, where he found a tub but no shower. The water worked, at least. But there was no stopper. So he was forced to take a strange combination shower-bath, twisting his body parts beneath the nozzle in a manner which would have challenged the most talented circus contortionist. He had finally completed the ordeal and was drying off when he heard the knock on the door. He immediately remembered the bellhop Wright had sent after ice for his ankle, and reminded himself to limp as soon as he'd opened the door.

Wrapping the towel around his waist, Bolan stepped out of the bathroom and twisted the door knob. But the man standing in there in the hall wasn't the bellhop who had carried his bags up the stairs and then been sent for ice. In fact, he wasn't a bellhop at all. This man was tall and broad with a blond beard and hair. And what he held in his hand was hardly an ice pack.

It was a cocked Colt 1911 Government Model .45 pistol.

NORRIS WRIGHT KNEW something was wrong but not exactly what it was. Only that it had to do with Special Agent Kenneth Clarke. The man might act like a doofus, but something told the SAC it was just that—an act.

Wright entered the outer office where the beautiful black secretary-receptionist sat. She was Yoruba by birth, and had come from the western part of Nigeria. The DEA man had given up trying to pronounce her name shortly after hiring her. It sounded somewhat like the Swahili name Mwanajuma—which he could pronounce—and they had settled on that as her appellation. Over the months she had been there, though, even the name had been shortened further for convenience.

"Juma," Wright said, stopping at her desk. "I suspect there'll be an agent calling here in a little while. Kenneth Clarke."

"The one from Washington?" Juma asked.

"Yes," Wright agreed. "Buzz me before you answer." He looked down at her desk. "You have a notepad handy?"

Juma reached into a drawer and pulled out a new yellow legal pad and a ballpoint pen. She set them on the desk.

"When he calls, put him on speakerphone so I can hear what he says, too. Tell him I'm out of the office. He'll ask you questions, and if there's a specific answer I want you to give him, I'll write it down. But act like the answers are your own. Got it?"

Juma nodded. "I take it you do not trust him?" she asked.

Wright smiled at the woman. She would need an answer that satisfied her curiosity without leading her to think too deeply. "I don't trust anybody who comes from the home office in Washington, Juma," he said. "They're all a bunch of upwardly mobile snakes who'll do anything to further their own careers. They don't care who they step on as they climb the ladder, and they aren't above twisting facts or just outright lying if serves their own purposes."

"I will be careful in what I tell him," she said.

Wright smiled again, then opened the door to his own office and entered, taking a seat behind the desk.

Wright picked up a pencil and began drumming it against the desk top, his thoughts returning to Clarke. What exactly was it about the man that didn't add up to the wimp he was trying to make himself out to be? Was it the way he carried himself—agile, as if he were some jungle cat ready to spring at a moment's notice? That could have come from tennis, or squash, he supposed. Or any other number of games the pansy-asses back in Washington, who were into health and diet, used to stay in shape. Was it the man's size? No, there were plenty of big sissies in the world. Size didn't always equate with manliness. How about Clarke's build? Even under the suit he had worn it had been apparent that the man had massive shoulders, a thin waist, and well-developed muscles. He supposed Clarke's physique could have come from some Nautilus machine in a Georgetown health spa—a lot of the home office boys were into that these days, too, as well as what they called executive boxing where they trained like real prize fighters in a boxing gym, and periodically pretended to fight each other with gloves so large that an injury was all but impossible.

Wright leaned back in his chair, put his feet up on the desk and tapped a pencil against the side of his cheek. There was a logical explanation for every single aspect that at first appeared to be a contradiction within Special Agent Kenneth Clarke. When he put them all together, however, the cumulative sum seemed to stretch credibility. But the icing on the cake was the scars.

The DEA man dropped the pencil onto his desk. Although Clarke had been wearing a suit, Wright had noticed what looked like an old knife scar on his wrist when he'd reached for one of the fifty-five-gallon drums on board the plane. And when he'd taken his fall, spraining his ankle, his pant leg had risen. Wright had gotten a brief view of what looked suspiciously like an old bullet wound just above the man's sock.

The DEA man squeezed his chin between his thumb and index finger. A person didn't get knife and bullet wounds sitting behind a desk in Washington, D.C. Or playing squash, or working out at a health club, or dancing around a boxing ring.

Wright was in the middle of his reverie when he heard the intercom buzzer sound on his desk phone. He glanced down at the blinking red light, pulled his shoes off the desk and jumped to his feet. Two seconds later he had transversed the short hallway between his office and Juma's reception area, and saw the woman with her finger on the button, ready to answer the call.

Wright nodded.

A moment later, Kenneth Clarke asked to speak to him.

"I'm sorry, he's out of the office right now," Juma said into the speakerphone.

Wright picked up the ballpoint pen, twisted the legal pad to an angle where he could both write and Juma could read, and waited.

There was some small talk about Clarke's sprained ankle, then he got to the point of the call. "I need to know where the wreckage from the airplane is being taken," he said. "Do you happen to know?"

Juma glanced up at him, and Wright hesitated. To refuse to tell him, or give him a bad location, or even stall, would add to any suspicion the man might already have. Besides, he could use Clarke's knowledge of the storage site to further his own attempt to learn the truth about the man.

Give it to him, Wright quickly scratched on the legal pad.

"There's a warehouse on the east end of the island," Juma spoke into the phone. "Not far from the racetrack. Do you need the address?"

"Yes, please," came over the speakerphone. "I'm in no condition to go there myself, but the big wigs in Washington are sticklers for such things."

While Juma gave him the address, Wright scribbled, *Ask him if he needs directions to the warehouse.*

"Do you know how to find it?" Juma asked.

"No, but I don't know how to find it," Bolan said. "He explained that he wouldn't be visiting the site himself. He just need the address for his report. He and Juma exchanged a few more mindless pleasantries, then the call ended.

"Good job," Wright said, as soon as she'd hung up.

Juma smiled.

Wright reentered his office and put his feet back up on the desk. He still didn't know exactly what to think about Clarke, or the real reason he had been sent to Lagos. But Wright's operations were getting too big to take chances. He lifted the pencil from the desktop again and held it to his lips. No, it would be far safer to make sure. Clarke needed to be out of the picture, once and for all. And he knew just the way to accomplish that—quick and easy. Lagos was famous for hotel robberies, and other street crime. What he had might still draw some suspicion from Washington, but it was a chance he would have to take.

Besides, by the time the rest of the DEA clowns put everything together, he'd have disappeared into thin air. Norris Wright would be nothing but a memory within the Drug Enforcement Administration. He'd have become the big one that got away.

Dropping his feet to the floor again, Wright lifted the telephone receiver and punched in a number.

A voice with a South African accent answered on the second ring. "Yes?"

"Van der Kirk," the DEA SAC said into the receiver, "get some of the men together. I've got a couple of jobs for you."

THE EXECUTIONER SAW two things at once.

The first was that while the .45 pistol was cocked, it was no longer locked. The thumb safety was down, and the weapon was ready to fire.

The second thing he saw was the man's knuckles turning white as his fist began to squeeze down around the pistol grip. And when that happened, the trigger would fall.

Bolan reached up instinctively, his right hand moving across his body to grasp the barrel of the weapon as his left came from the other direction, slapping into the wrist behind the gun. His thumb fell between the hammer and the firing pin a split second before the hammer fell to bit into his flesh.

The X-pattern formed by his hands bent the bearded man's wrist at an awkward angle, weakening his grip, and allowed the Executioner to rip the gun from his grasp. The trigger guard caught on the man's index finger and a loud snapping sound echoed sickeningly into the room as the bone broke. A loud scream of pain followed.

The Executioner jerked the weapon free with both hands, then pulled his left thumb from under the hammer. The movement tore his skin and left behind a trail of blood. The hammer fell forward against the slide but lacked the force to ignite the primer in the chambered round. Still holding the weapon by the barrel, Bolan drew it back over his shoulder and started to swing the butt at the man's face.

But the blonde had recovered from the shock of his broken finger quickly, and his other hand shot forward in a short jab. The blow was aimed at Bolan's nose. He had just enough time to move an inch, and it took him on the cheek.

The soldier's head rocked back. The man with the blond beard took advantage of the opening, and his good hand lunged for the .45 again. His finger found the grip, and he jerked back with all his strength.

But by now Bolan was ready. He held on, letting the bearded man's own strength pull him forward with the gun. At the last second, he bent his elbow and drove it into the hardman's face. A muffled grunt issued forth from the lips buried beneath the Executioner's forearm.

Still hanging on to the barrel, Bolan brought his left hand up in a short, chopping uppercut that caught the blonde squarely beneath the chin. His head rose with the force but he seemed to have an iron jaw, and his grip on the stock of the Government Model remained firm. With the roar of a bull, he brought his face back down, aiming a head strike at the bridge of the Executioner's nose.

Had it struck home, Bolan would have suffered a broken nose and likely have lost consciousness. But the soldier's reflexes had been whetted to perfection over the years, and he shifted to the side. By the time the other man's head struck the top of his shoulder, the blow had lost most of its force. Another roar—this time of anger and frustration rather than pain—shot from the attacker's mouth. His injured hand crossed his body, groping beneath the OD photojournalist's vest he wore over a white T-shirt.

But Bolan's dodge of the head strike had spun both men in the doorway, off balance. The attacker jerked his hand beneath his vest and waved it wildly in the air. The Executioner's back smashed into the door frame, and the tug of war for the pistol continued. For a second, the bearded man forgot about his broken finger and sent another punch at Bolan's head. The Executioner bobbed down and to the side, and the unknown attacker's fist hit the doorjamb behind him with a loud thump. The gunner howled in anguish as the broken finger was suddenly remembered.

Bolan rammed a knee into the man's groin, and yet another scream of misery issued forth from his open mouth. But the man still held on to the grip of the pistol as if rigor mortis had set into his hand.

Grabbing a handful of the blond hair, the Executioner twisted the man's neck down toward the gun, at the same time pulling the weapon toward the floor. The force of the sudden direction change caught the gunman flatfooted, and acted much like a judo takedown. Except that it took both men to the mat, for neither could afford to lose his grip on the pistol.

Both men continued to hold on to their end of the gun as if their lives depended on it. Which they did.

The bearded man hit the ground on his back. Bolan came down on top of him. But the attacker had obviously had some training in grappling, and shifted his weight the moment his shoulder blades struck the floor. Bolan was thrown off the man's chest. Now, both men faced each other once more, this time on their sides, both still struggling to gain control of the big Colt .45.

The bearded man's injured hand shot across his belly, again trying to reach whatever it was he had beneath the vest. Bolan didn't know what it was. A weapon of some sort? And if he

was successful at reaching it, it would likely tip the balance
of the fight in his favor.

And end the career of the man known as the Executioner.

Before the bearded man could get his hand under the vest,
Bolan worked his legs up under him, then drove forward on
top of the man again. The towel around the Executioner's
waist came untied, and was left behind on the floor as the two
figures began to roll over and over, first with one on top, then
the other. The whirling seesaw didn't stop until Bolan's back
hit the wall of the hotel room.

The blonde's face was now an inch from the Executioner's,
and his fetid breath was almost enough to end the fight right
there. Bolan felt the fingers of the man's injured hand wrap
around his throat. But there was no strength in the broken finger, and the Executioner brought his chin down hard against
the back of the man's hand. At least one of the fragile bones
located cracked, and the beared man screeched in new pain,
loosening his grip. Bolan kept the injured hand trapped between his chin and chest, and continued the downward pressure. More bones snapped like dried twigs.

The unknown attacker finally got his hand away. Again,
they rolled over each other on the floor, retracing the path
across which they had pitched only seconds before. They
came to a halt at almost the same spot where they'd started
with Bolan on the bottom and the big gunner on top.

Bolan still held the Colt's barrel in his iron grasp. The other
man held the stock. The barrel was jammed into the Executioner's ribs, directly over his heart, and at the awkward angle
at which he lay, he couldn't use his other hand to sweep it away.

The bearded man's face twisted into an almost unworldly
grimace of evil as the index finger of his good hand worked
itself into the trigger guard. Bolan felt him pull back on the
trigger with all his strength, apparently unaware that the hammer was still uncocked. But that wouldn't last long. He'd figure it out soon enough.

The Executioner extended his arm to the side in another attempt to strike the weapon hard enough to get it away from his chest. But as he did, the back of his hand brushed the crumpled towel on the floor. Changing tactics, he extended his arm to the side, swept the towel off the dirty carpet and found one of the corners. With a whiplike snap, he flipped up the opposite corner. It struck the blonde in the left eye, and his head snapped backward as if he'd been punched.

But still, he held on to the Colt.

The towel fell back and Bolan flipped it again. This time he let it loop across the back of the man's neck, the end falling to stop halfway between their faces. With a deep breath and a mighty heave, the Executioner drove his back off the ground and extended his arm. His fingers snagged the other end of the towel six inches below the man's throat.

Now the towel encircled the attacker's neck like a collar. And the Executioner began to twist.

Slowly, as the knot tightened, the face of the man began to turn red. His eyes bulged as he realized what was happening. He reached up with his injured hand, clawing ineffectually at the makeshift garrote around his neck. But the broken finger and the cracked bones in the back of his hand had rendered the hand useless. His eyes shot down to his other hand. Using it would mean he had to release his grip on the pistol.

Bolan continued to twist the towel tighter, watching as the attacker's neck began to spasm. His head began to jerk violently back and forth like a horse trying to throw its rider. The man opened his mouth and tried to cough but no air was available, and nothing came out. Again, his ballooning eyes glanced down to the other hand, which still held the grip of the .45 pistol.

He knew he had to make a decision. Fast. Did he want to die by strangulation? Or gunshot? The brain behind the white orbs set in his forehead had already figured out he was screwed either way. Damned if he did. Damned if he didn't.

Bolan twisted harder on the towel and watched it sink into

the soft flesh beneath the blond beard. The man on top of him finally jerked his hand away from the gun and clawed at the material pressing into his carotid arteries. But by then the towel was too tight, and he had lost too much strength and cognizance. Another thirty seconds went by, then the blonde closed his eyes and went limp. He fell forward on top of the Executioner.

Bolan kept the pressure on for another half minute in case the man was faking unconsciousness. Then, satisfied, he released his grip, and shifted his hips beneath him.

The corpse on top of him rolled off to the side.

Bolan lay there, the towel still clutched in one hand, the barrel of the .45-caliber in the other, staring at the ceiling and catching his breath. Then, rising slowly to his feet, he turned the gun around in his hand, drew the slide back to insure a round was chambered, then hurried to the door of his room. A quick glance up and down the hall told him there had been no witnesses to the fight. And the gun had never gone off to alert anyone. No one seemed to hear the screams. He closed the door, locked it and turned back to the body.

The corpse lay sprawled on its back on the dirty carpet. Bolan wrapped the towel around his waist once more, then knelt next to the body. Pulling back the OD vest the man wore, he saw the pancake-style hip holster for the Colt on the man's belt. On the other side of the body—the side that the man had clawed for several times during the encounter—was a black leather sheath. The Executioner flipped the retaining snap and withdrew a Cold Steel Tai Pan dagger. Even in the hotel room's bad lighting, the mirror-polished seven-and-one-half-inch blade gleamed its deadliness.

The Executioner tossed the knife across the room, onto the bed. Quickly, he searched the dead man's pockets. He found a package of condoms and a tin of snuff, but no clues to the man's identity. Tossing them onto the bed next to the knife, he stood.

Bolan didn't know the man's name. Maybe he never would. But he had a damn good idea of who had sent him.

NIGHT HAD FALLEN by the time the Executioner left the Bristol Hotel by the back entrance. He had quickly repacked all his equipment, and now carried it with him in his luggage. He had no time to dispose of the man's body, so he had simply rolled it beneath the bed where it wasn't likely to be discovered for several days. If the cleanliness of the room was any indication as to how often the maids arrived, he doubted anyone would notice anything amiss until the smell of death began to penetrate the walls and disturb the other guests. And considering the already rancid smell of the hotel room, even that might go unnoticed for weeks.

Bolan kept to an alley that paralleled Breadfruit Street, his eyes peeled for either a tail or other would-be assassins. He had to assume that the blonde had been told to report back to Wright after he'd killed Bolan. Since that wasn't going to happen now, there was every chance in the world that the DEA man had already sent someone to find out why.

And finish the job of killing Kenneth Clarke, if it hadn't already been accomplished.

The Executioner emerged from the shadows when he reached Nnamdi Azikiwe Street and flagged down the first cab he saw. "Racetrack," he said in English.

The cabbie had probably heard those words out of American tourists a million times in his career, and he nodded in boredom.

Bolan got into the back and the cab took off at breakneck speed. The driver skidded and squealed the tires through a turn at Tinubu Square onto Bambgose Street and started toward the east end of the island.

The Executioner settled into the seat for the ride. He wore a lightweight jacket and loose-fitting khaki slacks over his blacksuit. Both the Desert Eagle and Beretta rode in their respective rigs beneath the outer cover garments, and were backed up by the Applegate-Fairbairn fighting knife. In addition to the weapons, he carried a set of lock picks and a variety of other equipment.

Just before they reached Campos Square, the cab passed a bus station. Bolan leaned forward, tapping the driver on the shoulder. "I need to make a quick stop on the way," he said.

"Yes?"

"Take me back to the bus station for a moment. And wait. I'll only be a second or two."

The cabbie frowned. "I will have to leave the meter running," he warned.

"No problem," the Executioner said. "Just do it."

When the cabbie slowed but didn't turn, Bolan looked up and saw him squinting into the rearview mirror. It was obvious he was wondering if this was nothing more than a trick to skip out on payment—his passenger might enter the bus terminal, exit through another door and leave the cabdriver high and dry. To alleviate the man's worry, Bolan reached into his pocket and pulled out ten U.S. dollars. He reached over the front seat and dropped the money next to the man driving the cab.

The man made a lightninglike U-turn in the middle of the street. A moment later they pulled up in front of the bus station.

Bolan exited the vehicle with his bags, walking through the waiting room past a variety of poverty-stricken would-be travelers. Much like in America, the buses of Nigeria were the wheels of the poor, with the wealthier residents choosing faster, and more comfortable, means of transportation.

A row of lockers appeared at the rear of the waiting room. Bolan set his bags on the floor, reached into his pocket and pulled out a handful of coins. He dropped the coins into the slot of one of the large lockers at the bottom of the row, stashed his bags, then closed the door and removed the key. He reached beneath his jacket, dropping it into a small pocket in his hidden blacksuit as he returned to the cab.

At Campos Square, the driver angled over to Mission Street. Mission led them the rest of the way to Tafawa Balewa

Square, where the racetrack was located. The cabbie screeched to a halt in front of the main entrance.

Bolan got out, stuck another handful bills through the window and walked to the entrance, his eyes clandestinely watching behind the cab to check again for a tail. He saw nothing to make him suspicious. But just in case, he bought a ticket to the races at the window, passed inside the gate, then left again by a side exit.

When he reached the run-down warehouse, Bolan found the two-story structure dark. He crossed the street and slipped inside the entryway of another, similar structure where he removed both the jacket and the trousers that had covered his blacksuit. Patiently he waited, keeping surveillance on the building across the street for a good fifteen minutes. From his hidden vantage point in the shadowy entryway, he could see two doors leading into the warehouse. He had also spotted a double overhead loading entrance on the side, just off the parking lot, as he approached. The parking area looked as if it extended to the rear of the building. If so, and if another entrance was located there, it would be the least visible place to make his entry.

The Executioner checked the luminous dial on his watch, then took a final glance up and down the deserted street. Nothing. Crossing the street at a jog, Bolan cut around the side of the building into the lot, passing the loading door he had seen earlier. He turned the corner at the back, where the parking lot ended abruptly. An unkempt grassy area stood at the rear of the warehouse, and in the middle of it he saw another door. It was flanked by four windows, two on each side.

The soldier crouched in the shadows for a moment, again taking stock of the situation both in front and behind him. Nothing had changed. The only sound was a dog howling somewhere far in the distance. And like dogs the world over, the hound had soon recruited an entire canine chorus to join in his song.

Bolan stood and moved to the first window. It was painted shut. Entry wouldn't be difficult but it would be almost impossible without leaving telltale signs for anyone who saw the window later. And at this point, he still didn't want Wright or anyone in league with him knowing he was interested enough to break in.

Cupping his hands, Bolan could see only shadows through the dirty glass. He made out the wrecked Antonov in the middle of the large room, as well as several other unidentifiable shapes in what appeared to be the warehouse's only room.

Staying close to the wall, the soldier moved along the outside of the building and examined the other three windows that ran along the back. All were the same. Painted shut. He walked back to the door and glanced down at the knob. It consisted of a simple snap lock—a device anyone with a credit card could penetrate. In addition to the snap, he saw both a dead bolt set in the wood above the knob, and a large brass padlock that had been mounted on steel brackets.

Pulling out an ASP laser-beam flashlight, Bolan stuck it between his teeth and directed the beam down at the door. From another pocket in his blacksuit he pulled the lock pick case, unzipped it and went to work. The snap lock took three seconds. The dead bolt, forty-five. But when he came to the padlock, his first two tries failed to slip the tumblers correctly.

He was about to try a third time when he saw an easier way in. The steel braces had been screwed into the door and frame with simple Phillips head screws. Zipping the picks back into the case, he returned it to his blacksuit and pulled out a Spyderco SpydeWrench multi-tool. A moment later, he had attached the correct bit to the screwdriver shaft on the handy device, and gone to work on the screws. A minute after that, the brace that had been attached to the door frame swung free.

The Executioner pocketed the screws along with the SpydeWrench for replacement when he left. Twisting the doorknob, he entered the warehouse. As he crossed the threshold, it occurred to him that his entry had gone easily. Too easily.

A split second later, he found out why. The beam from the

ASP had just come to rest on the wrecked Antonov when the flashlight suddenly became a bull's-eye target.

The first shot came from the Executioner's left, threatening to burst his eardrums in the narrow confines of the warehouse at the same time it killed him. Black plastic exploded in his hand, and the parts of the ASP that hadn't been destroyed went flying from his fingers. The sting from a thousand bees shot from his hand up his arm. He hit the ground as the second shot flew over his head, this one coming from the other side of the huge room.

Two shots. From different directions. Two gunmen.

At least two.

The Beretta had found its way into his hand before he'd hit the ground, and now Bolan rolled to his side as he thumbed the selector switch to 3-round burst. He sent a trio of rounds flying at the muzzle-flash to his right but got no indication of whether they had hit home. Rolling again, he barely avoided the return fire that came from the left.

Then, all became silent. No one wanted to be the next to create a muzzle-flash, which would pinpoint his position. Bolan waited, unmoving. As his eyes adjusted to the darkness, he could make out the shadowy form of the airplane in the center of the room. Then the walls, and a few large storage crates took shape. He saw no human silhouettes in the darkness.

Only the plane, the crates and a few other items—still unidentifiable in the low light—were large enough to hide a man. Cover and concealment was limited. But it was there. At least enough to get him killed if he didn't watch himself.

The room remained silent, the roar from the earlier rounds dying in Bolan's ears. As his eyes became attuned to the environment, so did his hearing. Five minutes went by. Then ten. The Executioner began to hear what sounded like breathing coming from his right. His imagination? He didn't think so. As his ears grew more sensitive, he picked up the steady rhythmic breaths.

Slowly, he swung the Beretta toward the area from where

the breathing was coming. He listened further. When he felt as if he had pinpoint the breathing man's position as well as he possibly could, he pulled the trigger.

Three near-silent 9 mm rounds flew from the Beretta. Bolan heard a screeching moan as he rolled away from the return rounds he knew would fly at him. He twisted on the ground, firing another 3-round burst in the return of the flames those rounds created. As soon as the bullets had left the barrel, he crawled forward. But once again, he got no indication of whether or not his rounds had found their mark.

The Executioner wasn't in the mood for another waiting game. Firing another burst, he rolled to the side again and waited, aiming at the muzzle-flash of the return fire. As soon as he saw it, he fired once more, then repeated his change of tactics by crawling forward. But he got only two paces this time when he ran into something.

Something human.

The man on the warehouse floor let out a scream of surprise and terror, sounding like a schoolgirl who had just seen a black widow spider crawl up her dress. Bolan reached out with an open hand and made contact with what felt like the man's chest. Grabbing a handful of the shirt, he jerked the guy toward him and jammed the muzzle of the Beretta into the flesh just to the side of his fist.

The Executioner pulled the trigger and sent three more 9 mm rounds blasting into the man at contact range. Blood, organ parts and bone flew out of the man's back in the wake of the hollowpoint rounds. But the residual spray was almost as bad, and Bolan felt it drench him from the top of his head to his waist.

Not taking any chances, he rolled away from the man he had just killed. He had been fired upon by two men. And he had now killed—he thought—two men. But that didn't mean there had been only two men waiting to ambush him in the warehouse. There still might very well be more who had simply chosen to remain silent rather than expose themselves as targets. If that was the case, they might change their tactics and come out of hiding at any time.

Again, time went by slowly. As quietly as he could, Bolan ejected the near-empty magazine from the Beretta and inserted a fresh load. If there was one or more attackers still in hiding, they were keeping the same strategy now. Sooner or later, they knew—if they were there—that Bolan would begin to wonder. And sooner or later, he would have to find out. They held all the cards in this game.

The Executioner heard sirens in the distance. He didn't know if they were coming toward the warehouse or not. The area outside had appeared to be deserted for the night. Someone might have heard the gunfire, even inside the closed warehouse, and called the police. And the last thing he needed was to get tied up in jail while Hal Brognola tried to sort things out.

Bolan made his decision the same way he decided most things—suddenly, and with a certainty, which few men ever experienced. Without warning, he rose to his feet and pulled the trigger of the Beretta. As soon as the suppressed weapon had coughed out the first three rounds, he changed his point of aim and repeated the action. Working systematically, he showered the entire inside of the warehouse with a 360-degree storm of fire.

It was enough to flush out the man who had remained hidden behind the airplane. But it was also enough to make the man panic, and his shots flew wide of the Executioner. Bolan stood his ground, swinging the Beretta back toward the new muzzle-flashes and squeezing the trigger. He heard wet, squishy sounds above the cough of the sound suppressor as all three bullets struck flesh.

The sound of a body hitting concrete met his ears. Then all remained silent except for the ringing in his head.

Bolan felt certain now that he was alone. If there had been others with this last man, they, too, would have been flushed out. The ASP had been shot from his hand, but he still had a backup miniflashlight in his blacksuit, and he produced it now and twisted on the beam. The warehouse suddenly lit up.

The Executioner saw the three men he'd shot lying on the cold hard concrete. He moved from one to the next but recognized none of their faces. If they were associated with Wright, they hadn't been at the jungle site earlier in the day. And again, he found no identification papers on any of the bodies.

His disappointment came when he moved to the last man—the one who had hidden behind the plane. In the beam of the flashlight, the Executioner could see that he had been standing next to the cargo door when the Beretta had taken him down.

Bolan moved forward, more interested in the outside of the plane than the man on the ground. What he had seen earlier in the day, when the plane was still in the jungle, were reddish brown splotches on the side of the Antonov that looked like blood. His guess was that if it *was* blood, it had come from the pilot. No one else had been injured at the site.

All of which led Bolan to believe that the pilot hadn't died in the cockpit. None of the instruments or anything else in front of him matched the wound in the middle of his head. It was Bolan's guess that while the smaller gash above his eye probably had come from a bang on the head during the crash, the second had come from a blow delivered by a third party while the pilot was outside the plane. Then the body had been returned to the cockpit.ß

The soldier shone the flashlight on the area of the plane where he had seen the spots. He would never learn what they had actually been—not now. The blood from the last man he had killed still dripped down the wall of the plane. It now mixed, mingled, covered and contaminated the splotches he had seen earlier.

The sirens he had heard before were louder now. Maybe they were coming toward him, or maybe they were destined for some other crime or accident in the general vicinity. It didn't matter either way. It was time to get out of there.

He would learn nothing more in the warehouse.

4

The lobby of the Wayfarer's Hotel was deserted at the late hour Bolan strode through the front door check in. After the gunfight at the warehouse, he had returned to the entryway across the street, retrieved his jacket and slacks to cover his blacksuit, then walked the few blocks to where he'd flagged down another cab. The driver had taken him back to the bus station where he'd retrieved his equipment bags from the locker. Another cab had brought him to this hotel, which was located on the other side of Tafawa Balewa Square from the warehouse.

From there, he would be close enough to easily check on any activities involving the Antonov if he needed to do so. But he'd also be far enough away from the Bristol Hotel that he wasn't likely to be accidentally spotted by Wright, or any of the other DEA men he'd met in the jungle.

The Executioner took the key the desk clerk handed him. He helped the lone bellhop, still on duty at that late hour, down the hall with his bags. His room was on the ground floor this time, and unlike the Bristol, both the air-conditioning and telephone were in working order. After tipping the bellhop, Bolan closed the door, checked the locks, then stuffed his bags into the small alcove across from the bathroom that served as a closet. He doffed his jacket and outer pants, then sat on the bed. Sliding out of the Beretta's shoulder rig, he placed it next him and leaned forward, thinking.

He rested his elbows on his knees. He had caught a bit of sleep on the flight to Nigeria with Grimaldi, and even that hadn't been sound. He hadn't rested since arriving, and keeping his eyes open was beginning to become a full-time job in itself. He would have to sleep soon, he knew. No matter how much he wanted to keep working, keep moving, there came a time when the body simply said enough. When that happened, he either went to sleep or slowed to the point where he'd make mistakes. Mistakes that could get him or other innocent people killed.

Bolan rubbed his forehead for a moment, then looked at the telephone. Tired as he might be, he still had phone calls to make. The phone began to blur in his weary vision as he reached for it. This line, he knew, wasn't secure. But Norris Wright had no way of knowing where he was at the Wayfarer. And the DEA couldn't have taps on all of the telephones in Lagos. He picked up the receiver.

A moment later, Barbara Price said, "Hello, Striker."

Bolan frowned at the phone. Usually his cell phone number automatically came up when he called in, so it was no surprise that the Stony Man mission controller answered him by name. But Price should have had no more knowledge of where he was now than Wright, and that send a mild concern through his veins. "I'm not on the cell phone, Barbara," he said. "How'd you know it was me?"

Price laughed softly on the other end. "You been up without sleep again, Striker?" she asked good-naturedly.

"As usual," he said, rubbing his tired eyes.

"Ah," Price said. "Thought so. Well, I'll let you in on a little secret. We're equipped with the very latest in technology. Stuff the public only reads about in science-fiction novels." Her voice lowered to a mock-conspiratorial whisper. "Can you keep a secret?" she asked, then went on before he could answer. "We've named this secret device Caller ID. And our version is better than the phone company's."

Tired as he was, Bolan couldn't suppress a smile. "Are you trying to tell me I need some rest?" he said.

"Forty winks wouldn't hurt," Price said. "I've been with you when you were fresh, and I've been with you when you were so tired you could barely stand. Now, I'd have to say you function dead-on-your-feet better than any other man I've ever known on the best day of his life. But fresh and rested is always better. Even for you."

Price's voice had taken on a different tone with the last speech; a tone literally saturated with double meaning. Bolan pictured the beautiful honey blonde now, seated behind her desk in her office at the Farm. The life the Executioner led allowed no time for a true romance. Price knew this, and she accepted it. So there had been an unspoken understanding between them. When he was at the Farm, more often than not, he found himself sleeping in her room rather than his own. Another place, another time, and under different circumstances, Bolan knew the mutual affection they had for each other might well have led to something more traditional and permanent. But it was the here and now—reality—with which they were both forced to deal.

"I'll try to get some sleep before I get back to the Farm."

Price's laugh was now more of a giggle. "Then I guess I better do the same," she said.

"Is the big man there or in Wonderland?" the Executioner asked.

"Wonderland," Price said.

"Office or home?"

There was a short pause, and the Executioner knew Price would be glancing at the large clock mounted on the wall of her office. "He's probably still be at the office," she said. "Want me to try to get him?"

"No," Bolan said. "I'll call direct. You take care."

As professional as Price was—and there was no one better at what she did—she was still human. And that meant that she sometimes showed her humanity. Now, her tone changed again, and a hint of concern crept into it. "You do the same," she said. "Please be careful."

"Always," said the Executioner and hung up.

Bolan paused a moment to rub his weary eyes again. He glanced at the bed. Price was right. An hour or two of shut-eye was about to pass the "wouldn't hurt" mark and become absolutely mandatory whether he liked it or not. But it would still have to wait until he'd talked to Brognola.

Lifting the receiver once again, Bolan placed his call to the U.S. Department of Justice in Washington, D.C. When the switchboard operator answered, he said simply, "Hal Brognola."

"Whom may I say is calling?" the woman asked.

"Mike Belasko," Bolan said.

The Executioner heard a series of beeps and buzzes as the call was rerouted through the Justice Department phone lines, then Brognola's secretary answered. "Hello, Mr. Belasko," she said. "Mr. Brognola is in a meeting. Is this an emergency?"

Since the inception of their working relationship many years before, any call from the Executioner had been treated as an emergency whether it was or not. The reason was simple: Considering the way Bolan operated, there was no telling when he might have time to call again. Brognola's secretary at the Justice Department knew nothing about the big Fed's involvement with Stony Man Farm. In fact, like the rest of the world outside the Farm itself except for the President, she didn't even know Stony Man existed.

"Yes," Bolan said. "Please tell him it's me."

"Let me put you on hold."

Two minutes later, Brognola was on the line. "Afternoon, big guy," he said.

"For you, maybe," Bolan said. "For me, it's the middle of the night."

"So, what's up?" Brognola asked. "Don't worry, we're scrambled."

Bolan took a deep weary breath, then filled him on the events of the past twenty-four hours. He ended with the shoot-out at the warehouse.

"The guy who attacked you in your hotel room," Brognola said. "And the guys at the warehouse. Any of them DEA?"

"Not that I know of," Bolan said. "At least if they were, they weren't at the crash site. My guess at this point is no, they probably weren't." He paused to rub his forehead this time. "My guess is that Wright is living two separate lives. And running two totally separated groups of men."

"What makes you say that?" Brognola wanted to know.

"Remember you telling me you had an old cop's hunch?" Bolan asked.

"Yeah..."

"Well, call this the hunch of an old soldier. Wright has something going on the side—there's no other answer. He's the Lagos DEA SAC by day, and my guess is he's into the drug trade himself by night." He let his hand fall from his head and stared ahead at the wall. The cheap print of an ocean scene hung on the wall in front of him seemed to be shifting back and forth, as if the waves in the picture itself were rocking it. "I don't know the particulars yet," he continued. "Maybe Wright's simply on the payroll of one of the cartels and feeding them information. Maybe he's the kingpin himself. Or maybe he falls somewhere in between."

"But he's definitely dirty?" Brognola asked.

"As dirty as last week's laundry," Bolan fired back.

"So, what can I do for you on this end?"

The Executioner paused, thinking again. "Get hold of Bear," he said. "Earlier, he tapped into the DEA personnel files for me concerning Wright. Tell him I need him to do the same with every other DEA employee working out of the Lagos office. Both agents and non-commissioned support personnel. There's bound to be more shooting coming up. And I can't tell the players without a program."

"Separating the good guys from the bad may get a little tricky on this one," Brognola agreed. "How do you want Bear to get the information to you?"

Bolan glanced at the phone on the table next to the bed. "I've got the portable fax with me," he said.

"Consider it done," Brognola said. "But it could take some time. So use that time to get some sleep. You sound beat."

"You're the second person to tell me that in five minutes," Bolan said.

Brognola could guess who the other person was. "And we both know you well enough to tell when you need rest." There was a short pause, then the Stony Man director said, "Of course everyone knows people in different ways." The low chuckle that followed was neither lewd nor indecent. It was simply Brognola's way of acknowledging the relationship between Bolan and Price, which everyone knew about but had too much respect to talk about.

"Thanks, Hal," the Executioner said. "Get back to work."

"Call back when you can," Brognola said. "This has been a lot more interesting than the budget meeting you called me out of."

Bolan hung up again, rose from the bed and walked to the bags in the closet. A few minutes later, the portable fax machine was hooked into the telephone on the table. Unbuckling the gunbelt around his waist, he slipped out of the blacksuit and draped it over a desk chair at the foot of the bed. The Desert Eagle came out of the holster and went under his pillow.

The Executioner started to roll down the covers, then stopped, staring bleary-eyed downward. He was too tired to even do that, and he sprawled out next to the Beretta on top of the bedspread itself.

He was asleep before his head hit the pillow.

THE LIGHT OF EARLY morning drifted through the crack in the window curtains as the Executioner opened his eyes. His first act upon awakening was to turn toward the fax machine. It still stood where he'd left it, no different. He glanced at his watch. He'd been asleep almost three and half hours. But Brognola had warned him it might take awhile for Kurtzman to gather all of the information he'd requested.

Rising to his feet, Bolan looked toward the bathroom. As so often happened, he had gotten just enough sleep to make him want more. A shower while he waited on the fax might help him wake up. Remembering what had happened at the Bristol right after he'd bathed, he turned back to the bed and retrieved the Desert Eagle from under the pillow.

As soon as he'd showered, Bolan returned to the bed with the Desert Eagle. The fax still hadn't come, so he walked back to his bag and took out a small gun-cleaning kit. He returned to the bed, took a seat and dropped the cleaning kit and a rag down at his side.

Bolan looked up for a moment, staring at the painting of the ocean on the wall in front of him. More sleep might have been good, but at least the picture was no longer moving. He had the presence of mind now to think through where things stood and make plans for the rest of the mission.

For a moment, the Desert Eagle stayed frozen in his hand. "Kenneth Clarke" might have survived two assassination attempts, but for all practical purposes he was dead. Wright obviously suspected Clarke of having been a plant or he wouldn't have tried to have him killed. But the man Wright knew as Clarke hadn't only escaped, he had killed all of his would-be assassins in this process. His ability to pull that off should have more than confirmed the DEA man's suspicion that Clarke wasn't some wimpy, mild-mannered D.C. desk jockey. No, if he was any smarter than a fence post, Wright no longer had any doubt that Bolan had been sent to get him.

While cleaning the Desert Eagle his mind stayed on DEA

SAC Norris Wright. The man had taken quite a chance try-ing to have him killed. So he had to have had a reason that was big enough to warrant the risk. The death of a DEA agent didn't simply mean he'd be replaced—it met all hell would break loose in Washington and a veritable army of drug busters would be sent to Nigeria to find out what had hap-pened and see to it that the guilty party was punished. There would be repercussions. So the stakes had to be high. And he had to believe he was strong enough—insulated enough—to avoid the heat when that happened.

Bolan picked up the rag and began wiping down the Desert Eagle's frame. Maybe Wright didn't even care if investigative teams swooped down on Lagos, looking to go home with heads in their briefcases. Maybe his involvement with the peo-ple responsible for the downed aircraft was big enough that he could simply drop out of sight. Maybe he had already made so much money to disappear at a moment's notice.

There were several different approaches the Executioner could take at this point. First, he could go after Wright head-on. But killing the man would do little good. Even if he was top dog, there would be a dog number two to take over. Op-eration of whatever criminal organization he was hooked into would go on. If Bolan captured Wright alive, however, he could whisk him away for a very special interrogation in which the rights of the victim outweighed the rights of the guilty.

The problem with trying to capture Wright was that the man was likely to fight back. He knew he would face a stiff prison sentence if caught, convicted and returned to the States. And while prison was bad for anyone, it was especially hard on ex-cops. In the minienvironment behind the walls, the roles of cop and con were reversed, with the good guys being far outnumbered by the bad. Knowing this, many dirty cops chose to fight and die rather than go through that living hell. Bolan might have to kill the man in self-defense. Which again would mean he wouldn't learn what he needed to know.

He dropped the cleaning gear back into the small plastic container. And what was it he needed to know? Two things. First, what criminal enterprise was big enough to shoot down two planes, maybe sabotage a third so it would crash, and be organized enough to arrive on the scene and get rid of the crop eradication chemicals before the authorities arrived. He could come up with only one sensible reason for the truck tire tracks he had seen at the clearing in the jungle. A transport vehicle had arrived as soon as possible after the crash, taken the real chemicals off the plane, and on-loaded dummy drums. What group of men had enough money to pull all that off, as well as pay the informants who had obviously alerted them to the DEA-CDC ruse even before it happened? The second thing he needed to know was exactly what part Norris Wright had played in those events.

Bolan stood and walked to the closet, pulling a short-sleeved sport shirt, a light pair of cotton trousers and a khaki bush vest out of his suitcase. Wearing these, and the brown athletic sandals he pulled from another bag, he should look like any other American tourist who would go home a little disappointed that he'd picked Nigeria in which to waste his vacation days.

The Executioner's mind returned to the crop eradication chemicals as he began to dress. He didn't know what they had been replaced with. But at this point, it appeared that the real crop killers had been whisked away by the very men whose crops they had been meant to eliminate. Sure, eventually it would be discovered that what was in the fifty-five-gallon drums recovered from the crash was nothing more than water or some other substitute. But so what? By that time it would be all but impossible to determine where the switch had been made or who had made it.

Bolan shrugged into the shirt and slipped his weapons on over it. He covered them with the vest, then took one last look at the silent fax machine. Turning toward the door, he had already started to twist the knob when he heard it suddenly jolt, then begin to hum behind him.

Bolan turned back to the machine as the paper began to feed out of it.

Thirty minutes later, the Executioner had read the personnel files of every employee—both commissioned and civilian—who worked out of the Lagos DEA office. Rising again from the bed, he stuffed the pages into one of this suitcases in the closet, then pulled out a black velvet case that looked much like a jewelry box. Along with a larger cardboard container, he carried them through the door to the hallway.

Bolan waited until the door had swung closed behind him, then twisted the knob to make sure it had locked. A hard smile covered his face. He had seen the files, and while studying them, he had decided how he would proceed. His new course of action had now been determined.

NORRIS WRIGHT suspected if he got any more angry than he already was, the top of his head might blow off. Then the thought went away as he remembered he was in Lagos, where nothing was supposed to work right. Ever. Lagos was the most backward, dirtiest, godforsaken place he'd ever been in with the possible exception of Calcutta. His blood pressure wasn't going to go down until he got out because, no matter how calm he had learned to appear on the outside, he wasn't going to quit being pissed about something inwardly until he was out of this hellhole for good. He reminded himself that in two more days, this city would be nothing but a bad memory, and that knowledge helped.

When the rage coursing through his veins began to ebb, he looked across his desk at Dolph Van der Kirk. The South African was seated in an easy chair, the sides of which were all but invisible behind his powerful frame. Since his competitive power- lifting and bodybuilding days had ended, Van der Kirk had taken up smoking, and it seemed to Wright that he approached the vice with the same enthusiasm with which he had once tackled barbells. He was smoking an unfiltered cigarette as if it might somehow sprout legs and run away from him if he didn't hurry. With each deep inhalation the man took, the orange ember at the end brightened and doubled in size.

"You want to tell me what happened?" Wright asked the man across from him, forcing his voice to stay calm.

Van der Kirk shrugged. His enthusiastic smoking was just that—enthusiasm. Rather than reflect the nervousness it would have represented in most people, in the South African's case it was simply indicative of the way he approached life. Hard, fast, and head-on. He took a deep drag and let the smoke trickle slowly out of his mouth. He didn't answer.

"Let me make sure I've got this straight," Wright went on. "You sent Peterssen to kill Clarke in his hotel room. Peterssen didn't report back. So you sent Wilkinson, Schmidt and Togov to the plane to kill Clarke if he went there. Instead, we find our three men dead on the floor of gunshot wounds." Wright stared at Van der Kirk. Smoke was still trailing from his mouth and nostrils as if it might never stop. "That pretty much sum it all up?"

"That pretty much does," the South African agreed amiably, the smoke still coming.

Wright shook his head in disbelief. "Then I think it's safe to assume that Peterssen has shuffled off this mortal coil along with the other three, don't you? No one's found a body, but that's probably just a matter of time." He watched Van der Kirk draw down on the cigarette again, and wished for a moment he hadn't given up the habit himself several years before. "Wilkinson, Schmidt and Togov were damn good men. Anybody who could take them out—especially at the same time—should have been able to kill an idiot like Peterssen with both hands tied behind his back."

"Peterssen was a good man," Van der Kirk said, a new windstorm of smoke beginning to flow from his face.

Wright looked at the man's wide body and thought of a bull; a bull who could speak.

"You just didn't like him personally," the man finished.

"He was the stereotype big dumb Swede," Wright argued. "Stupid. A fucking cartoon come to life. In Technicolor. With Surround Sound."

Van der Kirk chuckled, deep in his massive chest. "He wasn't the brightest star in the sky, no," he said. "But Peterssen made up for his lack of intelligence with strength and enthusiasm."

Wright fell silent in thought for a few seconds. He knew he was overreacting. He might well have chosen Peterssen to kill Clarke himself if it had been his responsibility. But dammit, he wanted something or somebody concrete he could blame this mess on. "Any particular reason you picked him?" he asked.

Van der Kirk shrugged. "He seemed competent to perform such as easy task—it wasn't brain surgery we were asking of him. Knock on a door, then shoot the man who answers. Not too difficult." He finished the cigarette with one more deep inhalation, lit another off the end, then dropped the still-fiery stub of the old one into an ashtray on the table next to the chair. "And," he went on as smoke clouds circles his entire bull-looking head, "I knew that if Peterssen was apprehended by the police he wouldn't talk. He was as loyal as a sheep dog."

Wright nodded, still fascinated by the amount of smoke the other man could ingest. "Yes," he said. "Loyal as a sheep dog. Not quite as smart as one, but just as loyal."

"I also knew that if Peterssen was apprehended or killed, it would be no tremendous loss to our ranks."

Wright nodded. Okay. Peterssen had now been discussed, explained, exhausted, and it was time to move on. So he didn't object when Van der Kirk changed the subject.

"You said that whoever killed our men at the warehouse would have had an easy time with Peterssen. What makes you so sure the same man or *men* were responsible?"

Wright put his feet up on the desk. "Give me a cigarette," he said.

The South African's face reflected both surprise and bemusement. "You quit smoking."

"Dammit, Dolph, just give me one of your fucking cigarettes and let me worry about that!"

Van der Kirk laughed again, and for a moment Wright thought he looked more like Satan than a bull. He produced a crumpled soft pack of Camels from his shirt pocket and tossed it through the air. Wright caught it, shook one out and stuck it between his lips. The nearly forgotten taste of even the unlit tobacco was suddenly familiar again. And wonderful. There was a book of matches stuck between the plastic wrapper and the paper. He struck a match, lit the end of the cigarette, then dropped the matches and pack onto the top of his desk. He let the smoke enter his lungs like an old lover, then said, "I don't know how I know it was the same man," he said. "But I do. And I know who that man was. Kenneth Clarke. He's not the wimpy-assed little office boy he pretends to be."

Van der Kirk gave him a nod. "You're right," he said. "Who else would it have been? As to whether he's actually one of the pencil necks or just pretending to be one, I couldn't say. I didn't meet him."

"Take my world for it, Dolph," Wright said. He inhaled smoke until he thought his lungs might burst, then added, "He's got a knife scar on his wrist. One of his calves shows what looks like an old bullet wound."

"What did you do? Sleep with him?" Van der Kirk asked, smiling.

"I'll ignore that," Wright said. The cigarette was calming him, and he felt less like arguing. "I told you about his sprained ankle. I saw the scar when he fell. I bought his act myself at the time, but now I think it was nothing more than a ploy so he could ask about the truck tracks. He's a cagey one. I'll grant him that."

"Where is he now?"

"I don't know," Wright said. "I sent one of the field agents over to his room this morning to pick him up. Keep in mind I assumed Peterssen had killed him during the night. I figured my man would knock, no one would answer, he'd get a maid or the hotel manager to open the door. Then they'd find the body and we'd go from there." He paused and looked at Van der Kirk's burning cigarette, then took the one out of his own mouth and stared at it for a moment. "That's exactly how it went. Except there wasn't a body. And all of Clarke's luggage was gone."

Van der Kirk nodded. "If someone tried to kill me, I'd leave too. Wouldn't you? Have you checked with the airlines to see if he's flown out again?"

"Yeah. But as far as they could tell, he never even flew in."

Van der Kirk leaned forward slightly in his chair. "What does that mean?"

"He came on a private flight. I suppose he could have come by sea. But private aircraft is more likely."

"Well, doesn't the DEA have their own private planes for such things?"

"Of course they do," Wright snapped. "But they wouldn't fly in some flunky number cruncher on one. It would be cheaper just to buy him a commercial ticket." The smoke trailing up off the end of Van der Kirk's cigarette was beginning to make shapes that for some strange reason annoyed him. He took a final drag off his own half-burned smoke, then looked around for some place to extinguish it. The ashtrays he had used in the past had been moved away from the desk when he quit smoking.

"Are you sure he's even DEA?" Van der Kirk asked, as he lifted the ashtray from the table at his side, leaned forward and placed it on the desk.

Wright smashed the butt into the clay dish. "I don't know. I E-mailed the home office, asking a couple of inane questions and mentioning his name. If he isn't, we should find out."

"Unless they've sent someone from outside your agency to check on you. They could know more than we suspect." Van der Kirk finished another cigarette, leaned forward and dropped it next to the others in the ashtray on Wright's desk. "The might be covering for him."

"That's always possible."

"The real question is," the muscle man said, "what do we do about Kenneth Clarke now? Do you still want me to try to find and kill him? My guess is he's figured out he's not real popular and decided to hide out somewhere until he thinks the heat's off. Then he'll stick his tail between his legs and head back to Washington."

Wright looked up from the spot on the desk where his gaze had been. "If that's the case, you and I will be long gone."

"Correct," Van der Kirk said. "Why don't we do this? If we see him, we'll kill him. But we've got more important things to take care of at the moment." He stood. "Speaking of which, we have shipments flying out of both Ghana and the Cameroons today. And there is a minor peasant uprising among some of the field workers in Chad."

Wright frowned. "Anything important?"

"Nothing that can't be handled with a few AK-47 rounds," Van der Kirk said. "We'll kill a few. The others will fall back in line." He smiled. "I keep forgetting. None of that will mean jack shit in a few days."

"No," Wright said. "But we should keep up appearances until then. By the way, I heard from our friend."

The nonchalant attitude Van der Kirk had exhibited throughout the meeting suddenly vanished and was replaced by a no-nonsense earnestness. "And?"

"He's not coming."

"You didn't think he would, did you?"

"No, of course not. He'll be flying three of his top guys in a day early, though."

Van der Kirk turned toward the door. "You baby-sit them,"

he said. "They make me want to puke. They always smell like curry, and they're almost as bad as kaffirs." He started to open the door.

Norris Wright lifted the pack of Camels from his desk and held it in the air. "You forgot these," he said with a trace of regret in his heart at he looked at the cigarettes.

Van der Kirk turned. "I have others," he said. "You will need those."

Before Wright could argue, he left the office.

FINDING SOMEONE in Lagos who was willing to take chance to make a buck would be no problem, the Executioner knew. Poverty in this city of ten million was rampant. Bad enough that it had often been compared to that of Haiti, with Haiti usually coming out sounding like a paradise at the end of the discussion. The city was also noted as one of the great crime centers of the world. It was from this latter group of people that Bolan knew he would have to recruit the person he needed. He wanted someone who could do what he wanted done, and not look suspicious or get caught while doing it. At the same time, he needed someone he could, at least partially, trust.

And therein lay the issue in question. Finding both qualities in the same person might not be easy.

The club was on Pepu Street near the Sheraton Hotel. Things didn't kick off until around eleven o'clock every night, and it was closer to that hour in the morning when Bolan arrived. But while the club was closed, the streets never did. He walked along the sidewalk, his eyes skirting the drunks who lay sleeping it off in the stairwells and gutters, ignoring the panhandlers who beckoned for money that would be spent on suya, wine and drugs, and looking more carefully at the street hustlers, corner drug dealers, pimps and prostitutes. They eyed him, as well. He was in an area of the city where white men rarely went at that time of day. They came at night for the music and when they came they stayed all night, not wanting to risk the dangerous streets before daylight. It was rare to see light skin in the area as the clock neared midday, and the street people had to assume any white man there at noon had to be desperate for either drugs or a woman.

The Executioner looked far too healthy for a drug addict, and he knew it. So it didn't surprise him when a black woman wearing a bright orange halter top, short shorts and a garter belt that extended blatantly from under the shorts stepped out from a doorway when he passed by.

"Hey," the woman said, giving him a smile that promised whatever perversions he could dream up. "It's a little early. But I'm always willing to make few naira."

For a moment, Bolan was taken aback. The woman's accent was American. He studied her, head to foot. Attached to her garter belt were black fishnet nylons that led down long slender legs to spike heels. In turn, the woman watched him with a wariness that said she had been on the streets long enough to be careful. But while she sized him up in return, she became an animated advertisement of what she was offering, striking several different poses. "I can do anything you want, baby," she said.

Bolan nodded. "Come with me," he said.

It had been too easy, and now, the woman grew suddenly wary. "Where?" she asked. "Look, there's a perfectly good alley right back—"

"You can't do what I want you to do in the alley," he said, interrupting her. "We need to go to my car." He pointed down the street in the general direction of the black Ford Nissan he'd rented just before coming to this area.

"We going to do it in your car?" the woman asked.

"Part of it," Bolan answered.

"Huh?" There was a look of bewilderment on the prostitute's face.

Bolan stepped forward. "Look," he said, "what I want you to do has nothing to do with sex. And it won't hurt you. I'll pay triple your normal rate, and all you have to do is perform a simple little task in which nobody even touches you."

"What the hell you talking about?" the woman said. "You sound crazy. I'm not listening to any more of this." She started to turn her back to him.

"Come to my car," Bolan said. I'll give you a hundred naira just for that."

The woman swung back around. "I'm listening again," she said. She reached out and snatched the bills Bolan had taken from his pocket and stuffed them into the front of her shorts. She was still slightly wary as she took him by the arm and they started off down the street.

Bolan opened the Nissan's passenger's door for her, and she stared at him as if he were from another planet. "Man, you sure are a gentleman. Damn sure hope you aren't some no crazy-ass strangler or something, too. You don't strangle people, do you?"

The Executioner thought of the blond man who had tried to kill him in his room at the Bristol, and the towel he had used to end the assassination attempt. Rather than answer, he just closed the door, then circled the car and got in behind the wheel. For the moment, he left the keys where they were—in his pocket. "What's your name?" he asked the woman.

"Amanda."

"Pretty name. You're American, Amanda," Bolan said.

"Well, aren't you the regular little James Bond." Amanda smiled, showing an even row of beautiful white teeth.

Bolan studied her closer now. While she had been on the streets long enough to be wary, she couldn't have been there too long. She still looked too good and had a keen wit. And she really was attractive. He glanced down at her arms. No needle tracks. That didn't mean she wasn't hooked on drugs of some kind—she might still be in the pill-popping or sorting stages of the habit. Or she might even have progressed to the needle but fired up in areas of her body that were covered by the scanty clothing she wore.

But the Executioner's instincts told him that wasn't the case. Her eyes were clear, and she just didn't have the feel of a junkie. "How'd you wind up here, Amanda?" Bolan asked.

Amanda laughed. "Are you asking me 'what's a nice girl like me doing in a place like this'?" she asked.

"Pretty much."

"Well," Amanda said, shaking her head to get the hair that had fallen over her eyes out of the way. "It's a long damn story, and you don't want to hear it. It involves a man. But enough about me. Let's talk about you. What do you want? A little head? That'll cost you—"

Bolan held up his hand. "I already told you, I don't want sex."

"You queer?"

The soldier laughed and shook his head.

"Didn't think you looked like a twinky-boy," Amanda said. "But you don't look like the kind of man who needs to buy sex, either. I'd think the girls would be lining up at your bed with their panties already down around their ankles."

"I'm going to tell you this one more time, Amanda, then I want to move on with this conversation. I don't want any type of sexual act out of you. Is that clear?"

"Okay. Got it."

"Good. Now answer me this. Why are you walking the streets in this hellhole?"

"Because I don't have the money for a ticket back to Detroit," Amanda said. "Soon as I get it, it's adios Lagos. Goodbye, and good riddance, Nigeria."

"I offered you triple your going rate for the simple favor I'm about to ask of you. What if I changed that offer to an airline ticket home, and gave you enough money for food and other expenses?"

Amanda might not have been a whore in Lagos very long, and she might not have been a drug addict. And she wasn't naive. She'd been around long enough to know few men were going to do anything for her unless there was something in it for them. "What would I say to that? First, I'd say that's a lot more than three times the price I charge." She giggled like a little girl, then added, "I'm good baby. But nobody is *that* good." When Bolan's face remained impassive, she went on. "Second, I'd say this simple favor isn't likely to turn out as simple as you make it sound."

"Listen to what I want you to do, then decide. If you say no, I'll buy you the ticket home anyway."

Amanda's surprise became shock. A tear began to form in one of her eyes. "Don't play games with me," she said. "Please. You don't know what it's been like out here and—"

Bolan cut her off. "I'm not playing games," he said. "You're going home before the day is out, Amanda. Whether you help me or not. All I ask is that if you turn me down, you help me find someone else you think can do the job I need done."

The woman's eyes were threatening to overflow now. Hope had returned to her life. "It's a deal," she said. Her next question was more curious than skeptical but she asked it anyway. "If this is so simple, how come you don't just do it yourself?"

"Because it involves people who know me. And I don't want them to see me." He explained in great detail what he wanted her to do. When he had finished, he said, "You're going to need some different clothes to play this part. A new dress, I think. I'll buy it."

"Do I get to keep it, too?" Amanda asked.

"Yes. What do you say, Amanda? You want to do this? My offer still stands—you're going home, one way or the other."

"It's a done deal," Amanda said quickly. "You ready to do it now?"

"The sooner the better."

"Then let's go shopping," Amanda said. "I intend to look like one fine lady when I get back to Motown." She sat back against the seat and puffed her chest out with an exaggerated air of importance as Bolan inserted the key and started the ignition. Amanda glanced at him with a devilish smile. "You don't mind if I call you James, do you? Like James Bond."

"It's as good a name as any."

HAD HE NOT SEEN HER before on the street, Bolan wouldn't have believed it was the same woman.

Amanda came out of the dressing room wearing a skirt, jacket, shoes and ruffled blouse that made her look more like the attractive young president of her first-grader's Parent-Teacher's Association than a Lagos street prostitute. Bolan, sitting impatiently on a chair surrounded by mirrors in the up-scale dress shop, saw her look up at him questioningly. "Yes," he said, answering the question he knew was coming for the third time. "I like this one, too. You look beautiful."

Amanda smiled, then stepped into the half circle of mirrors, staring critically at herself from every possible angle. She stepped back and forth, striking a number of poses. But they were completely different poses than those she had struck on the street when she'd thought Bolan was just another john looking for a good time. Finally, she looked at the Executioner and asked timidly, "You don't think this skirt makes by butt look too big?"

Bolan kept his smile hidden. "No. You look perfect." He glanced at his watch. "Now, let me pay for it, and the other outfits, and let's go."

Amanda gave him another big smile. "Which one do you want me to wear now?" she asked.

"That one," the Executioner said, standing. "Just have the lady cut the price tags off and let's go."

Amanda turned to the middle-aged saleswoman who had waited on her for the past hour. The woman had appeared shocked when Amanda first walked through the door in her short-shorts with the garter belt hanging out beneath them. She had been about to try to dissuade her from entering when Bolan had appeared in the doorway behind her. At that point, she had quickly summed up the situation. Black whore. Stupid white man. He'd fallen in love with her. That meant sales, and sales meant commissions. And while commissions might not have changed the condescending attitude throughout the fitting process, she had at least become civil.

"So, you like this one, too?" the woman asked Amanda with a forced wooden smile.

"Yes, and I'll wear it out," Amanda told her. "Wrap the rest of them up, honey."

The saleslady glanced at the dressing room Amanda had used. "And the...clothing you were wearing when you arrived?" she asked, wrinkling her nose in disdain at the memory.

Amanda glanced at the Executioner and winked. Although no words had passed between the two of them on the subject, each had sensed the other's distaste for the saleslady's snobbery. Turning back to the middle-aged woman, Amanda said, "Oh, you mean my whore costume? Keep it. It'll look great on you."

The woman's bottom lip dropped open in shock.

Five minutes later, Bolan and Amanda left the store with the packages. "We ready for the main show, now?" the young woman asked.

Bolan nodded. "Yes. Then, when you're finished, I'll see that you get to the airport with enough money for a ticket on the first plane headed west." He unlocked the passenger's door and opened it for her.

Amanda got in, her movements more that of a lady now than a prostitute. But as the Executioner started to close the door for her, she reached up and wrapped her fingers around his arm, stopping him. Tears suddenly filled the beautiful chocolate-brown eyes as she said, "Thank you, James."

"You don't have to thank me," Bolan said. "You'll be earning both the ticket and the clothes."

Amanda shook her head, and her eyes grew even more moist. "That's not what I meant."

The Executioner felt his eyebrows lower in a puzzled look.

"For just a few minutes back there," Amanda went on. "I was a rich woman. And I had a husband who loved me enough to buy me expensive clothes." Like they had earlier in the car, the tears threatened to spill over. She bit her bottom lip lightly to stop them. When she had control over her emotions once more, she said, "And a very handsome husband, at that."

Bolan didn't know how to respond. So he just nodded.

The drive to the Lagos DEA office took a little over fifteen minutes. Bolan had no intention of getting close enough to be spotted. But to be on the safe side, he had changed his looks as well. Gone were the wire-rimmed spectacles and every other component that had made up the illusion that he was a bureaucratic goon. He had added a large pair of sunglasses and a white straw hat to his face, and while it might not fool anyone who knew him at close range, at a distance, he looked like a completely different man than Kenneth Clarke had been.

The Executioner pulled into a parking space a block from the office, threw the car into park, but left the engine running. "You know what to do?" he asked.

Amanda nodded, and for the first time since he'd met her less than two hours earlier, he saw a trace of concern in her eyes.

"I'll be near," he said. "We need one inside the office. His office. And the other on his vehicle." He reached into his pocket and pulled out the velvet box he had taken from his luggage earlier. Opening the lid, he said, "You remember which goes where?"

Amanda looked into the box. "The bigger one goes on the car," she said. "The little one in the office."

Bolan nodded. "Right. They're both magnetic. Put the big one under the bumper of the car. It should be no problem. The office could be trickier. Get it as close to his desk chair as possible. You may have to use your imagination."

Amanda turned away from him and looked out the side window of the vehicle. "It's been well developed over the past few months," she mumbled miserably.

A wave of sympathy washed over the Executioner. He didn't know the story of how she'd become stranded in Nigeria, and he didn't want to. But Amanda had been forced into prostitution as her only option for survival. Her situation brought back painful, long-ago-but-never-to-be-forgotten memories. Bolan's own sister had once been forced to sell herself by the Mafia, and the result had been the tragic deaths of most of the Executioner's family.

Bolan reached out and placed a hand on Amanda's shoulder. "Let's get it over with and get you started home," he said. "As soon as you're finished in the building, go to the parking lot. It's a big, dark blue, fully equipped Land Rover you're looking for, and it'll probably be parked in a reserved space. Got it?"

Amanda wiped the tears from her eyes. Then, for just a moment, the hard-core street prostitute came back.

"Don't you worry about me, Mr. James Bond," she said. "The day I can't trick and manipulate a man will be the day after I'm buried six feet deep in the ground." She opened the door and got out.

The Executioner watched her take off down the sidewalk. Her experiences over the past few months had been a living hell, and they would always be with her. But in Amanda he saw a strength that would enable her to overcome them and move on with her life.

Bolan let her get halfway down the block before he backed out of the parking spot. Driving slowly, he timed it so he drove past the DEA office just as she entered the front door. He saw Wright's blue Land Rover parked just around the corner of the building in the parking lot. She should have no trouble finding it when she came out of the office.

Driving a block down, the Executioner pulled into another open space and turned back to watch. With one hand, he reached over the seat and grabbed the larger box he'd taken from his bags that morning. Placing it on the seat where Amanda had been moments earlier, he opened it.

Inside, the soldier went to work activating the battery-powered receiving unit. It wouldn't pick anything up until Amanda had planted the transmitter in Wright's office. But then he should be able to hear any dialogue that remained between them. Turning the dial to the same frequency at which the transmitter was set, he settled back into the seat to wait.

The Executioner realized that, without thinking, his right hand had slipped under his jacket to rest on the butt of the Beretta 93-R.

It had been a long time since Amanda Freeman Ironsi had worn panty hose, and the soft sound they made swishing between her legs as she walked was somehow comforting. It brought back memories of the days right after she'd graduated from business school and taken the secretarial job with one of Detroit's biggest law firms, days when she dressed for work in very much the same way she was dressed now. A sick feeling suddenly hit her stomach as she realized that had been before she'd met Murtala Ironsi, and lost her heart, and all her common sense, to the man.

Amanda's high heels clicked along the sidewalk toward the DEA office, but she was careful not to let the exaggerated hip-sway she had developed over the past few months creep into her gait. She had to look the part she was playing. But she had no doubt she could be convincing. She was a good, if not great, actress. She had gotten rave reviews in her high school newspaper for her part in *Raisin in the Sun,* and had she been able to go on to college she might have studied drama. Her acting skills, instead, had been honed more through her time as a prostitute while she'd been stranded in Nigeria. She had played many parts to satisfy the odd, and often perverse, desires of men. And while her memories were shameful and filled her with pain, perhaps she could now turn that experience into something good.

Amanda passed a ground-floor office a block from her destination, and looked through the window. Inside, she saw a man and a woman seated at desks facing the street. The woman was typing, as she herself had once done. The man sat idly in his chair, staring off into space. He looked nothing like Murtala Ironsi, but he made her think of her former husband just the same.

Ironsi had been a foreign exchange student at one of the many schools that were all grouped under the heading Cranbrook Institutions in Bloomfield Hills, just outside Detroit. She had met him after work one night, when against her better judgment she had taken up a fellow female law office employee's offer to get a drink at a local singles' bar. According to Ironsi, he was the grandson of a Nigerian general who had put a halt to a 1966 military coupe in which the country's prime minister had been assassinated. The grateful Nigerian Cabinet had quickly given General Ironsi the reins of the government. But he, too, had been toppled and murdered a few months later, and his wife and Ironsi's father—then a teenager—had been forced to flee the country. They had lived in exile in several other African countries while Nigeria suffered changes of government more frequently than most people in the impoverished land could afford to change clothes.

Amanda passed the window and walked on. She wondered now if anything at all of what Ironsi had told her had been true. She wasn't even sure any more that Murtala Ironsi was even his real name. He had brought her to Nigeria with the promise that he had secured a high position in one of the larger businesses. Well, she thought, as she crossed the street and neared the front doors to the DEA office, at least *that* was true. But he had forgotten to mention that the business was the growing and distribution of heroin, marijuana and cocaine. And then one day, Ironsi had simply disappeared, never to be seen again.

With no living family in the U.S. to call for help, she had been stranded.

Amanda stepped up on the curb and walked on. Her thoughts turned to the big man she was about to help, and who would then help her. She had been promised many things by many men since her husband had disappeared, but none of those promises had been kept after the men had gotten what they wanted from her. She instinctively trusted the man she called James Bond. She couldn't put her finger on exactly why she trusted him, but she did. A basic "good" just seemed to emanate from the very pores of his body. She had no doubt that he was capable of violence. But he was incapable of evil, of that she was sure. He was the total opposite of Murtala Ironsi, and the men she had known on the streets of Lagos since. Not only did she know he would stand by his word, he had gone a long way toward restoring her faith in the males of the human race.

So, Amanda thought as she neared the front door of the DEA office, pull this off, honey, and you'll be back in Detroit again looking for a job—a legitimate job—before the week is out. She reached out for the steel bar that would open the glass door, and once again remembered her role in *Raisin in the Sun*. It was a more pleasant memory than some of the stranger roles she had played for smaller audiences of men over the past few months. But both experiences would help her now.

Get in character, girl, Amanda told herself. The rest of your life, and maybe even the life of the man who's saving you, depends on this performance.

Entering the reception area, Amanda saw a Nigerian woman seated inside a circular desk against the far wall. She walked stiffly forward and said in a stern voice, "I wish to speak to Special Agent in Charge Norris Wright."

The woman looked up from the papers in front of her, and Amanda saw her fingers tighten around the pen she was holding. "Excuse me?" she said.

"I said, I wish to speak to United States Drug Enforcement Administration Special Agent in Charge Norris Wright," Amanda repeated in a louder voice. "It is my understanding that he leads the Lagos field office."

"Your name?" the woman, clearly surprised and somewhat intimidated, asked.

"Amanda Ojukwu," Amanda said. "Mrs. Amanda Ojukwu."

"Do you have an appointment?" the receptionist asked.

"No, I do not."

"Then I'm afraid you'll have to—"

"You be afraid all you want to," Amanda said. She turned quickly and strode toward the door she saw in the wall to the side of the reception area. "I intend to speak with Mr. Wright, and I intend to speak with him now!"

"Mrs. Ojukwu, you can't just—"

"Watch me," Amanda said, and opened the door. She found herself inside a short hallway. Directly ahead was one lone, closed door. "Where is Special Agent in Charge Norris Wright?" she called out in a loud voice. She stepped on to the door in front of her. "I wish to speak to Norris Wright, and I wish to speak to him right now!"

Behind her, Amanda heard hurried footsteps. Then the meek voice of the secretary called out, "Mrs. Ojukwu, please! You can't—"

"I can, and I am," Amanda shouted over her shoulder. "Norris Wright, where are you?"

The door in front of her opened and a figure appeared. Behind Amanda, the secretary said, "Mr. Wright, I tried to stop her but she wouldn't—"

"It's okay, Juma," the man in the doorway said. Amanda could see that one of his hands was hidden behind his back. Even a year ago, she wouldn't have noticed such a minor detail, and wouldn't have known what it indicated even if she had. But she had picked up more than a few things on the streets. She knew that Wright had come to the door not knowing what to expect. He didn't know if the loud voice he heard just outside his office was a threat or just some crazy woman. And until that had been determined, he was keeping a hand on his gun.

"Is there a problem I can help you with?" Wright asked, as Amanda took a step toward him.

"Are you Special Agent in Charge Norris Wright?" Amanda demanded.

"Yes, ma'am, I am."

"Then there is indeed a problem with which you may help me, Mr. Wright," she said, stopping angrily with her own face less than a foot from his.

The serious expression the DEA man had worn up until now slowly melted into a patronizing smile. Good, Amanda thought. He's decided I'm just some crazy, irritating, black woman. In just a second here, his hand will drop away from the gun behind his back.

It did.

"Won't you step into my office?" Wright said. "We can discuss whatever it is there. Juma, could you bring two cups of coffee in, please."

"I require no coffee," Amanda said. "Or anything else except your prompt action in regard to the situation about which I am about to tell you."

Wright kept the phony smile on his face. "Then please," he said, "come in." He stepped back and waved a hand through the doorway.

Amanda's eyes skirted the room as she stalked importantly into it. She saw the desk—wood. She saw the chair in front of the desk where she knew she was about to be asked to sit— also wood. She scouted the area farther, hoping to find something metal that would be within her reach once she was seated. Something on which she could stick the magnetized thing James had given her.

"Please, have a seat, "Norris Wright said, indicating the chair with another sweep of his hand.

Amanda sat down.

Wright walked around his desk, and as he turned the corner Amanda saw the gun she had known was there sticking up out of the back of his pants. He dropped into the desk chair, then said, "How may I be of service, Mrs. Ojukwu?"

Amanda placed her new alligator purse in her lap and leaned slightly forward. She had palmed the smaller of the two devices he had given her—the one which went in the office rather than on the car—as she entered. Now, she said, "I shall get right to the point, Special Agent in Charge Wright. My seven-year-old son attends a private school for boys here in the city. Last night, I found a plastic bag of what I am certain was marijuana in the backpack in which he carries his schoolbooks."

The expression on Wright's face turned weary, telling Amanda he had indeed fallen for her act. To him, she was just another angry mother who thought her problems were the only ones in the world.

"I'm very sorry to here that, Mrs. Ojukwu," Wright said. "But I'm afraid that would be a matter for the local Nigerian police rather than the DEA. You see, we have no jurisdiction in this country except for—"

Amanda's eyes had continued to search for a place to plant the transmitter, and as she started to respond to the statement, they suddenly fell on a thin metal reinforcement strip running along the front of the desk, just below the overhanging top. "Special Agent in Charge Wright," she said in exasperation, "perhaps you have noticed by my accent that I am *not* Nigerian by birth?"

"Of course," Wright said smiling patiently.

"I am an American," Amanda said. "You are American, and the Drug Enforcement Administration is an American law-enforcement agency, is it not?"

"Yes, but—"

"There is something else of which you should be aware," Amanda said, straightening in her chair. "While I am an

American citizen, my husband is Nigerian. Perhaps you are familiar with him? He is a member of the cabinet." Now, she puffed up as importantly. "His name is Yakubu Ojukwu." She had pulled the name Ojukwu off the top of her head as she walked through the front door of the building, and had no idea if there was anyone in the Nigerian cabinet by that name.

"Of course I know Mr. Ojukwu," Wright said. "But—"

Amanda leaned suddenly forward with her arms, holding the purse in her lap with her breasts. Both of her hands reached under the desk top as if to brace herself. "Every sentence you speak to me begins with the word 'but,' Special Agent in Charge Wright," she said. "Am I to assume this means you do not intend to check into this matter? It is of grave concern, I assure you. Not only to me and my family but to children all over this nation."

"I will pass this information on to the local Nigerian police, Mrs. Ojukwu," Wright said.

Amanda sat back in her chair and forced a frightful face of anger across her features. Suddenly, she stood. "You may rest assured that Mr. Ojukwu shall hear of the fact that you refuse to act on this matter," she said. "As will the American consulate, and the director of the Drug Enforcement Administration in Washington."

Wright rose behind his desk. "Do what you feel you must do, Mrs. Ojukwu," he said. "I'm sorry I couldn't have been of more direct help." He smiled again, then said, "May I see you to the door?"

"I know the way!" Amanda snapped. She turned and stalked out of the office, through the short hall and past the secretary to the sidewalk. She cast a quick glance over her shoulder to make sure no one had followed, then turned the corner to the parking lot where the DEA vehicles stood. James Bond had described the vehicle she was looking for, and it was easy to find in the place reserved for it nearest the door. She walked nonchalantly that way, and seeing no one else in the lot, pulled the other device he had given her from her purse. As she reached the rear bumper of the blue Land Rover, she bent at the waist, reached under it and let the magnet attach itself to the metal.

Amanda Freeman Ironsi had just straightened back up when she felt the strong hands grab her shoulders from behind.

BOLAN WATCHED the few people on the sidewalk who walked by in front him. Unlike the vast majority of Lagos, which bustled with the activity of an overpopulated beehive, this strip of offices was an anomaly. It set away from the main areas of business activity, and few people seemed to frequent it except those who worked inside the buildings. Which was why the DEA had chosen the site, he suspected.

Amanda didn't take long to find a place to plant the transmitter. The Executioner heard a soft click over the receiver, then the woman's voice said in a haughty tone, "Am I to assume this means you do not intend to check into this matter? It is of grave concern, I assure you not only to me and my family but to children all over this nation."

A few more words were exchanged, then Bolan saw Amanda emerge onto the sidewalk. She turned away from where he was parked, back in the direction from which she had come, then suddenly disappeared around the corner into the parking lot.

Bolan backed out of the parking space. Over the receiver on the seat, he heard Norris Wright mutter under his breath, "Stupid bitch." Then the sounds of papers shuffling became the only sound from the DEA office.

Not wanting to back across traffic and draw attention, Bolan circled the block. He came up on the parking lot in time to see a man hurrying up behind Amanda. Even though the man's back was to him, he recognized him. Dirk Woodsen— the same young agent who had picked him up the day before, and driven him and Wright into the jungle.

Bolan increased his speed as Woodsen grabbed Amanda a second after she'd planted the homing device on the bumper. From all he'd seen of the young DEA agent, the man was honest. The Executioner would have bet his right arm that Woodsen wasn't involved with Wright and his enterprises outside the DEA office. But he'd also bet the Woodsen didn't know anything about Wright's illegal transactions, and he would see this situation as a stranger messing with his supervisor's vehicle. That was enough to arouse his suspicion for any number of logical reasons.

Woodsen had seen her at the bumper. In a moment, he'd check and find the homing device. Then he'd march Amanda back into the office building, where if Wright had the sense God gave a goose he'd also check his office for bugs.

And the Executioner couldn't afford to let that happen.

Amanda helped him more than she knew. Bolan pulled into the parking lot as the beautiful woman began flailing at Woodsen's face with both arms and screaming, "Rape! Rape! Somebody help me!"

Woodsen was blocking her blows as fast as they came, his mind on the attack and not what was taking place behind him. The Executioner drove right up behind him, rolling down his window a second before his foot stomped the brake and threw the vehicle into Park. Reaching through the opening, he circled his left arm around Woodsen's throat and jerked the man back against the Chevy. He continued to choke the young agent until the man's body went limp in his arm. Then, reaching behind him with his left hand, he lifted the case that housed the portable receiver and twisted, returning it to the back seat. Twisting, he used both hands to drag Woodsen's unconscious body through the window as he scooted across the seat to the passenger's side.

The Executioner glanced around the parking lot. As far as he could see, there was no one on the street to have observed what had just occurred.

Amanda stood frozen just outside the car. Bolan leaned

around Woodsen's sleeping form and said, "Get behind the wheel. You can drive, can't you?"

His words snapped the woman out of her momentary traumatic trance. "What a question," she said, as she opened the door and took the driver's seat. "I told you I was from Detroit, didn't I?"

"Prove it," Bolan said. "Before somebody comes out here and sees what's going on."

Amanda stayed cool, driving out of the parking lot to the street on the other side of the block quickly but without any tire screeching or other recklessness that might have drawn unwanted attention. "Where we going?" she asked once they were headed down the street.

"Just like I promised you," Bolan said. "To the airport."

Amanda gave him a quick sideways glance. "I hope you aren't expecting me to take him home with me," she said.

"No, I promised the ticket, the clothes and some traveling money," he said. "You're on your own when it comes to finding a new boyfriend."

Woodsen was wearing another of the baggy batik shirts he seemed to favor, and Bolan reached beneath the tail, running his hand around the man's belt until he found a S16-Sauer P-226 in an inside-the-waistband holster. He pulled it out and jammed it into his own belt, then searched further and came up with a set of handcuffs. It wasn't easy, as they drove along with all three in the front seat, but he finally managed to get Woodsen's hands cuffed behind his back. A second after that, the young agent regained consciousness.

Dirk Woodsen came to and immediately tried to draw his gun. He found he couldn't move his hand far enough to find the empty holster. His eyes were bleary but as they began to focus he looked at the Executioner next to him and said, "Clarke …?"

"Sort of," Bolan said.

The words only puzzled the man further. "What's going on?" he asked.

While Bolan was ninety-nine-percent certain Woodsen wasn't mixed up with Wright, this was a good chance to add the extra one percent. "You tell me," he said.

"There was this chick messing with Norris's car," Woodsen said. "I grabbed her and—" He glanced up into the rearview mirror, then jerked his head to the other side. "Hey! That's her! Clarke, what the hell—"

"Woodsen," Bolan said, and the sound of his name turned the young man back to face the Executioner. "You seem like a good kid with a great career ahead of you. But you're not going to understand much, if any, of this until it's over. So I'm not going to waste both of our time even trying to explain it."

Woodsen sat in dismay for a few seconds, then finally nodded in resignation. "You've sold out," he said. "Well, I hope they paid you enough to live with yourself." He stared at the Executioner, and now his eyes grew hard with hatred. "I suppose you're going to kill me now?"

Bolan shook his head. "No. But I'm going to have to keep you off the ground for a few days." He returned the man's stare but left the hatred out of his own eyes. "Take my word for it, Woodsen," he said. "When the dust settles, and the heads within the DEA start to roll, you'll be happy to have a good alibi to prove you weren't involved."

"Involved in what?" Woodsen asked.

"Your boss, Mr. Wright, is smack dab in the middle of the downed planes and an ongoing criminal drug enterprise."

Part of youthful morality, the Executioner knew, was an almost blind loyalty to those one respected. "You're a liar," Woodsen shouted. "Norris would never sell out." He shook his head. "No. I don't believe you. It's you who's crossed the fence. You're behind this mess."

"That belief is exactly why I've got to put you on ice for a few days," the Executioner answered. "You're a good man. But you're ignorant of the truth. And you'd go straight to Wright if I let you go."

Woodsen fell silent. Bolan pulled the cellular phone from his pocket and tapped in a number. When Grimaldi answered, he said simply, "Where are you, Jack?"

The pilot gave him a hangar number and directions to find it. By the time Bolan hung up they had reached the airport. The Executioner repeated what Grimaldi had told him, directing Amanda through a labyrinth of service roads that ran around the runways and buildings. When they reached the hangar, he took a quick glance around to make sure no one was watching, then pulled the handcuffed DEA agent out of the car before pushing him up into the jet. Amanda followed.

Grimaldi was in the back, reading a paperback novel. He looked up as they boarded the craft. "Well, well," the ace pilot said. "I'm drawing jailer duties again, am I?"

"Just for a little while," Bolan said. He explained who Woodsen was, then said, "Make him as comfortable as you can, Jack. He's okay. But he hasn't figured out who the good guys are in this game yet."

Grimaldi rose and walked to the lockers on the wall. He opened one of the green steel doors, and clanking sounds echoed inside the cabin as he pulled out a set of leg irons. Bolan seated Woodsen in one of the chairs bolted to the floor, and Grimaldi ran the leg irons around the legs of the chair before fastening them to the young DEA man's ankles. He unlocked the cuff on Woodsen's right wrist, then fastened it around the chair's armrest. "Want something to read before I sit back down?" he asked.

Woodsen just sulked without answering.

Grimaldi seemed to notice Amanda for the first time now. "Whoa, son," he said. "I hope you're planning to leave her, too." A wide grin covered his face ear to ear.

Amanda returned the smile.

"She's heading back for the States, Jack."

"Nah, that's no good," Grimaldi said. Still grinning like a

Cheshire cat, he pointed to Woodsen. "If you've got to send someone back, send him. I'd rather keep an eye on this beauty."

Amanda's smile became an almost girlish giggle of appreciation. She knew Grimaldi was kidding. But she also knew he appreciated her for her beauty. And he had no idea who, or what, she'd been only a few hours earlier. In short, both Bolan and Grimaldi had treated her like a beautiful woman, not a whore.

Bolan took the keys from Amanda and drove to the main terminal. He found a parking spot and escorted her quickly to the ticket counter. There was a plane leaving for Paris in half an hour with good connections to New York, and then Detroit. Setting the boxes containing the rest of her new clothes on the floor, the Executioner bought her ticket, then stuck the rest of the naira bills back into his pocket. From another pocket, he produced a roll of American money. "You'll need some bucks to eat on," he said. He pulled ten hundred dollar bills off the roll and handed them to her.

Amanda's eyes widened. "How much do you think I eat?" she asked as she took the money.

"And you'll need something to live on while you find a job," he said, handing her a thousand dollars more.

"Wow," Amanda said, taking those bills, too. "You need any more magnet deals stuck any place, you know the girl to call." New tears of happiness suddenly flooded her eyes, and a moment later she flung her arms around Bolan's neck, her face against his chest, her own chest heaving back and forth in sobs of gratitude.

Amanda wiped her face with the back of her wrist. "Thank you, James," she said. "Thank you with all my heart. You saved me."

Bolan shook his head. "You saved yourself by being what you are." He tapped his chest. "In here. You saved yourself by never giving up. Never telling yourself you were stuck where you were with no way out. You're a fighter, Amanda. And you're a winner."

Amanda opened her mouth to say something. But before she could, the Executioner had turned his back and walked away.

RAIN CLOUDS were gathering over Lagos by the time Bolan got back to the DEA office. He drove slowly past the parking lot, noting that Wright's Land Rover was no longer there. The portable radio receiver and homing device monitor was now on the seat next to him, and he unbuckled the snaps and lifted the lid. The battery-powered unit hummed for a few seconds as it warmed up, then several colored lights twittered on the various screens before settling into a steady glow. The Executioner adjusted the volume control that led to the bug in Wright's office. Nothing but static. He turned to the dial that led through the airwaves to the "homer" Amanda had mounted inside the Land Rover's bumper. It was equally dead.

Wherever Norris Wright and his Land Rover were, they were outside of the unit's reception area.

Bolan glanced at his watch. It was only midafternoon. That meant there was still a good chance Wright would return to the DEA office before the day was out. The best thing for the Executioner to do would be to find a nice, quiet, out-of-the-way place to park and wait. He needed somewhere where he wouldn't draw attention, where he could set up and wait for Wright to come back.

The same spot where Bolan had waited for Amanda was still vacant, and the Executioner pulled the rental car into the slot again. There had been little traffic—either street or side-walk—around this small office complex when the beautiful black woman had planted the devices. But if anything, the area was even more deserted now.

Bolan needed a reason to be where he was, a reason that would be passed over and not questioned by the small number of drivers and pedestrians who came down the street.

The Executioner got out of the car, walked to the front bumper and opened the hood. Leaning forward, he busied himself checking hoses and other components of the engine. From this vantage point, he could look to the sides of the car and see the street, or glance either way and watch the sidewalk. But he was all but shielded from the automobile traffic, and would appear to pedestrians to be just another man dealing with minor car trouble.

Bolan fiddled with the engine for fifteen minutes, then decided it was time to change spots. By now, any problem that he could have taken care of himself would have been fixed. If it was more serious, a normal driver would have given up and gone looking for a phone to call a tow truck. It was time to find a new place to set up. He slammed the hood and started back toward the door. He was just about to open it when he heard the voice.

"Hey, man, you have any spare change?"

Bolan looked up at the sidewalk and saw three young men in their early twenties standing there, grinning at him. Two were white, the third black. It was one of the white men, a tall lanky individual, who had spoken. When Bolan didn't answer, he took a step forward. "Hey, are you deaf?" he said. "I asked you if you had any spare change."

Bolan sighed as he looked down the street to make sure they hadn't drawn the attention of any of the DEA agents who might have chanced to choose that moment to exit the office. This was a complication he didn't need. "Yeah," he said. He reached into his pocket. "Take this." He pulled out two hundred naira in bills and extended his hand.

The lanky man closed the rest of the gap between them and ripped the money from the Executioner's fingers. All would have been fine had he turned with his friends to leave. Instead, he made a serious judgmental error. Mistaking the Executioner's gift as the payoff from a frightened foreigner, he said, "You sound American."

"I am," Bolan said, as he started to get into his car again.

"Then you have more money than this." The tall man

opened his mouth in another leering grin. Closer now, Bolan could see yellow teeth, and smell the malodorous breath they created. Behind him, the other two moved into the narrow area between Bolan's car and the one next to it.

The Executioner looked the lanky man in the eye, and what he saw told him there would be no getting rid of this trio of street punks by giving them more money. They wanted everything and had decided he was an easy mark. He had no time for this juvenile drivel, and it could do nothing but cause him trouble by drawing attention to him along the street. But these guys weren't going to go away on their own.

By now, the black man and the other white were directly behind their leader. Bolan saw that the other white man's face looked like a map of the moon—marred by the scars from teenaged acne. The black man wore his hair in a long Afro, the likes of which had rarely been seen since the 1970s. His hairy head moved forward behind the lanky man, and he mumbled something Bolan couldn't hear. The lanky leader nodded, and suddenly produced what looked like a chef's butcher knife from behind his back.

Bolan didn't hesitate. As the knife came around the man's side, he reached across his body and grasped the wrist holding it. Before the lanky man could cut downward at the Executioner's own wrist—a simple technique even the most rudimentarily trained knife fighter knew how to perform—he brought his opposite forearm across and slammed it against the flat of the blade. The big knife flew from the hand of the surprised man's fingers.

A short backfist from the Executioner sent two of the yellow-brown teeth dropping from the lanky man's mouth. A right cross dropped him to the pavement after them. Behind him, the black man had drawn an old-fashioned leather sap from his pocket. It was already over his head. Bolan took a half-step back as it arched down through the air at his head. With the clean miss, the man's own momentum carried his arm down and threw him off balance, leaning forward. Bolan reached out and grabbed a handful of hair and jerked him further forward. He tripped over his already downed leader and sprawled facedown between the cars.

The Executioner raised his fist over his head and brought it down in a hammer-hand that struck the man right where his neck joined his head. He was out before Bolan could look up. When he did, he saw that the other white man was already a half-block away, and running as fast as his legs could churn.

Rising above the Chevy's rooftop, the Executioner looked back down the street just in time to see two middle-aged DEA agents come out of the office. He ducked back down, rising again until only his eyes peered over the roof of the car. The two men paused in front of the building to light cigarettes, then turned the corner into the parking lot.

The only emotion the Executioner felt as he looked back down at the two unconscious street hoodlums at his feet was disgust. Had this altercation begun five seconds later, the DEA men couldn't have missed it. As it stood now, he had two unconscious little punks he'd have to do something with before Wright returned to the office or other DEA agents came out.

Hurrying to the trunk, Bolan inserted the key and lifted it. He rummaged inside one of his equipment bags until he'd found the roll of duct tape, then returned to where the black man lay on top of his white cohort in crime. Thirty seconds later, both men's legs were taped together and their arms were secured behind their backs. Wide strips of silver tape covered their mouths and eyes. The lanky man was coming around again now, and Bolan leaned in close to his ear. "You make one noise and I'll kill you," he said. "You understand me?"

The bound, gagged and blindfolded man nodded.

"Then go back to sleep for a while," Bolan said, and sent another right cross solidly into the man's jaw. He took another quick glance around the area before stuffing both men into the trunk and slamming it shut again. He got back in the car and started backing out of the parking space.

The Executioner had cleared the other parked cars and was about to turn the wheels when he heard a faint beep come from the receiver on the seat next to him. He switched his foot from the accelerator to the brake and waited. A second later, the sound returned a tiny bit louder. Then a steady series of beeps, growing gradually louder, begin to emanate from the speaker. He pulled back into the parking space and turned to look at the monitor. The fact that the sounds were growing in volume, with shorter intervals between them, meant the transmitter was getting closer to the receiver. Wherever he'd been, Norris Wright was coming back to the DEA office.

Bolan looked at the screen. While it was incapable of specifics, it did show general directions. And it indicated now that the Land Rover was approaching from the southeast.

The Executioner slumped low behind the wheel, but twisted to look out the rear windshield. Thirty second later, the dark blue Land Rover drove by less than three feet from his rear bumper. Wright was driving. But there was someone in the passenger's seat. A shorter man. The Land Rover continued down the street, turning back into the parking lot by the DEA office and disappearing around the corner.

Bolan rose behind the wheel, leaning slightly forward to look down the sidewalk. A minute or so later, Wright rounded the corner of the building on foot. With him was a man dressed in a light off-white suit that couldn't have possibly come off any rack. The suit, and the man wearing it, was almost as wide as it was tall. But even beneath the baggy material, the Executioner could tell that the man's width didn't come from obesity. He walked with the confidence, balance, and even grace of a well-trained athlete. Bolan squinted, studying the man's face. He hadn't been at the crash site in the jungle, and the Executioner didn't recognize him from anywhere else, either. Not that the face mattered in this case. The powerful shoulders, arms and legs would have been unforgettable even if a face had never been seen to go with them.

The two men disappeared inside the DEA office's front doors.

From the bug Amanda had planted, the Executioner heard the sounds of them entering Wright's private office. The SAC called out, "Juma, hold my calls." There was a muffled female response from somewhere in the background, then a door closed.

Wheels squeaked—a desk chair rolling on its rollers. Bolan visualized Wright taking a seat behind his desk. Then a gruff laugh sounded over the radio monitor, and a gravelly voice said, "Your girl there, Juma, she still thinks I'm a paid DEA informant?"

Wright was the one who laughed this time. "Oh, yes, my personal informant who won't deal with anyone but me," he said. "The other agents think the same thing."

"You told them that?" the gravelly voice asked. The accent was South African rather than Nigerian.

"No, I let them come to that conclusion on their own," Wright snickered. "Far more effective that way." He paused, then went on. "You've never been on this side of the desk in the drug trade, Dolph. So I don't expect you to understand the subtleties involved. But your comings and goings, with no explanation, are identical to what an informant might do. And it would be considered very bad form indeed for any of the other agents to get too nosy about someone's private snitch. Especially one who reported straight to the boss."

The laugh the South African gave now sounded like rocks going through a blender. "Very convenient," he said.

"Hey, you use what works, right?"

The muscular South African Bolan had seen on the street didn't respond. But the Executioner could almost see him nod. Instead, he said, "Where are the drums we took off the plane?"

"They're safe," Wright said. "And it's not that I don't trust you. But the fewer people who know where we stored them the better."

"You better not try to fuck me over on this, Norris."

"You know me better than that," Wright said. "There's more than enough money in this for both of us. Besides, it's worth it to be square with you. You think I want to spend the rest of my life looking over my shoulder to see if you're there?"

"You wouldn't have to look long."

Wright either didn't notice the implied threat or didn't take it seriously. "When the time comes, you'll be with me," he said.

Bolan frowned. The time? What time? he wondered.

"What about this Kenneth Clarke asshole, by the way?" the South African asked. "What's become of him?"

"I don't know," Wright said. "He's simply disappeared."

"I don't like that, Norris. It's a loose end we don't need. It's the kind of thing that can come back later and bite you in the ass." He grunted. "He doesn't sound like the wimp he tried to make you think he was."

"No," Wright said. "That was an act. He was definitely sent to snoop around, and I don't like it any better than you do." The DEA man cleared his throat. "But what's the worst-case scenario? He's figured things out and reports back to Washington that I'm playing for the other team? They take a long time, and go through more red tape than you can dream of before they get the okay to act on something like that. Our deal goes down tomorrow. We'll be long gone before they try anything."

The thick man grunted his agreement.

Bolan frowned harder, his eyebrows almost touching his nose. Wright had just admitted he was in the illegal drug trade. But what was the deal they were talking about? If Bolan was reading it right, it sounded like something separate from the drugs. The Executioner heard a click. He frowned, wondering what it was. Then, a second later, there was the sound of a deep breath being expelled. One of the men had just lit a cigarette with a lighter. As it turned out, it had to have been the South African because Wright's voice said, "Let me have one of those."

A shuffling sound, like something being pushed across a desk, came over the receiver. Then the man with the gravelly voice said, "It's probably time to start buying your own again, Norris."

Wright chuckled, and when he spoke he sounded somewhat like Hal Brognola when the Stony Man director had one of his cigars clamped in his teeth. "I'll buy you some," the DEA man said. "If I buy my own, I won't be able to lie to myself about taking up the habit again."

"Have you talked to our kaffir friend today?" the South African asked.

Wright laughed. "He's not a kaffir," he said.

Bolan frowned again. Kaffir was a derogatory term for black man used by racist South Africans.

"Sand kaffir?" the muscle man asked, and both of them laughed again.

"I'll be talking to him tonight. He's getting the money together."

"I suppose that takes a little doing. Even for him."

"Yeah," Wright said. "Not even he finds that kind of cash accidentally fallen under the cushions of his sofa. But he'll have it, and have it here, by tomorrow." The long draw on a cigarette came over the radio waves. "Suppose you come over tonight while I call him. After that, I'm out of my house for good," Wright said.

Bolan didn't know what the South African's answer was because no words came over the receiver. He had either nodded or shaken his head for yes or no.

There was a shuffling sound as one of the men inside the office stood. "I'd better get back," the South African said. He paused. "I rode here with you. You have a car I can take?"

A click came over the radio waves. "Juma?" Wright asked.

The female voice that came back was obviously on an office speakerphone. "Yes, sir, Mr. Wright?"

"Where's Woodsen?"

There was a short pause and the rustling of papers. "I don't really know, sir. He hasn't checked out, but he's not in his office," she answered.

"Probably in the can," Wright said. "Give this gentleman who's about to leave my office a set of keys to his car, and tell Woodsen he'll need to grab a ride home with one of the other agents."

"Yes, sir."

The click sounded again.

"Do any of your agents suspect anything?" the South African asked.

"No," Wright said. Bolan heard the soft sounds of their feet on the carpet as they made their way toward the door. "Especially Woodsen. He's young. And he thinks I hung the moon."

The now-familiar gravel-grunt issued forth again from the South African. Then a door opened and closed. Bolan heard Wright sit back down behind his desk.

The Executioner reached for his cell phone. At about the same time the man called Dolph emerged from the front of the building before disappearing around the corner into the parking lot. And over the receiver, Bolan heard Wright lift the telephone on his desk and tap numbers into the instrument. His own phone in hand, he waited. A moment later, Wright began to speak into the phone.

In Arabic.

The Executioner mentally kicked himself for not connecting a recorder to the monitor on the seat next to him. He didn't speak Arabic and had no idea what the call was about. But when he added it to the South African's derogatory joke about sand kaffirs, it became obvious the call had to do with whatever the other deal was the two men had going.

Bolan twisted in his seat and jerked a tape recorder and wire connection from his equipment. But by the time he had it plugged in, Wright was hanging up.

A different Land Rover—rust colored and a year older than

the new one Wright had commandeered for himself—pulled out of the parking lot and drove past the Executioner. Bolan watched it. He could try to follow the South African, but there was every chance of losing the man once they got out of this quiet area and entered the chaotic traffic found in most of Lagos. No, he'd stick with Wright. Not only was the bug planted on the man's Land Rover, the Executioner's instincts told him the DEA man was the person to watch. This Dolph might be a partner in both the drug business and whatever this "other deal" was they were planning, but Wright was the key.

The sounds of paper shuffling told the Executioner that Wright was busy at his desk. He took advantage of the brief respite in the action to finally use the cellular phone that had been in his hand. Tapping in the number to Stony Man Farm, he told Kurtzman he needed an ID on a short stocky South African named Dolph, and passed on the rest of what he'd learned.

"The big question, Bear," Bolan said, "is what's really in the fifty-five-gallon drums they took off the plane. Until now, I thought it was the eradication chemicals they mix into the spray. I assumed they switched the drums with fakes, and shot down the other planes carrying the same chemicals, so their crops wouldn't be killed. But after hearing this, I'm not so sure." He stopped talking for a moment and scratched his head. "Do you have any way of finding out if the FAA people have tested the contents of the containers that were on the plane when it was checked?"

"Let me see what I can do," the Stony Man computer wizard said. Bolan heard the tapping of keyboard keys in the background. A moment later, Kurtzman said, "I've got a copy of a report by some guy named Charles in front of me on the screen," he said.

"Ryan Charles," Bolan said. "I met him at the crash site. From Morocco."

"That's him. They tested the drums once they had them back in a controlled environment. Tested positive." Kurtzman paused. "It really was eradication chemicals on the plane when it crashed."

"I don't think so," the Executioner said. "But I think it really was eradication chemicals on the plane by the time the FAA and DEA got to it." He scratched his head again. "We've been working under the assumption that Wright took the chemicals off the plane so they couldn't be used to destroy his drug fields. I think that's a faulty assumption. It's beginning to look like he put real chemicals *back on*."

"Why would anyone—" Kurtzman began.

"Because they made an initial switch before the plane took off from the States," Bolan said. "They took the real chemicals off and put something else they wanted transported to Lagos in its place. Then, when the plane went down, they had to cover it by making a second switch and putting real chemicals back on."

"Then what was it they flew to Africa after they made the first switch?" Kurtzman asked. "And if they left the real chemicals in the U.S., how did they get them to Africa in time to make the second swap in the jungle?"

"They didn't get the real chemicals from America to Africa that fast, Bear," Bolan said. "They didn't have to. They used eradication drums they'd taken from the first two planes. The ones they shot down."

"Okay, I'm with you so far," Kurtzman said. "But you still haven't answered my other question. What was it that came over on the plane and they took out of the jungle?"

"That's the sixty-four-thousand-dollar question," the Executioner said. "We find the answer to that, we'll have the key to whatever this 'other deal' is Wright and Dolph have set up."

"Let me get off here so I can find out just who Dolph actually is," Kurtzman said.

"Thanks, Bear," the Executioner said and hung up.

Bolan waited patiently, listening to the bug in Wright's office, but hearing nothing more of interest for another hour.

When Wright left the office just before five o'clock, the Executioner used the homer attached to the Land Rover's bumper to follow the man. The Land Rover led him into one of Lagos's few wealthy residential areas. But, able to stay much farther behind than he would had he been forced to tail the DEA man visually, Wright had already parked the Land Rover and entered the house by the time Bolan drove past a few minutes later.

The Executioner parked down the street, wishing he had a bug inside Wright's house as well as his office. On the other hand, it appeared Wright was alone so he wasn't likely to learn much more. Maybe Dolph was joining him for the phone call later, maybe he wasn't. But it made no difference at that point. Even if the Executioner snuck up and taped into the phone lines, the call would be in Arabic. There wasn't time to record it, get it back to Stony Man Farm for translation and find out what it had been about. Not when Wright had been clear that their other deal was going down tomorrow.

Bolan turned the ignition back on. There were other ways to get more information. Pulling away from the house, he started back toward his room at the Wayfarers Hotel. He was halfway there when he remembered the street punks in the trunk and pulled into an alley.

They were still unconscious as he dropped them over the side of the trash bin and closed the lid.

The rain clouds that had formed earlier began to break as Bolan neared the airport. By the time he reached the hangar again, a light drizzle was falling. He braked to a halt, cut the engine and got out. Two steps later he was out of the rain and beneath the hangar's metal covering. As he approached the Lear jet, the raindrops made quiet, restful, pings on the corrugated roof overhead Their tranquillity seemed to be the opposite polarity to what was going on in Lagos in regard to Wright and his partner, Dolph.

The soldier boarded the plane through the cabin door. It was empty, but he heard voices coming from the back. He turned that way and found Grimaldi seated in the rear of the aircraft. A wry grin was on the pilot's face as he listened good-naturedly to a threat-filled moralization by Dirk Woodsen. The young DEA man was telling Grimaldi about the horrors of prison life, and just what awaited both him and Kenneth Clarke once Woodsen was again free. Bolan passed the young man handcuffed to the seat across from Grimaldi. The Executioner's primary reason for returning to the airport was to pick up a specific piece of equipment. But a secondary motive was to insure that the young agent wasn't suffering psychologically any more than necessary. Woodsen's attitude proved that. The only thing that had been hurt was his pride—and nobody had ever died from that. The young man had figured out that he wasn't going to be killed, and probably even suspected by now that the agent he'd known as Kenneth Clarke, and this pilot, were actually good guys rather than bad. But that didn't mean he liked being held prisoner. He was young, and being in such a helpless situation bruised his dignity as a man.

Woodsen turned his threats Bolan's way as the Executioner appeared. Ignoring them, Bolan strode to the row of lockers on the wall and opened one near the middle. He breathed a silent sigh of relief when he saw the black leather case. During the hours he'd spent waiting outside the DEA office—first for Amanda while she planted the bug, then later for Wright to return—he'd had time to study the burglar alarm system on the building. While he was confident that he could disarm the unit manually, doing so would mean he would have to leave it unengaged while he searched the premises. That could cause problems. Many modern alarms systems automatically sent out a signal the moment they were disarmed by any but conventional means. Therefore, it would be much safer to enter the building just like one of the agents—by using the code. Bolan unzipped the case and looked inside, making sure what he needed was there. His problem was that he didn't know the code. That problem was about to be solved with the very special piece of equipment he now held in his hands.

Zipping the case back up, the Executioner turned to Grimaldi. "Everything okay?" he asked.

"A-okay," he said. Then his face took on a grimace of mock fear as he nodded toward Woodsen. "But it sure sounds like we're in for hell when this is over." The fear faded from his features and he winked at the Executioner.

Bolan nodded. He turned to Woodsen. "I don't have time to explain it all to you now," he said. "But when this is over, you'll understand why I had to do this. And you'll be glad I did."

Woodsen's chin shot out defiantly. "Fuck you."

Jack Grimaldi burst out laughing.

The Executioner looked at the young DEA agent, more convinced than ever that Woodsen was a good man. Who could blame him for being confused at this point? Bolan's eyes narrowed. He could use someone watching his back if the young man could be trusted. He didn't have time to explain things well enough to develop that trust right now. And for what he was about to do, he didn't need his back watched, either.

Bolan shoved the idea of turning Woodsen from enemy to ally onto the back burner. It would have to wait. He started to leave the plane.

"Nice of you to drop by, Striker," Grimaldi said. "Before the sermon began, I was just trying to interest our new friend here in a game of pinochle. Sure you don't have time to join us?" The question, like Grimaldi's feigned fear, was made in jest. Stony Man Farm's number-one pilot knew the answer to that question.

"Maybe some other time," Bolan said, as he dropped down off the plane. With the black case under his arm, he jogged back through the rain to the car.

The sprinkle had become a shower, and was threatening to become a full-fledged storm by the time the Executioner reached the DEA office again. He parked the Chevy on a side street where he could see both the parking lot and front entrance, then doffed the pants and jacket he had again used to conceal his weapons and blacksuit. There were still lights on inside the building so he waited.

Bolan's eyebrows lowered in thought. It had become blatantly obvious that Norris Wright led a double life. He was the special agent in charge of this DEA foreign field office. But when he put on his other hat, he was a major player—maybe *the* major player—in what appeared to be one of the biggest drug syndicates in Africa. The Executioner didn't know for sure, but he suspected it was the mysterious organization law-enforcement agencies had dubbed the Ivory Coast cartel. Wright had gone out of his way earlier to play down the Ivory Coast's significance. In any case, the name made little difference. It was an organization big enough to have its own air force that could shoot down DEA planes.

The Executioner turned his attention back to his immediate plans. What all this meant to him right now was that Wright led two very distinct groups of men. One group was made up of good men—the DEA agents. The other group was scum—the drug-dealing, murdering employees of the Ivory Coast cartel. But he had seen Dolph at the DEA office earlier in the day, and that meant that bad guys as well as good guys went there. And that, in turn, meant he might encounter men from either group once he'd penetrated the security system and began searching the office. If he was discovered while inside the building, he would have to make a decision, and he was likely to have to to do it in a microsecond. Anyone—good guy or bad—who came upon him during the soft probe would regard him as an intruder.

Bolan's jaw set hard, his teeth tight together. Handling the druggies would be easy—he'd kill them and go on about his business. If he met up with any honest DEA agents, the situation could become dangerous very quickly. They'd shoot him as fast as the cartel men. But he had no intention of shooting back. So how would he handle such a situation?

The truth was, he didn't know. And he wouldn't until it happened.

The last DEA agent left the office at a little after 8:00 p.m. Through the glass door Bolan watched him turn off the lights, set the alarm by punching in the code, and then twist his key in the door lock after he left the building. A final shake of the door insured him it was secure, and he circled the corner of the building to the parking lot.

The Executioner's eyes focused intently on the man as he got into one of the DEA SUVs. He was of medium height with a sturdy build, and had short hair that looked like it would turn wavy if he let it grow longer. Bolan had carefully studied the personnel files faxed to him by Kurtzman, and the man's face fit the picture in one of those files. His name was Wojtowicz. John Henry Wojtowicz, and he had been born in Beaver Falls, Pennsylvania. The dossier also mentioned, as might well have been predicted, that his nickname was "Wojo."

Bolan watched the man drive away, gave it another five minutes, then got out of the car. Flashes of lightning now filled the sky, followed by booms of thunder. Few people had been on the streets during the day in the sunshine, but now, at night during a thunderstorm, the entire area was deserted.

The Executioner grabbed the black leather case, tucked it under his arm like a football and sprinted across the street like a tailback hitting open field. From one of the pockets of his blacksuit, he produced his set of picks. A moment later, the tumblers in the door lock had rolled into place and the lock clicked open.

The low-pitched buzz of the alerted alarm system hummed softly amid the sounds of the storm outside. Bolan knew he had only thirty seconds to enter the code before the device sent out word that it had been violated. He had already unzipped the case, and now he pulled out an instrument that looked somewhat like a small notebook computer. Three color-coded wires extended from the back of the unit, and all three had a suction cup attached to the end. Placing the suction cups at strategic spots on the face of the alarm control, Bolan unfolded the small machine to expose a tiny screen. He flipped the switch on the side of the device marked On and glanced at his watch.

Fifteen seconds had gone by since he'd opened the door.

Bolan waited. A second later, a red digit appeared on the screen. His thoughts traveled to the creators of the device in his hands. The code-finder had been a joint effort between Aaron Kurtzman, the Stony Man Farm computer wizard, and Hermann "Gadgets" Schwarz, the Able Team warrior who was equally talented in the electronics field.

Another number appeared on the screen, then two more. Bolan's watch told him he had nine seconds left.

The second hand on the Executioner's watch continued to revolve, and he saw that only four seconds remained before entering the code would be useless. And he had no way of knowing if it was a four-, five-, or even a six-digit code that the alarm required. All he did know what that he was running out of time. Every second counted now, and he had to get started.

Reaching up to the alarm, he quickly tapped in the sequence. At the same time his trigger finger pushed the code, another digit appeared on the code-finder screen. He jabbed his finger over and up, and pressed the corresponding number at the same moment his watch told him he as out of time.

Bolan held his breath. He had entered five digits. If the code took six, he was out of luck, and all hell was about to break loose.

But he wasn't. The words Code Complete appeared in electronic red lights.

The Executioner reset the alarm, then stuffed his equipment back in the case and slung it over his shoulder on the carry strap. He looked down at the floor and saw the wet spots he had brought in from the rain. But there was no time, and little reason, to go looking for a mop. If anyone saw it, they'd simply assume the water had come from the wet shoes and clothing of one of the other agents.

Bolan moved away from the glass doorway, where even through the falling thunderstorm he suspected he might be visible from the street. Turning, he found himself in an outer office-reception area. The light filtering in through the door from the street was dim, but he could make out the form of a circular desk and computer hutch. And each time lightning flashed outside, more details became visible. Details such as the framed photographs and potted plants that littered the desktop.

The ASP laser flashlight had been shot to pieces at the warehouse, but the Executioner had his backup—a mini-flashlight. He would have chosen it over the ASP under these conditions anyway because it cast a faint glow that would be adequate for his search but harder to spot from the street. His first task was a quick security check of the entire building to assure that he was indeed alone. In doing so, he found that the complex consisted of two hallways leading off the reception area. The first corridor, to the left, led to a long hallway where the agents assigned to this foreign field office worked. All of their offices were empty, and Bolan saw no reason to waste time in a more thorough search. Ninety-nine percent of the Drug Enforcement Administration agents he had known over the years were good men and women, risking their lives to serve their country. He strongly doubted they were involved with Wright other than through the DEA.

Moving back past the reception area, Bolan entered the other hall. It led to a single door that opened to the largest office in the complex. It would be that of the special agent in charge. Wright. Moving silently across the carpet in the wake of the miniflashlight's beam, Bolan stopped in front of the desk. He ran his hand just below the overhang of the desktop. The transmitter was exactly where Amanda had said it would be.

The device had been in place less than a day, but the batteries in such units had disappointingly short life spans. Swiftly, Bolan replaced them, then moved back to the doorway. Starting on the right-hand side of the door, he worked his way around the office in a counterclockwise direction, shining the beam along the wall. He saw the usual male decorations. Certificates, photos and various other honors the SAC had received. A framed degree from Louisiana State University told the Executioner that Wright had double majored in history and political science, and matched the information Bolan had learned from the DEA personnel file. He moved the light on. Several African tribal masks and a spear had been mounted on the rear wall, and the final wall consisted of a painting by some local artist, which hung over a couch.

His perimeter search complete, the Executioner moved directly to the desk. It was a large mahogany piece that Bolan guessed had been purchased by the SAC himself—the DEA wasn't likely to have wasted money on it. Next to the desk was a less elaborate computer hutch that housed a Compaq Presario. A large filing cabinet set opposite the hutch.

Bolan began his search with the desk, finding nothing more interesting than paperclips and the type of aboveboard DEA paperwork he would have expected. He was trying to decide which to search next—filing cabinet or computer—when he heard the sounds from the front of the building.

A key had been inserted into the lock on the glass door. A moment later, the door opened and the hum of the alarm sounded in the entryway.

Voices and laughter drifted back to him as the Executioner moved quickly across the office to the hallway door. He had left it open as he had found it, and he pressed his back to the wall at the side. Peering around the corner, he saw the faces of two agents he recognized from the personnel files. Both were middle-aged and slightly overweight. He remembered their names. Richard Morris and Tim Morgan.

But the two men weren't alone. Three young women with Nigerian accents accompanied them, and they had obviously all imbibed more than their fair share of alcohol during the past few hours. Morgan moved to the alarm as he slurred, "Don't look, now." The women laughed and dramatically turned their backs and shielded their eyes with their hands. "Yes, Sahib," one of them said, and the other two seemed to think the comment worthy of gales of more laughter. Morgan entered the code and the buzzing stopped.

The fumes of alcoholic beverages wafted across the reception to Bolan as the Nigerian girls continued to giggle drunkenly. They were still facing away from the two men, and Morris reached out and pinched the nearest girl. She squealed and jumped into the air, then turned and began to swing her fists halfheartedly at the man amid a new explosion of cackles.

Bolan stayed to the side of the door as the party of four stumbled toward the hall leading to the agents' offices, then he made his way back to the desk. Morris and Morgan weren't there in response to an intruder call, and they had obviously not come to the office to work. The chances of them entering the room he was in were slim. In fact, they showed all the indications of two men who were about to be preoccupied with other pursuits for quite some time.

The Executioner dropped into the seat at the computer hutch and checked the files on the machine's hard drive. He shook his head. There were more documents than he could ever hope to search in one night here. Rising, he moved quickly back across the office to the reception area, then walked quietly to the door leading down the other hall. From one of the offices halfway down, he could hear a chorus of moans, heavy breathing and an occasional slapping sound. The orgy was in progress. The agents weren't about to interrupt him for a while. He closed both the reception area door and the door to Wright's office behind him as he returned to the computer. Bolan lifted the phone. A moment later he had Kurtzman on the line. "I'm about to send you a present, Bear," he said. "I'll need you to erase the trail of both it and this call."

"No problem," Kurtzman said. "Can you tell me what it is or do I have to wait for Christmas to open it?"

"I'm about to send you all the documents on Wright's computer," Bolan answered. "I don't have time to look them over here. I'm going to need to know what you've found as soon as possible."

"Okay. Shoot it through. I'll get on it ASAP."

Bolan hung up and turned his attention back to the computer. A few minutes later, he had connected the hard drive to the line at Stony Man Farm, and the files were on the way. He stood and hurried back to the other part of the building.

Again, the moans, screeches, shrieks and a few unidentifiable sounds assured him that Morgan and Morris were busy. He entered Wright's office once again and took a seat in front of the filing cabinet.

Starting with the top drawer, the Executioner used the flashlight to search the alphabetized labels on the manila file folders. All pertained to DEA managerial business. He spot-checked a few to make sure the labels weren't a ruse, then closed the drawer and opened the one beneath it. These files were alphabetized as well. They concerned specific cases rather than management. Bolan did the same spot check, coming up with nothing of interest. He was about to close that drawer, too, when a small cream-colored spot caught his eye against the gunmetal gray at the rear of the drawer.

The Executioner pulled the drawer all the way out of the cabinet and set it on the floor. Another of the manila file folders fell haphazardly inside the opening. It had been hidden behind the back of the drawer. It bore no label. He opened the file and trained the flashlight on its contents, finding two stacks of documents, a rubber band holding each stack together. In the first stack he found roughly two years' worth of monthly rental receipts for an office at another location in Lagos. The second stack was made up of canceled checks that corresponded to the receipts. The checks had all been signed by Wright.

The Executioner squinted at the two piles. He had come across canceled checks in the other drawers, but they had all been written on accounts in the DEA's name printed across the checks. The canceled documents he saw before him now were from a private account in Wright's name, and bore no indication of his association with the Drug Enforcement Administration.

The address of the other office was printed on the receipts. Bolan memorized it, then wrapped the rubber bands around the stacks again and dropped them back into the folder before replacing it inside the filing cabinet. He had just slid the drawer back into place when he heard the drunken laughter in the hallway just outside the office.

Already on his knees in front of the filing cabinet, it was a short twist and into the chair well beneath the desk. The Executioner had just pulled his boots in out of sight and killed the light from the flashlight, when the door to the office opened.

"I want to do it on his desk," an unseen feminine voice said, giggling. "I want to do it on the big man's desk."

"Your wish is my command," answered a male. Bolan didn't know if it was Morris or Morgan. And he didn't care. All he knew was that he was about to experience a delay he didn't need. But as he heard the two drunks climb onto the desktop above him, he knew he was stuck where he was. He wouldn't be leaving the offices until the two sated their lust and went on to find other amusement.

Bolan could only pray it didn't take too long.

Unfortunately, his prayer went unanswered—the alcohol in the DEA agent's system made sure of that. But if the noises issuing forth from the mouth of the woman above him were any indication, she didn't seem to mind. Bolan accepted the inevitable, and leaned back against the underside of the desk to wait it out. His thoughts returned to what he had found in the back of the filing cabinet.

Wright had been renting a second office for the past two years. And he had used a private account to pay the rent. Why? Why hadn't he used one of the regular DEA accounts? There were two possible reasons. This office complex might see little traffic, but it wouldn't have been kept secret from the Nigerian underworld for very long. Maybe Wright had decided his agents needed an unknown spot to meet with informants—a place where snitches and undercover officers wouldn't be spotted and identified. If that was the case, Wright might have used his personal account in order to additionally cloak the office's purposes from the landlord. He could have made arrangements to be reimbursed by the DEA for the expense. Such things were not uncommon.

But Bolan knew in his heart that wasn't the case. Not in this instance.

Bolan's instincts told him that wasn't the reason for the second office. What would have been the point in hiding the file behind the drawer in the cabinet if that was the case? No, the other office wasn't for DEA use. In fact, no one within the DEA, other than Wright, was even aware of its existence. The other office was the place out of which Wright and his friend Dolph conducted their drug cartel business.

Finally, the man and woman rolled off the desk and lumbered back out of the office. As soon as he heard the door slam, Bolan emerged from under the desk and rose to his feet. A quick final scan of the office with the flashlight assured him he had left no traces of his presence. Then he crept out into the short hall between Wright's office and the outer area. The door from the hall to the reception area had been left wide open, and he stopped, listening.

The orgy down the other hall sounded as if it had resumed. At least the same type of noises he had heard while hiding below the desk filled the air.

Bolan crept to the alarm system, entered the code to deactivate the alarm, then set it again. The hum returned, telling him he had thirty seconds to get through the door. He wasted no time locking it behind him—it would take too long using the picks, and if the humming sound happened to be heard amid the grunts, groans, moans and other wailing that echoed off the walls in the agents' wing of the complex, Morris and Morgan might come out to see what was going on. But unless they actually saw him there, Bolan foresaw no problem. According to the personnel files, both men were not only married, they were violating DEA policy by bringing the girls to the office as they had done. The guilty consciences of men in such circumstances—especially when drunk—tended to blame their own mistakes for anything out of the ordinary. They would think they'd simply forgotten to relock the door upon entering, and by the time they got out to the alarm it would be reset. The hum would go down as nothing but their culpable imagination.

The rain had stopped but deep puddles still remained in the street. The Executioner jogged through them, his boots sending splashes to both his sides. He unlocked the Chevy's door, slid behind the wheel and reached back into his memory for the address he'd found on the receipts.

A moment later, he was on his way to Norris Wright's covert office.

THE OTHER OFFICE was in a run-down, two-story building in the Yaba section of Lagos, a block and a half from an entertainment area where two local bars of renown were located. As he opened the door and got out of the rented Chevy, the jazz music from Art's Place met his ears. Drifting in from a slightly different direction, he could hear the more traditional African chords of Yoruba Chief Ebenezer Obey, the musician who headlined at Melki's Spot.

The Executioner locked the car and looked up at the building. It looked deserted. Not just for the night but for eternity. And it looked as if that desertion had taken place years ago.

Bolan had once again thrown on the light jacket and baggy khakis over his blacksuit, and looked like any other man heading toward the nightlife and a good time. He followed the sidewalk to the front of the building, keeping his gaze straight ahead and watching the place out of the corner of his eye. At the end of the block, he ducked into the alley and stayed in the shadows as he made his way past trash containers. A ragged, gray-and-yellow tiger-striped cat darted out past him, then stopped and followed him down the alley to the rear of the building.

From what Bolan could see, the structure had once been a

two-story office complex, and from the rear, it looked even more run-down than before. As the cat began to softly mew and rub against the soldier's calf, his eyes searched the building for any signs of an alarm system such as he'd dealt with at the DEA office. He saw none. At this location it appeared that Wright's security system consisted of anonymity rather than electronics.

Several windows ran along the back, with an ancient wooden door in the center of the structure. Bolan walked forward. The cat, appearing to have adopted him for the time being, kept pace at his side. The doorknob was gone from the door and he pushed it open. The cat darted between his legs into a common hallway and disappeared into the darkness. The Executioner followed it inside the building.

Dust from years of neglect and the stench of rotting wood filled the Executioner's nostrils. He walked along the hallway with the flashlight as his guide, casting the beam ahead of him. In the center of the hall, he saw steps leading to the second floor. Three formerly occupied office complexes sat on one side of the steps, three on the other. Bolan cast the light back and forth across the hall, checking the doors as he passed. Some were old and as decrepit as the rest of the building. Other doors were missing all together. He caught the cat in the beam as the animal darted inside one such open entryway. Then the feline disappeared amid a muddle of wine bottles, beer cans, torn and mangy mattresses, and other tracks left by Lagos street people who had obviously taken up squatters' rights there sometime in the past. But now, even the homeless had abandoned this building for greener pastures.

For a moment, the Executioner wondered if the address on the receipts in Wright's hidden file had been wrong—a foul-up at the printer's that the owner of the building didn't think worth the hassle of changing. It was a possible. But since he was already there he might as well check out the upper floor before regrouping.

Bolan stayed to one edge of the rickety steps as he mounted the stairs, hoping that the decayed wood wouldn't give way beneath his weight. He felt a presence to his rear, then the dirty tiger-striped cat bounded confidently past him to disappear once more in the darkness of the second floor. Once he reached the top, the Executioner repeated the process of checking the doorways. He found what he was looking for on the second door to his right.

A new brass lock and doorknob gleamed under the glow from the flashlight. Above it was a dead bolt. When he raised the light over the door, floor to ceiling, he saw that the whole door was new. A wood-grain pattern covered the front. Stepping forward, Bolan rapped lightly on the door and heard a hard pinging sound rather than the thud that should have been produced. No one answered his knock. He hadn't expected them to, and that hadn't been the reason behind the action. He had learned what he needed to know. The wood-grain pattern on the front was nothing but a plastic veneer. The door behind it was steel.

He'd found the right place.

The cat joined him again, dropping to its side and dividing its time between a lick-bath and watching the Executioner as he produced the lock picks and dropped to one knee. Bolan made short work of both locks. A moment later, he was inside.

What he found looked like it belonged in another building. As the cat walked in behind him and began to explore the area on its own, the Executioner directed the flashlight's beam around the room. Unlike what he had seen through the missing doors of some of the other complexes, this space had been remodeled within the past few years. Walls had been knocked down to create one large space. It was elaborately decorated, and if Bolan still had any reservations as to whether it was Wright who had rented the office, they left him when the light fell on the rear wall. African masks, spears and other tribal weapons—almost identical to those on Wright's DEA office wall—hung behind the desk, which was the twin to the expensive mahogany piece behind which Wright sat at his other location. Equally high-priced easy chairs and other furniture was spread out around the room, and when the light fell to the side wall Bolan saw a brass and leather sofa. The cat had already claimed it as its own and appeared to be dozing.

Bolan went to work immediately, rummaging through the desk. But as he had found at the DEA office, there was little of interest. The drawers were filled with office supplies. It was obvious that this was a place where Wright came to work. But once that work was accomplished, he took all evidence of what he had done there away with him.

One yellow legal pad, however, sat on top of the desk and had been used. The Executioner could see the ragged yellow stubs at the top of the pad where pages had been torn off. He found a pencil in the desk's middle drawer, and under the beam of his flashlight, he lightly shaded in the top sheet on the pad. He had hoped an impression of what had been written on the previous page would appear, but it didn't. Wright was obviously well acquainted with this technique and, in addition to the page on which he had last written, had torn off several more below it.

Bolan replaced the legal pad and pencil where he'd found them and opened the bottom left-hand drawer. More yet-to-be-used office supplies met his eyes. Running his hand over the bottom of the drawer just above the one he'd opened, his fingers struck something taped inside. Squatting, he angled the flashlight's beam up into the desk. A key.

The cat rose from his nap on the couch, stretched and yawned, then dropped lightly to the carpet and walked over to check on the Executioner's progress.

Bolan pulled the key away from the tape and held it under the light. He frowned. It was the key to a safe, but he hadn't seen a safe in this office or at the DEA headquarters. Of course the safe the key fit didn't have to be at either place.

There could easily be a third location. Wright might keep the key here, away from the safe, for additional safety.

Bolan examined the object in his hand. His instincts told him that wasn't the case. The inconvenience associated with such an arrangement outweighed the practical security advantage.

Casting the flashlight's beam at the wall, the Executioner began searching for any hidden compartment where a safe might be concealed. He checked behind the several paintings, all the African masks, and every other item large enough to secret even a small safe. He found nothing. Which left the floor and ceiling as the only other possibilities, and the ceiling seemed almost as impractical as a separate site. Starting at the door to the hall, he began walking counterclockwise around the perimeter of the room, casting the light at the wainscoting that joined the floor to the wall. The cat followed at his heels. The two found what they were looking for in the rear right-hand corner of the office. The carpet along the floorboard looked loose. And was. When Bolan pulled at the corner, it rose easily and the gleaming silver steel door to a shallow firebox set into the floor looked back at him.

The key fit perfectly in the lock. To his side, the cat mewed, as if congratulating the soldier on a job well done.

Bolan was about to open the door when he heard the sounds of creaking footsteps on the steps outside. He had just enough time to drop the carpet back in place before the door to the hallway opened.

In the doorway, he saw a man holding a key in one hand, a gun in the other. Behind him in the hall were innumerable other men.

At least too many to count as the lead man raised his gun and aimed it at the Executioner.

THE EROTIC VOICE of the South American songstress Noelia floated from the speakers of Norris Wright's stereo. He poured another two fingers of ten-year-old whiskey into his highball glass and looked across the glass coffee table at Dolph Van der Kirk, who looked at the bottle, shrugged his massive shoulders and said in his gravelly voice, "Why not? We have nothing else to do tonight besides the final confirmation call." He scooted his glass closer to Wright.

The DEA man poured Van der Kirk another drink, then set the bottle back on the glass. "I like her," he said.

The South American looked up. "You like who?"

"Her," Wright said, jerking his head toward the stereo. "Noelia. And she looks as good as she sounds. If I were ten years younger...no, make that five, I think I'd go find her and make her mine."

Van der Kirk gave out an unfavorable grunt that might as well have shouted, "Fat chance."

Wright chuckled and took a sip of his whiskey. He had started to speak again when his words were cut off by the ringing telephone on the table between the two men. Both jumped as if bitten by snakes. Then both men laughed softly.

"As the end nears, the stakes grow higher," Van der Kirk said.

"And the tension mounts," Wright added, as he lifted the receiver to his ear.

"Hello?" he said.

"Salaam."

Wright nodded toward Van der Kirk, which was another way of saying, "Yes, it's him."

"How are you, sir?" Wright said into the phone.

The heavily accented Arab voice switched to impeccable British-boarding-school English. "I am well," he said. "And you?"

"Fine, just fine," Wright replied. "And we're all ready to do business."

There was a short pause on the other end. Then Wright heard the man say, "I received word that the plane had gone down in the jungle."

"Yes it did," Wright said. "But that hardly even slowed us

down." He paused himself, then went on. "We switched drums. I had my men in and out before anyone was the wiser. What you want is in my hands. Safe and secure. We're just waiting on you now."

"My people should arrive in Lagos sometime late tomorrow morning," the voice said. "The transfer must be made tomorrow night. As soon as it is concluded, I want my representatives to be able to leave the country."

"I understand completely," Wright said. "It should be no problem. Where would you like us to deliver your...product?"

The voice on the other end told him. The conversation continued as the two men worked out the few remaining minor details. Finally, Wright said, "Yes, thank you, sir, and goodbye."

He hung up and looked across the table to Van der Kirk.

"This is really the perfect crime, you know," he told the South African. "Who would ever suspect it?"

Van der Kirk nodded, took a gulp from his whiskey glass, then said, "Yes, we set up a multimillion-dollar illegal drug operation, control everything from growing the crops through wholesale distribution and we remain mysterious. No one knows who we are."

Wright chuckled softly, taking up the story. "They even come up with a name for us—the Ivory Coast cartel. I like it. But it's ironic. I've never even been to the Ivory Coast. Have you?"

"No," Van der Kirk said, shaking his head. "Having a name adds to the mystery." He clasped his hands over his head and stretched his bulky arms. "The beauty of the whole thing is, we set up such an organization, skim everything off the top at the last minute, then simply walk away. Police the world over will assume we were killed by competitors."

Wright agreed, then added, "Within a few weeks, our whole infrastructure—the whole cartel—will unravel. Gone. My people, the Nigerian government, everyone concerned will eventually put it all together and realize you and I were behind it. But they will still think we're dead. No one will ever suspect we simply left of our own accord." He lifted his glass to his lips once more. "How many men have the self-discipline to walk away from billions of dollars of annual income?"

Van der Kirk slipped out of the Italian loafers he wore and put his stockinged feet on the glass table. "None," he said. "Unless they already each had five billion tucked safely away and were guaranteed another final billion apiece from another source."

Wright set his glass on the table and stared at the thin wet ring that formed around it. "Few men are as wise as we are, Dolph," he said. "And I don't just mean the business acumen we've demonstrated during the past two years. What I mean is that few men ever realize that there's a point past which money becomes meaningless. Enough actually does become enough."

"What could we possibly do with a trillion dollars that we can't do with six billion?" he said. "How much expensive whiskey can a man drink? How many whores can he fuck?"

"Precisely," Wright said. He glanced at the other man's stockinged feet on his table. He didn't like the sight, but it was hardly worth mentioning at this stage of the game. Van der Kirk was crude and hadn't been pleasant to deal with during the past two years, but he was good at what he did, and it had been worth it. Besides, they'd soon be separating forever. "Neither of us can spend money fast enough to justify any further risk," he said. "It's time to retire."

Van der Kirk nodded and sent out another of his signature gravelly-grunts.

"Do you find it ironic," Wright asked, lifting his whiskey once more and taking another sip, "that the drug business was what got us together and made us rich? But that this final score has absolutely nothing to do with drugs?" The questions had been rhetorical, and he hadn't expected more than another of Van der Kirk's coarse rumbles.

"I try not to think that deeply," the South African said, draining what remained in his glass. "It gives me a headache."

"Well, by tomorrow night the headaches will be gone," Wright told him. He poured his glass full from the bottle again but when he looked at Van der Kirk, the muscle man shook his head. "But first, one of us needs to run by the office and get the passports and other ID."

"I can do it tomorrow morning," Van der Kirk suggested.

"Good," Wright said. "Why don't you do that while I'll pick up our friends at the airport."

"I would hardly call them friends."

"Well, I wouldn't call anyone about to hand us two billion bucks an enemy, would you?"

The South African came out with another of his guttural groans, which Wright was beginning to find annoying. "We can settle on acquaintants," he said.

Wright frowned at him. "I know you don't like anyone with skin even a half-shade darker than yours, Dolph," he said, "but let's not make any of them mad at us. This guy could be a formidable enemy, and I don't want to have to look over my shoulder for the rest of my life wondering when one of his religious-nut zealots is going to stab me in the name of Allah."

Van der Kirk sighed. "I suppose you are right," he said. "And while it looks now as if we will never have to work another day in our lives and can disappear into luxury, who knows what the future will bring? One of us might find a need for him again some day."

"My sentiments exactly," Wright said. "Never burn your bridges."

The South African raised his glass. "To health, wealth and unburned bridges," he said. Both men took a drink. Wright was the first to finish and set his glass on the table. Van der Kirk leaned forward and pushed what remained of his drink up next to the other man's. "Now it's time for me to go home and get packed."

Wright smiled. He was mildly curious as to where Van der Kirk planned to spend the rest of his days in leisure. But they had both decided it would be better if neither man told the other his plans. After this final score went down the following night, they never planned to see each other again. The DEA man glanced around at his living room. He was about to see the last of this house, too. He would abandon it as soon as he'd packed the few things he intended to take with him, then he'd get a hotel room somewhere near the docks. There was no point in taking chances at this stage of the game.

Van der Kirk pulled his feet off the table, stood and slipped back into his loafers. He had turned toward the door when the phone suddenly rang again. He froze in place and turned back. "You were expecting someone else to call tonight?" he asked.

Wright shook his head. "No, but it's probably just one of the agents. Once in a while one of the younger ones gets into something and has to call at night. And once in a while Morris or Morgan get their load on and call to complain about their marriages."

He lifted the receiver. "Yes?" he said into the instrument.

"Mr. Wright," the voice on the other end said, "this is Mary at the alarm company. Have you been to the office without telling us tonight?"

THE ODDS AGAINST the Executioner had been stacked far higher than six-to-one innumerable occasions in the past. He was still walking, talking and breathing while the men who had stacked those odds were not. But he had rarely been so outnumbered in such narrow confines, with so few objects that could offer concealment, let alone cover.

As the door to the office burst open and Bolan looked up from the floor safe, his eyes caught the glimmer of red coming from the right front corner of the room. A tiny electronic eye stared across the doorway from one wall to the other at knee level. He had missed it as he entered the room. And he had found the safe in the opposite corner before he'd come to the corner from which the tiny light shone. Had he searched the floor in the opposite direction, he would have discovered the electric eye before the safe and known that the office was wired for intruders.

But that wasn't the way Lady Luck had chosen for it all to go down, which meant the gunmen now entering the office had caught him by surprise.

The first man through the door, however, appeared even more surprised than the Executioner. He and the other men had obviously been sent to check out the signal from the electronic eye, and by the look of shock on his face Bolan suspected they had answered numerous false alarms in the past. Such invalid alerts were far more common than the real thing, and after a few, complacency set into the minds of those who did the checking.

The cat smelled upcoming danger and had no qualms about deserting his new friend. It disappeared under the desk as Bolan jerked the Beretta 93-R from his shoulder rig. His thumb fell automatically onto the safety selector switch, and he dropped the lever into burst mode.

A trio of semijacketed 9 mm hollowpoint rounds spurted almost noiselessly from the Beretta. The three rounds made the pattern of an isosceles triangle in the chest of the man in the doorway. His face already reflected shock, so it didn't have to change. He had been surprised to actually see anyone in the room when he entered, and he died still surprised as his reflexes threw him back through the doorway into the hall. His body drove the man directly behind him backward, as well.

Bolan dived behind the desk, and his knee brushed up against the dirty fur of the alley cat. The cat hissed but had no intention of sharing his hiding spot. He streaked out from under the desk toward a chair.

The Executioner knew the desk wasn't thick enough to stop any major caliber rounds from the gunmen. But it was the only thing he had, so he would utilize it as best he could. All he could hope for was that by moving back and forth behind the concealment he could use the desk to hide his exact location from return fire. No matter how skillfully he followed such a strategy, sooner or later, the bullets of the enemy would find him.

He couldn't fight a defensive war in these narrow confines. He would have to take the initiative if he wanted to survive.

Rising to his knees, Bolan leveled the Beretta over the desktop and waited. Excited voices chattered in hushed tones in the hallway. He couldn't make out the words. A second later, a face that looked to be in its early thirties, with prematurely gray hair above it, looked timidly around the corner of the doorway.

The Beretta spit again, and when the 9 mm rounds were finished the face no longer looked young nor old, nor like a face at all. Another man, foolish to the core, stuck his own head around the other side of the door to see what had happened.

Bolan blew it off, too.

The Executioner moved to the other end of the desk. He didn't know exactly how many men were in the hall, but he knew he was still vastly outnumbered. He had, however, accomplished the first part of his quickly conceived battle plan—none of the men in the hallway appeared too anxious to enter the office after what they'd seen happen to the first three. Rather than more heads appearing in the doorway, it remained clear. Anxious chattering whispers drifted in through the hall as the men tried to decide what to do next.

Bolan waited. Finally, the babble abruptly halted. Which told the Executioner all he needed to know.

Another attack was about to come.

The next man to try to get through the doorway sported bright red hair and a matching beard. He appeared suddenly, squatting on his haunches. In one hand he gripped a mini-Uzi as the other braced the door frame for balance. At the same moment, a clean-shaven man in a navy blue T-shirt came around the opposite side of the doorway, standing upright, with a British Sten submachine gun. A second after that, a gunman with a .357 Magnum Colt Python gripped in both hands suddenly took up position between the other two in the center of the opening.

They were covering all the bases, coming in high, middle and low. Bolan knew the technique. Each man would be responsible for one-third of the room. It wasn't bad strategy and would have worked against many men—even experienced gunfighters.

Such tactics did not, however, work on the Executioner.

A steady stream of fire shot from the mini-Uzi's barrel, blanketing the room to Bolan's left. But the Executioner wasn't inside the redhead's assigned zone, and the rounds missed him by a good ten feet. The man with the Sten did the same to his left, wasting his ammo on the other side. The man with the Colt had been assigned the center third of the room, and it was he who pinpointed the Executioner's position behind the desk first.

So he was the first to die.

Switching the Beretta to single shot mode, he pulled the trigger and the first 9 mm round struck the man with the revolver full in the face. He flew backward, all the way across the hall into the opposite wall.

The Executioner shifted his point of aim a fraction of an inch to the left and lowered it slightly. The next round caught the squatting man squarely between the eyes and turned the bright red hair of his head and face a far darker shade. He fell where he had squatted in the doorway.

Rather than fight the recoil, Bolan let it raise the gun for him. As it did, he moved the machine pistol back to his right. Round three from the 93-R's triple-tap caught the Sten-gunner on the side of the throat, ripping a hole through his jugular vein. Bright crimson blood shot out, and the British subgun fell to the ground just inside the office on the carpet.

Bolan let up on the trigger and waited. He didn't have to wait long.

With a loud banshee cry, a gunner with a shaven black

skull tried a different strategy. He appeared on the other side of the hallway, partially hidden by the staircase railing between him and the office. A burst of autofire roared from his AK-47, the 7.62 mm rounds peppering the desk just to Bolan's side. The Executioner switched back to burst mode, raised the Beretta and fired. He felt the three bullets leave the barrel and watched the bannister splinter as one of the rounds drilled through it. The other two sailed past and into the bald black man, striking him squarely in the heart and a lung.

Bolan heard footsteps running in the hall. Yet even as he did, another gunman with a death wish appeared in the doorway. Bolan hoped Wright had paid these men well. They were giving their lives for the crooked DEA man.

Another AK-47 panned back and forth across the room as the newest Norris Wright sacrificial lamb scanned frantically for the source of the death all around him. He saw the Executioner behind the desk a split second before the Beretta coughed once more. His head jerked backward as if pulled by the hair from the rear. Then his head bounced back just as fast and stared at Bolan in amazement. But only with the left eye. A 9 mm hollowpoint round had blown the right from the man's face.

Slowly, the one-eyed man's fingers relaxed. The AK-47 seemed to be in slow motion as it slid from his grip and fell to the floor at his feet. A moment later, the man's legs gave out. He slithered down the door frame, his Cyclops face still looking straight at the Executioner. He dropped to his knees and stopped again. Then, with one final breath, his eye closed and he fell forward into the office on his face.

Outside the office, somewhere in the building, the Executioner heard a hysterical shriek. It came from farther away than just beyond the doorway. His eyebrows lowered in question. He didn't have long to ponder the source of the scream.

"Hey!" screamed a voice just outside the door. "Don't shoot any more!"

"How many of you are left?" Bolan demanded in a loud voice.

"Just me!" came the trembling voice again. "I give up! Don't shoot! Please don't shoot!"

Bolan hesitated for a moment, thinking. It could easily be a trick. "What was that scream I just heard?" he yelled.

"I don't know!" said the quavering, unseen voice. "It come from Randy. He ran off! Just don't shoot *me,* okay?"

The Executioner took a deep breath. "Drop any weapons you have and come in," he said, as he shifted his position behind the desk once more. "Keep your hands high and clear. One move I don't like earns you bullets." He hoped the man would accede to his words. At this point, he'd rather have a live enemy who could give him information than just another dead body incapable of speech.

Two loud clanks sounded in the hallway just to the right of the door. "I'm gonna come in there now if that's okay," he called out. "I threw down my guns so don't shoot me. Okay?"

"Let me warn you before you come in," the Executioner growled, barely loud enough to be heard. "The first thing I'm going to do is search you. If I find any hideouts on you, I'll not only kill you, I'll kill you slowly." Bolan wouldn't resort to torture right now, but it wouldn't hurt the man in the hall to think he might.

There was a long silent pause. Then another clank sounded outside.

A moment later, a reed-thin man of medium height stepped timidly into the doorway, his skinny arms held high over his head. He wore a white T-shirt, now stained with blood from his fallen comrades, and ragged blue jeans. Brown hair, just over the ears, shot from his head at unruly angles.

"Facedown on the ground," the Executioner ordered. "Spread your legs and keep your arms out." When the man hesitated, he barked out, "Now!"

The skinny man dived forward to the carpet.

Bolan had traded the near-empty Beretta for the Desert Eagle, and he held the mammoth .44 Magnum pistol on the prostrate form as he walked around him to the door. Satisfying himself that there were indeed no more live attackers in the hall, he moved back to the thin man and dropped to one knee next to him. A quick frisk found no hidden weapons. Bolan pulled a role of electrical tape from his blacksuit. "Put your hands behind your back," he ordered. "Cross your wrists."

The man did as he was told without hesitation.

The Executioner ran several figure eights around the man's wrists, then cut away the remaining tape with the Applegate-Fairbairn knife. He sheathed it once more, then said, "Stay where you are. You move, and I'll kill you."

"Yes, sir," the man said.

Moving quickly back to the corner of the room, Bolan pulled the carpet back and saw the key still in the safe where he'd left it. He opened the door, directed the flashlight's beam downward, and saw a large yellow envelope. It was packed to the point of tearing. It was the safe's only contents. He pulled it out.

After a quick glance at the thin man on the floor to insure he wasn't up to something, Bolan opened the envelope. Inside, he found two passports. The first he opened was South African. The photo inside was of the broad-shouldered muscle man he had seen with Wright, named Dolph. The name in the document was Robert Jennings.

The other passport was American, and it came as no surprise to the Executioner when he opened it and saw Norris Wright's smiling face looking back at him. Wright was about to take on a new name, too—Alfred Blanchard.

Bolan felt the same strange feeling come over him he had felt earlier, when he realized he was familiar with the name Norris Wright but couldn't remember how. Alfred Blanchard was logged somewhere in his mental files, too. But again, he couldn't place it.

The rest of the envelope contained driver's licenses, credit cards and other support ID for the passports. All were in the names Robert Jennings and Alfred Blanchard. Bolan gave them a quick once-over, then returned them to the envelope, unzipped a large pocket across the back of his blacksuit and stuck the envelope inside. He moved back to the man in the middle of the floor and reached down, grabbing the taped wrists and jerking him to his feet. "Let's go," he said.

"Where?" the man asked.

Bolan slapped him across the face. Not hard enough to injure him but enough to get his attention. And enough to split his lip and send a trickle of blood drooling down his chin.

"When I want you to speak," he said, "I'll ask you a direct question. You got that?"

The man started to answer, then stopped, wondering if he should. But the man hedged his bet by answering wordlessly with only a nod.

With the Desert Eagle still in one hand, the taped wrists in the other, Bolan pushed his prisoner through the door to the hall. They walked to the top of the steps, then stopped. Bolan looked down. He had heard someone running, then he had heard the scream. What he saw below explained both. The man he had now taken into custody had called him Randy.

Randy had made it only halfway down the steps in his attempt to escape. The decomposing wood had given way beneath his running feet, and he had fallen through the staircase. His chin had caught on the step in front of him and snapped his neck as cleanly as a hangman could have done with a well-tied noose.

Randy still swung gently back and forth beneath the staircase, his head wedged in the sharp wooden shards of the shattered step, as Bolan guided his prisoner down past him.

BOLAN CAME TO A HALT on the concrete in front of the hangar, killed the Chevy's engine and got out of the car. He took a quick glance around the area, making sure there were no curious eyes, then opened the passenger's door and reached in, jerking his prisoner out by the hair. Five seconds later they were inside the hangar and boarding the Lear jet.

Dirk Woodsen's attitude still wasn't that of a loyal Eagle Scout, but it had softened somewhat since the Executioner's last visit to the hangar. As Bolan pushed the man in his custody into the rear of the plane, he saw that Grimaldi had placed a small metal folding table between the seats, and that he and the young DEA agent were engaged in a game of cards.

"Blackjack!" the pilot said, as Bolan and the other man entered the area. He slapped the ace of hearts and king of spades onto the table faceup, and grinned as he took a pen and a small notepad from his shirt pocket, made a note, then stuck them back into his pocket. "Sorry, Dirk," he said. "There goes your government retirement." He looked up at Bolan as the Executioner pushed his prisoner into the cabin area. "That's a little over three million dollars our new friend here owes me."

Dirk Woodsen didn't comment. But he looked like he was fighting an urge to smile.

Bolan still had hold of the other man's hair, and he slammed him down into the seat next to Woodsen. Bolan glanced at the DEA agent. He had a hunch things were about to heat up and knew he could use some help during the remainder of this mission. It was too late to ask Stony Man for Able Team, Phoenix Force, or even a team of blacksuits to help. They'd never arrive in Africa in time.

The Executioner turned his eyes to Grimaldi. He was a good man on the ground as well as in the air and had watched the soldier's back more than once. But Bolan wanted Grimaldi with the plane. He didn't yet know exactly what was going down, and he might need to be airborne at a moment's notice.

Bolan looked back to Woodsen. "How'd you like to help me?" he asked.

Woodsen stared straight into the Executioner's eyes. "Are

you crazy?" he asked, although his tone didn't hold the same conviction he'd had earlier. He was wavering in who he believed were the good guys and the bad guys in this little game.

Bolan glanced at his watch, then gave the man a quick summary of what was going on. He finished by saying, "Here it is in a nutshell. Wright and this Dolph character had the drums containing the eradication chemicals switched with something else before the plane took off from America."

"Dope?" Woodsen asked, frowning.

Bolan shook his head. "No. That wouldn't make sense. The drug buyers are in America. The Ivory Coast cartel ships drugs *out* of Africa."

"Then what?"

"We don't know yet," Bolan said. "But let me continue. They loaded the plane with identical drums that contained whatever it is that's at the heart of this other deal. Then the plane went down in the jungle."

"It wasn't shot down like the others? Or sabotaged?" Woodsen asked.

"No, I don't think so. I think it was just pure bad luck on Wright and Dolph's part." Bolan let that sink in, then continued. "This meant they had to make another switch in the jungle—they not only wanted whatever it was they'd flown over disguised as eradication chemicals, the FAA and the Nigerian officials needed to find eradication chemicals in the wreckage. So that's what they did—swapped out again, leaving eradication chemicals they'd taken from the planes they shot down earlier at the crash site."

Woodsen's eyes told Bolan the young man was still not convinced.

"You know this Dolph?" the Executioner asked.

Woodsen shook his head. "Never heard of anybody by that name."

"He's almost as wide as he is tall," Bolan said. "And not an ounce of it's fat."

Woodsen's eyes suddenly flickered. "I know who you're

talking about," he said. "I've seen him with Wright. But they aren't partners. The guy you call Dolph is a snitch of Wright's."

"I'm sure that's what he wanted you and everyone else in the DEA office to think," he said. "But ask yourself, have you ever seen any proof that he's an informant? Or did you just assume it?"

Woodsen didn't respond. Bolan got the answer from his eyes. "You listen while I question this man," the Executioner said, nodding toward the seat next to Woodsen. "Then tell me what you decide." He turned his attention back to the gunman who had surrendered to him at the run-down office building. The man sat where Bolan had thrown him, the blood on his T-shirt now dried a rusty brown, strands of his wild hair still pointed off toward the corners of the universe.

The thin man's eyes were frightened. They also held a dullness, as if he wasn't entirely sure where he was, what had happened to get him there, or maybe even who he was. "You have a name?" the Executioner demanded.

"Yes, sir."

Bolan waited. But when the man didn't respond further, he frowned. The expression on the face of the man in the blood-caked T-shirt had changed slightly but he didn't look as if he were trying to be a smart-ass. He looked more like he had just answered the question which had been asked of him, and answered it correctly.

A sick feeling began to creep over the Executioner. Obstinance, cockiness, angry resistance to questioning—he knew how to deal with those things when interrogating someone. But he realized what he was about to face was a trait found in some individuals that made them the hardest of all men to successfully question. Stupidity.

"Okay," he said. "What is your name?" He paused a second then, realizing he was dealing with a four-year-old in a man's body, and would have to be specific about every detail, added, "Give me all your full name. First, middle and last."

"Rupert Dunn Shelton," the man answered.

Bolan nodded. "What do people call you?" he asked.

"Rupe, usually. Sometimes they call me—"

"I'll call you Rupe," Bolan interrupted. "Who do you work for?"

Shelton looked up at him with innocent eyes. "I don't know, really," he said.

The Executioner sighed inwardly again. He was ninety-nine-percent certain the man was telling the truth. He was simple, and Bolan would have preferred facing a battalion of armed terrorists to trying to talk to him. But he had no choice. "Who pays you?" he asked.

"Well," Shelton said. "I don't know anymore."

"What does that mean?"

"The guy who used to pay me—every week—was Doug."

"And who's Doug?" Bolan asked.

"One of the guys you killed back there at the office. I don't know who'll pay me now. I hope somebody will."

Bolan had been watching Woodsen out of the corner of his eye and could see the amusement on the young DEA agent's face. He was enjoying the difficulty thoroughly.

The Executioner was about to speak again when the cell phone began to vibrate in his pocket. Pulling it out, he thumbed the switch and said, "Yeah?"

Aaron Kurtzman's voice came over the line from Stony Man Farm. "Got some info for you, Striker," he said.

"Let's have it."

"Okay, first, it looks like this Dolph character is Dolph Van der Kirk. Former South African Recce Commando. Court-marshaled and dishonorably discharged for black-market sales of military arms. You want the details?"

"Van der Kirk," Bolan said out loud, and looked at Woodsen.

The young DEA man shook his head. He didn't recognize that name either.

"Go on, Bear."

"That was almost ten years ago," Kurtzman said. "No civilian convictions since the military bust. Everyone from South Africa to Interpol seem to have files open on him. There's some suspicion that he might be involved with this bunch they're calling the Ivory Coast cartel. Anyway, some of the intel reports also mention an unidentified partner in the cartel. No one seems to know who he is, though."

Bolan nodded. "They don't," he said. "I do." A picture of Norris Wright formed in his mind.

"Yeah, "Kurtzman came back. "Norris Wright. By the way, pertaining to the hard drive files you sent from the DEA office? We found several dozen numbered bank accounts scattered all over the world. Most of them in Switzerland, the Caymans and other countries famous for confidentiality."

"That's probably where the money on this deal is going to show up," the Executioner said. "Keep an eye on them. The Treasury Department or someone can go after what's in them when this is all over. Nothing else of interest?"

"Not unless you consider routine DEA business, and a few thousand downloaded porno pictures interesting."

Bolan nodded. It had been worth a try, sending the files to Stony Man. But after learning of the second office Wright had rented, he'd have been shocked to find the man taking the chance of leaving incriminating evidence on his computer.

"But speaking of the name, Norris Wright," Kurtzman continued. "You said it rang a bell somewhere you couldn't place. So I ran it through the machines every which way to Sunday, and there are more Norris Wrights in the world than you'd guess. But no one besides our DEA–Ivory Coast boy who you're likely to have ever met, or even heard of."

"No, but I have heard the name before," Bolan insisted.

Kurtzman chuckled. "That's because you're warrior, my friend, and you've studied historical battles both large and small."

"You're leading up to something, Bear," the Executioner said. He glanced to his watch. "Let's get to it."

The Stony Man computer wizard's tone of voice reflected that he hadn't taken Bolan's words offensively but rather as a reminder that the clock was running. "The only Norris Wright I found who was even mildly interesting was when I ran a historical check on the name." He paused to clear his throat before continuing. "A Major Norris Wright was one of the men at the Vidalia sandbar fight way back in 1829."

A light bulb flashed in the Executioner's brain. "That's where I remember it," he said. "Jim Bowie."

"Right," Kurtzman said. "Wright stabbed Bowie in the chest with a sword cane during the melee that followed the duel between Samuel Levi Wells and Dr. Maddox—neither of whom got hurt in the duel. But all hell broke loose between their friends a soon as it was over."

Bolan remembered the story now. "After Wright stabbed Bowie, Bowie killed him."

"Correct, sir," Kurtzman said. "The sword cane got stuck in Bowie's chest. Wright was trying to pull it out, and Bowie reached up, grabbed him, then gutted him with the big butcher knife he was carrying in those days."

The Executioner nodded. The bowie knife itself wasn't to be invented for a couple more years, if he remembered correctly.

"In addition to the sword in his chest," Kurtzman went on, "Bowie had been shot twice and hit over the head with a pistol before he disemboweled Wright. Then he cut some other guy before he finally collapsed." Kurtzman chuckled softly. "Tough hombre, old Jim. Reminds me of someone else I know. But he usually carries a Desert Eagle instead of a bowie knife."

The odd feeling Bolan had experienced from not being able to remember where he'd heard the name Norris Wright should have been gone now, he knew, but it wasn't. In fact, it had intensified. "Bear," he said. "You have the whole story of the Vidalia fight there in front of you?"

"Sure do," Kurtzman said. "When the name hit, I pulled up everything I could about it off the Internet."

Bolan could feel the yellow envelope against his back in the pocket of his blacksuit. "Is the name Alfred Blanchard in there anywhere?" he asked.

"Just a second..." Kurtzman's voice trailed off. Bolan could heard the clicks of the man's computer mouse as he scanned the document on the screen in front of him. A few seconds later, Kurtzman said, "Sure is. Alfred Blanchard was the guy who Bowie attacked after he killed Wright. Cut him on the arm. Blanchard escaped."

The strange feeling was suddenly gone. Bolan remembered the degree from the University of Louisiana that had hung on Wright's wall at the DEA office. The man had a double major—political science and *history*. From a university only a few miles from the site of the famous sandbar fight. If he hadn't known the story before, he would have learned it in college, and also remembered the man involved because of the name. In fact, having another Norris Wright in the history classes would have been a subject for discussion and probably more than a few jokes between him and his classmates.

It wasn't any coincidence that Norris Wright had picked the name Alfred Blanchard as his new identity once this big deal he was planning was over. Right now, however, it didn't seem too important how Wright had come up with his new name—just an irrelevant bit of random information that was mildly interesting.

When Bolan said no more about the matter, Kurtzman took it as a good time to change the subject. "I've got one more item you might be interested in. Although it may not have any direct relationship to your current mission, either."

"What's that?"

"We ran our daily scan of all the world's top intel groups," the computer genius said. "The Israeli Mossad and British M-16 both had reports of three suspected terrorists getting off a plane in Lagos an hour ago." He paused, then went on. "Arabs. Known associates of Osama Bin Laden."

Bolan gripped the phone a little tighter. Osama bin Laden. The millionaire sheikh had taken the place of Carlos the Jackal as the world's most wanted man. Financed by his own incredible wealth, he was responsible for acts of terror and mayhem all across the globe. Was it just a coincidence that his men were in Nigeria now? Or did it have to do with this mysterious deal Wright and Van der Kirk had talked about?

It had to. It couldn't be coincidence. Lagos was hardly the garden spot of the world. Certainly not the sort of place to which anyone—including terrorists—came unless they had business that forced them there.

"Okay," Bolan said. He glanced to his side and saw that Woodsen had been listening attentively to the half of the call he could hear. Seated next to the young DEA agent, Rupert Shelton seemed interested, as well. The Executioner stared into the dim-witted man's eyes. They still had a dull cast to them, but they seemed to have taken on at least a little more alertness. Even so, he wasn't looking forward to resuming the questions he had for the man, which would have to be phrased for a five-year-old. "Anything else, Bear?" he said into the phone.

"Nope. But I'll call you back if we get anything."

Bolan hung up and turned back to where Shelton was leaning forward in his chair. The man was smiling like a kid on his way to a birthday party. Bolan felt sorry for him. He didn't seem like a particularly bad man—just not a very bright one. Of course it didn't take a Mensa membership to pull the trigger of a gun. Doug, was who had paid him before Bolan killed the man—undoubtedly an underling of Wright's and Van der Kirk's—had used Shelton's mental deficiencies to his own advantage. The Executioner didn't expect to get much information out of the simple man now.

Looking down at Shelton, Bolan had to resist the urge to pat him on the head like one would a puppy. "Hear something that made you happy?" he asked.

Shelton nodded, the moronic lopsided grin still on his face. "A name," he said.

The soldier tensed. "What name?" he asked.

"Van der Kirk," Shelton said.

"Yeah," Bolan said, looking at the man below him intently. "Do you know someone named Van der Kirk?"

"Not very well," Shelton said. "But I've met him. He was a friend of Doug's."

The soldier nodded. For a moment there, he had thought he might get lucky. But it had been too much to ask to think that Shelton would have known either Wright or Van der Kirk well enough to provide anything useful. Doug had paid him. And Doug was as far up the ladder of the Ivory Coast cartel as Shelton's connections would have gone.

Before the Executioner could speak again, Shelton offered the first words yet that hadn't had to be dragged out of him. "I don't know Mr. Van der Kirk very well," he repeated. Then, almost as an afterthought, he added, "In fact, I've only been at his house once."

The three dark-skinned men who got off the early-morning flight from Cairo all had short hair, neatly trimmed beards, wore expensively tailored business suits and carried black leather briefcases. Anyone watching, who didn't know who they were, would have guessed they were Middle Eastern men in the oil business.

Norris Wright knew that they were, indeed, Middle Eastern. And that they were in business. But that business wasn't oil.

It was terror.

Wright stepped forward and shook hands all around. His DEA credentials had gotten him past the security barrier into the precustoms check area, and would help get the men out again with nothing more than a cursory check of their baggage. He walked them to the front of the line, where they cut in ahead of the other tired, irritated travelers who had come in on the same flight and couldn't understand why these men merited special privileges. Wright smiled back at a few sarcastic comments, held up his badge case, but offered no other explanation.

The uniformed Nigerian customs agent took a superficial glance at the three men's passports, their cards identifying them as Egyptian drug enforcement agents, then passed them through without even a pretext of checking their bags. Ten minutes later, they were all in Wright's Land Rover. They had introduced themselves simply as Mohammed, Moe and Ali.

"Want to take a ride down to the wharf?" Wright asked, as he pulled away from the airport.

"It would be a meaningless gesture," said the man called Moe, slightly taller than the other two. He was seated directly behind Wright in the back seat. "The vessel isn't yet here, and won't be until midafternoon."

Wright nodded. "Then how about a little entertainment?" he said. "I could take you guys to—"

The man who had introduced himself as Ali rode in the shotgun seat. "Thank you, no," he said, turning toward Wright. "We have no taste for your decadent Western pastimes." He glanced at his watch. "You have arranged for us a place to stay?"

"Of course," Wright said.

"Then please take us there," Ali said, turning back to face the windshield. "It is time we prepare for the afternoon prayers."

Wright nodded his head. "I understand," he said. "And I respect your beliefs," while thinking, *you're a bunch of mother-fucking radical asshole fools.*

"Thank you," Ali said, showing that he had heard the other man's words. But he gave the other man a quick glance, and when he did the expression on his face suggested he suspected Wright's thoughts, as well.

"You'll be staying at the Excelsior," Wright said. He didn't bother to tell them he had a room at the same hotel. He wanted to keep an eye on them until the deal was done, but he also wanted to vacate his house a day early. And he had taken a sick day from the DEA office. There was no sense taking any chances at this stage in the game.

Wright cleared his throat. "There are a few minor last-minute details we should get out of the way."

Ali, who was beginning to look like the man in charge, anticipated Wright's next question. "Your money is ready," he said. "One-half will be sent out from Switzerland. The other half from the Cayman Islands. We have broken it into the amounts you requested, and it will be deposited into the various accounts you supplied us, under the names you also gave."

"Excellent," Wright said. He took the bridge from Lagos Island to the neighboring island of Apapa where the Excelsior was located. "Then allow me to suggest the following scenario. My truck, guarded by my men—to insure your product arrives to you safely—will arrive at the ship tonight precisely at nine o'clock." He had put emphasis on "guarded by my men" to remind the three Arabs not to try a rip-off. The "insure it arrives" had been nothing but window-dressing courtesy to soften the threat. Out of the corner of his eye, he saw Ali's face and knew that the subtle message hadn't been lost on him. In any case, Wright wasn't worried. The man Ali and the other two served wasn't known for double-crossing people. He didn't have to do such things. A couple billion bucks, here and there, was pocket change to him.

Traffic on the islands that made up the city of Lagos was never light. But it wasn't as bad today as usual, and Wright had learned to cut in and out of lanes with a hairbreadth of room like a native. Leaning on the horn every ten seconds or so, he guided the Land Rover through the streets to the hotel, pulling onto the circular drive to the front door. He threw the vehicle into Park and set the brake, then turned to Ali. "As soon as the truck arrives," he said, "you are welcome to test the contents of the drums. I will make a few phone calls to insure that the banks have made no mistakes." Again, he was too smart to directly accuse the men of trying to rip him off. But he wanted them to know he was paying attention, too. "Then, as soon as we're all happy, we can load your cargo onto the ship."

"After we have tested the contents of the drums," Ali said. "To make sure that there was no accidental mix-up on the part of one of your employees, we will make our own phone calls. That is when the money will be transferred." His dark eyes flickered in mild amusement, letting Wright know he was mocking the Westerner's own indirect approach. "Not until then will you be able to make *your* calls."

"Of course," Wright said. He glanced out the window as several bellhops came out of the lobby. "Would you like me to see you to your rooms?"

"That will not be necessary," Ali said. He, Moe and Mohammed got out of the Land Rover.

The three men disappeared through the Excelsior's door with the bellhops. He was so close, Norris Wright told himself. Only a few more hours, and it would be whiskey and soda or margaritas or whatever else he wanted on the beach every day. And he'd buy a new woman, or two or three new ones, every night. Of course he couldn't do that all the time. So what else would he do?

Wright smiled. Any damn thing he wanted.

The DEA man took his badge case out of his pocket and glanced at the gleaming gold shield as he pulled the Land Rover away from the hotel. The badge had been good to him. It had gotten him what he wanted. Should he throw it in the ocean now that he wouldn't need it any more? No, he thought, he might as well keep it as a souvenir.

It would be good to pull out for a laugh now and then when he didn't have anything else to do with his time.

THE CITY OF LAGOS was a city of islands, and so far Bolan had spent the majority of his time on Lagos Island and Ikoyi. But now, Rupert Shelton directed him onto the bridge over Five Cowrie Creek and the Chevy emerged onto Victoria Island. With Shelton riding shotgun, and Dirk Woodsen in the back seat, they took Akin Adesola Street toward Bar Beach, which was bordered by the waters of the Bight of Benin.

The Executioner glanced into the rearview mirror and saw the still confused face of Woodsen seated behind him. He felt sorry for the young DEA man. Woodsen was learning a hard lesson that every man had to come to terms with, sooner or later. And it was a lesson that was never easy for good men to stomach.

Not everyone who wore a badge was a good person.

Woodsen had already been questioning things on his own. But after the interview with Shelton, Bolan had come upon an easy solution to wipe away the young man's final doubts. He had called Hal Brognola. While Brognola's association with Stony Man Farm was top secret, he was nevertheless widely known in law-enforcement circles in his high-ranking role with the U.S. Department of Justice. Once Brognola was on the line, the Executioner had explained the situation to him in the presence of the young DEA agent. He had then handed the phone to Woodsen, who spoke to Brognola.

Woodsen had impressed both Bolan and Brognola even further. To insure that the call wasn't a setup, he had insisted on hanging up, then getting the Justice Department's phone number from the information operator. He had then returned the call and asked the switchboard operator for Brognola himself. Only then was he satisfied that both men were on the level.

Brognola had given Woodsen a direct order to abandon his ties to Wright and assist Bolan. It was now official. Although that didn't mean the young man wasn't still a little confused about everything.

"Turn left," Shelton said, when they reached Bishop Oluwola Street. Bolan did, and then followed further directions, jogging onto another short avenue that led to the road along the beach. Beside them, the gentle waves lapped inland onto the sands. Scattered along the beach were a variety of houses, some new, some looking as if they had been there almost as long as the beach itself.

Shelton leaned forward against his seat belt, as he tried to remember which house belonged to Van der Kirk. "I was only here one time," he reminded the Executioner. "I hope I can remember it."

Bolan had developed a large quantity of compassion for the man, who had been a victim of birth. True, he had tried to kill the Executioner. And he had more than likely killed other men while in the employee of Wright and Van der Kirk. On the other hand, his sluggish brain meant he was easily misled, and Bolan doubted he really knew what he was doing half the time. Yes, he had to be held responsible for his actions. The fact was, Bolan was having a hard time trying to figure out just what to do with Shelton after the man led him to Van der Kirk's house.

Bolan continued to drive. A few minutes later, Shelton said, "I think that was it."

The Executioner glanced to the house they were passing. Nothing but a shack—hardly the kind of place he'd expect for a cartel kingpin to live. He wondered if Shelton was unintentionally leading him on a wild-goose chase. He didn't think the man was smart enough to do such a thing on purpose. But regardless of his motives, they were wasting valuable time. "That one?" he asked.

"No, not that house," Shelton said. "The good one we passed before."

"Which good one?" the Executioner asked.

"The one right before this one. It had the red windows."

Bolan remembered a house that had reddish-brown shutters. It hadn't been the last one they'd passed but had been within the past few minutes. He made a U-turn and started back. They retraced their path along the beach road until the Executioner saw the shutters once more. It was a fairly elaborate western ranch style one-story dwelling that looked as if it probably had four to five bedrooms inside. A double garage was attached to the side. Both garage doors were closed. And Shelton had mentioned a fence earlier when some of his rambling thoughts had come out of his mouth. This house didn't have a fence. A low rock wall ran along the front of the property. "Is that it, Rupert?" he asked.

Shelton squinted hard at the house,. "I don't think so, no," he said. "I don't think so. Not anymore, I don't."

The Executioner suppressed a sigh, reminding himself that he had to make special provisions in interpreting everything Shelton told him. "Okay," he said patiently, as they passed the house again. "Let me ask you this. You thought that might be the house. Then you saw it again, and don't think it is anymore. What changed your mind, Rupert?"

Shelton turned to face him. "There ain't no dogs barking down the street," he said with the innocence of a child. "And Mr. Van der Kirk, he had a car he kept in the driveway. It's not there, either."

It took a few seconds for Bolan to explain how things change to Shelton. As soon as he understood, Shelton said, "Yeah! That's the house!" He pointed toward the rock wall. "And there's the fence!"

Bolan drove on, looking at his watch again. It would be dark in another hour. They would have to wait until then. He didn't know what time this deal of Wright's and Van der Kirk's was coming off. All he knew was they'd be cutting things close.

But working on the edge was hardly a new experience for the Executioner.

Dusk HAD JUST TURNED to darkness when Bolan and Woodsen crept to the side of Van der Kirk's house. The rented Chevy was parked half a mile down the beach. Shelton, after being awake all night, had fallen asleep in the back. Bolan had un-taped his wrists even before they had left the airport, and knew there was a chance he might wake up and walk away, but he didn't see that as a problem. Things were about to go down, and when they did, they would go down fast. They were about to take Van der Kirk into custody, and even if he were of a mind to do so, Shelton wouldn't have time to get word to Wright. Bolan seriously doubted the slow man would even know how to contact the DEA SAC. Shelton was a simple man who was only dangerous when steered the wrong way by evil-but-smarter men. He had been born with mental disabilities, and through Doug, Wright and Van der Kirk had taken advantage of those disabilities.

Bolan cut to the side of Van der Kirk's house and stopped, holding up a hand to halt Woodsen at his rear. He turned to the man. "Stay here," he whispered. "Let me scout the perimeter and see what I find."

Woodsen nodded. His hand slipped under his batik shirt and came to rest on the SIG-Sauer Bolan had returned to him.

The Executioner moved along the side of the house, stopping at each window. Some of the shades and curtains were open, and inside he saw empty bedrooms that looked as if they were rarely, if ever, used. One window showed a study, with the dark forms of a desk, book cases, a couch and a reclining armchair. He moved across a patio that faced the waters of the Bight of Benin, weaving his way through white cast iron chairs, several padded loungers and a wet bar that stood alone to the side of the concrete slab. Through the glass in the top half of the back door, he could see the kitchen. A light was on above the stove, and it cast a dull glow over the predominantly stainless-steel room. The Executioner moved off the patio and around the corner to the other side of the house.

Through the first window he came to he saw a large bathroom. A shower stood against one wall, a large wooden hot tub against the other next to the sink. The toilet appeared to be hidden in its own closet behind a closed door. Next to that door was another, which was open. Bolan could see both men's and women's clothing hanging from rods. He moved on.

As he neared the next window on that side of the house, he heard a loud, irregular buzzing noise. Edging closer, he identified the sound as a man's snoring. Ducking beneath the sill, he raised his head slowly until his eyes could peer through the corner of the opening. Across the bedroom, he could see three forms, asleep in the huge king-size bed. Nearest the window, a head, shoulders and one naked female breast were visible above the covers. The woman's eyes were closed in sleep. On the other edge of the bed, another nude black woman had rolled completely out from under the blanket and bedspread, and lay curled on her side in a fetal position.

In the middle was the man Bolan had seen earlier with Wright—Dolph Van der Kirk. He lay flat on his back, and the periodic roars issuing from his nose and open mouth threatened to break the room's furniture and cave in the ceiling.

It was vital that Van der Kirk be captured alive rather than killed. A plan to accomplish that objective was already forming in Bolan's head. The South African was sleeping before his big night. The Executioner couldn't have asked for a better time to take the man down.

Dropping beneath the window again, Bolan moved to the side, stood then sprinted back to where Woodsen was waiting. Quickly, he explained the situation to the young DEA man. "The back door's the closest to the bedroom," he said. "I'll go in that way. As soon as you hear my kick, you go in the front."

Woodsen nodded.

"We've got to take him alive," the Executioner stressed. "Otherwise, we won't know what he and Wright have going down tonight, and Wright will carry it out on his own."

Woodsen nodded again, then took off toward the front of the house.

Bolan circled around the back again, hearing the surf as the waves rolled in and lapped up over the sand not twenty yards beyond the patio. Again, he was struck by the seeming contradiction between what nature had awarded Lagos, and what people like Wright and Van der Kirk had made it. When he reached the door, he drew the Beretta and reached out, trying the doorknob. Locked. He took a half step back with his left leg, raised his right and sent the heel of his leather and nylon combat boot thrusting out against the wood.

The splintering lock sounded almost like the crack of a baseball against a wooden bat. The door flew inward, the top hinge flying off and into the stove opposite it with a loud clank. Bolan darted into the kitchen, dipped his right shoulder and moved past the stainless-steel sink against the wall. As he entered, he heard another crash as Woodsen kicked his way into the front of the house. Ahead, he saw a door leading out into a hallway. As he reached it, his heart sank.

The sound of a toilet flushing reverberated through the plumbing in the walls.

The Executioner cut right again and sprinted three paces down the hall to where he knew the bedroom had to be. The door was open, and he dropped into a combat crouch, the Beretta ready, as he hit the opening. Once inside, he took a step to the left, leveling the Beretta at the bed.

But there were only two people on the king-size mattress now. The two women. Both held the sheet up to their throats to cover their breasts and stared back at him with wild, terrified eyes.

Bolan's gaze shot to the side of the room where, from behind the closed bathroom door, he could still hear the toilet as it wound down, finishing its flushing cycle. Van der Kirk was awake and inside. But he couldn't have helped hearing the doors crash open.

Was he armed? Maybe, maybe not.

As it turned out, Dolph Van der Kirk was well armed.

The bathroom door suddenly swung back and Van der Kirk, completely nude, stood in the opening. An Uzi was gripped in both of his big fists, and a steady stream of 9 mm fire blasted from the barrel of the Israeli-made subgun. He had misjudged where Bolan would be by only a fraction of an inch, and the rounds sailed by just over the Executioner's right shoulder. One bullet seared across the top of his blacksuit, ripping the material and scorching the flesh beneath, but doing no serious damage.

Bolan was driven back through the doorway out of sight.

The bombardment of 9 mm rounds suddenly ended. Silence fell over the house. Then the Executioner heard soft footsteps shuffling down the hallway to his side. He glanced that way to see Woodsen, SIG-Sauer in hand, coming toward him. He held up a palm and Woodsen stopped.

"Van der Kirk!" the Executioner shouted through the open door. "Drop the Uzi and come out with your hands behind your head! You do, and you'll live. You don't, and you'll die!"

His answer was another stream of fire that blew through the doorway into the hall. From the bed came the low moans of one woman, the high-pitched shrieks of the other. From the angle at which he stood, the Executioner could see them, huddled together in each other's arms, trembling. He extended a hand toward them, then waved it up and back over his shoulder several times. "Go on," he whispered. "Get out of here."

The women were as frozen in place as statues.

"Now!" the Executioner shouted angrily. He turned the Beretta toward them and the two nude women leaped from the bed and ran toward him. They raced past Bolan and Woodsen, down the hall and out of sight. A moment later, Bolan heard a door slam behind them.

Bolan hesitated only a second. He had to return fire or the South African would quickly figure out that he was bluffing, that he needed Van der Kirk alive. That knowledge would give the man a tremendous advantage. Dropping to one knee, he slammed the Beretta back into his shoulder rig and drew the big Desert Eagle. Then, leaning low around the door frame, he saw that the bathroom entryway was empty. All he could see was part of the hot tub and the wall behind it.

The Executioner fired a double-tap of .44 Magnum rounds into the tub and the holes appeared in the wood. Water began pouring out, soaking the carpet. Then a flash of flesh appeared again, and another burst from the Uzi sent Bolan diving back away from the door. He waited two seconds, then peered back around the corner to see that Van der Kirk, too, had returned to concealment. Firing one more round into the hot tub, he ducked back and turned to Woodsen. "Take this," he whispered to the young DEA agent.

Woodsen transferred his SIG-Sauer to his left hand and reached for the Desert Eagle. "What do you want me to do?"

"Take my place at the door," the Executioner said. "Fire every once in a while. Make him think I'm still there. But don't kill him."

The young DEA man frowned. "What are you going to do?"

Bolan couldn't answer. He was already down the hall and heading for the front of the house. Woodsen had opened the storm door before kicking the main entryway, and now Bolan did the same as quietly as he could. Cutting across the front yard, he sprinted around the side of the house toward the master bedroom, hearing another exchange of gunfire from within the dwelling as he ran. But the shots were barely audible outside and wouldn't be heard by the neighbors, the nearest of whom was at least a quarter mile away.

That was good. The Executioner didn't need to deal with Nigerian cops at the same time he tried to do what might already prove to be impossible—take Dolph Van der Kirk alive without getting himself and Woodsen killed in the process.

Bolan slumped low as he neared the bedroom window, his head rising only long enough to catch a glimpse of the doorway leading to the hall. It was empty. Woodsen had ducked back around the corner again. Bolan walked along the side of the house to the window leading to the bathroom and raised his head slower, more cautiously.

With his eyes and forehead just above the sill, the Executioner could see the bathroom clearly now. Dolph Van der Kirk stood between the shower and the door leading to the bedroom. As Bolan watched, he dropped a spent magazine from the Uzi and replaced it with a fresh one. A half-dozen more high capacity mags were scattered at the muscleman's feet on the carpet.

He wasn't going to run out of ammo soon, that was for certain.

Bolan heard the familiar boom of his Desert Eagle and a big 44 Magnum round flew into the bathroom at over 1400 feet per second. It thudded into the wall, shaking the very foundation of the house but being stopped by the bricks on the outside of the house. The Executioner watched Van der Kirk's lips move as the man counted, "One, two, three," then leaned around the corner and cut loose with another burst of 9 mm autofire from the Uzi.

The South African was a good eight feet away from the window. Examining the glass itself, the Executioner saw it was slightly tinted and set into a stainless steel frame. There was no way he could get through it without alerting Van der Kirk, and giving the man more than enough time to shoot him while he crawled awkwardly through the opening. If he broke the windowpane, the muscleman would hear it. Even if the window happened to be unlocked, and he could slide it up, the odds were stacked in favor of the South African hearing or even seeing him. Each time Van der Kirk ducked away from Woodsen's return fire, he turned sideways and the window entered his field of vision.

Bolan dropped below the window again, concentrating on the problem as Woodsen and Van der Kirk exchanged another volley of fire. Somehow, he had to get closer to the muscleman.

Quickly, the Executioner reached into a pocket of his blacksuit and pulled out a pair of thin black leather shooting gloves. The yellow Kevlar lining reminded him they were cut resistant as he slipped them over his fingers. Then, carefully, he unthreaded the sound suppressor from the barrel of the Beretta 93-R and dropped the device into long narrow pocket along the leg of his blacksuit.

Squatting next to the window with the Beretta in his left hand, Bolan took a final look inside. Van der Kirk was firing through the door again into the hall on the other side of the bedroom. Good. Woodsen was doing his job. And so far, Van der Kirk had heard no rounds fired except the loud distinctive scream of the Desert Eagle. One gun. He would have assumed he was under attack by only one man.

It was time to shock him into reality.

Bolan aimed the unsuppressed 93-R at the ground with his left hand and pulled the trigger. A quick burst of hollowpoints shot from the barrel into the grass. Instead of the whispering sputter that usually accompanied the Beretta when it spoke, the now-unsuppressed weapon sounded more like 9 mm thunder clapping just outside the house.

The Executioner waited a second, then repeated the process, sending another trio of loud rounds from the Beretta. He jammed the Beretta back into his shoulder rig, then waited, poised, until he saw a flicker appear at the window. A split second later, he caught what looked like the general shape of a man's head.

Bolan's legs drove him upward in one smooth fluid motion. He twisted at the waist, and his gloved fist came around in a vicious right hook that shattered the glass and sent the razor-edged shards flying as if a bomb had exploded on the windowsill.

The Executioner's gloved fist traveled through the glass, his arm coming to full extension just to the left side of Dolph Van der Kirk's surprised face. Bolan shot his other hand inside the bathroom over the massive shoulder on the other side of the South African's head. His fingers clasped behind Van der Kirk's overdeveloped neck like a Thai boxer preparing to lower his opponent's head for a knee strike. He jerked violently forward and down.

But it wasn't his knee against which the Executioner snapped Van der Kirk's face but rather the windowsill beneath the shattered glass pane. The South African's head shot down against the wooden pane, and blood erupted from the corners of his mouth. His arms, still grasping the Uzi, were suddenly trapped between his chest and the wall beneath the window.

Van der Kirk roared with the rage of the bull he resembled, lifting his face off the windowsill. A bloody tooth blew from his mouth with the sound, and he stared at the Executioner with venom-filled eyes. A tug of war now began, with Bolan continuing to pull downward with all the strength in his arms and shoulders, bracing the front of his thighs against the bricks below the window outside the house. On his end, Van der Kirk used the inside wall below the opening against which to prop his chest for leverage as he pulled backward with his broad neck. It was a neck that had benefited from years of both power lifting and bodybuilding, and the tendons and veins stood out in bold relief on top of the straining muscles. Blood rushed to the area between his chest and chin, turning the skin a deep red. The Ivory Coast cartel man grunted and cursed with the effort. Bolan remained silent, concentrating on pulling the man down.

For perhaps half a minute they were at a stalemate; neither man could move the other more than an inch. Then, slowly, inch by inch, Bolan felt his interlaced fingers begin to slip away from each other inside the smooth leather gloves. It was no longer a battle of will, strength, or leverage but one of equipment. And while the leather over his fists had kept him from severing his own arteries when he broke the window, their slippery texture now worked against him.

Knowing that in seconds his hands would part and Van der Kirk would jerk back, then bring up the Uzi, the Executioner changed strategy. He gave one final pull downward, then suddenly relaxed his arms and straightened his knees.

Van der Kirk grunted again, but this time it was a grumble of surprise. As the resistance against his neck suddenly evaporated, his head shot back away from the window. Bolan kept both hands on the back of the man's head and let the South African's own strength pull him up, through the window and into the bathroom.

Glass, still protruding from the edges of the window, sliced through the Executioner's blacksuit, tearing at his flesh, as he shot into the house. The Uzi flew from the muscleman's hands and he fell to his back. The carpet was now soaked from the bullet-ridden hot tub, and water splashed to their sides as Bolan came down on top of the other man with his knees to the sides of Van der Kirk's mammoth chest. The man bellowed again then cursed and spit at Bolan's eyes. The Executioner dodged the flying saliva and raised his fist high over his head.

When he brought it down, the knuckles beneath the black leather glove drove into the "button" at the end of the South African's chin.

Dolph Van der Kirk suddenly quit struggling and went limp.

Bolan rose from his knees to his feet, catching his breath. He drew the Beretta, ready to use it as a club should the man at his feet suddenly return to consciousness. Finally, Woodsen appeared in the doorway to the bathroom. He had the Desert Eagle in one hand, the SIG-Sauer in the other.

Bolan took back the Eagle and rammed it into his holster. "Get you handcuffs out," he ordered the young DEA agent. Stooping, he helped Woodsen roll the South African onto his face on the soggy carpet. The cuffs were barely large enough to fit around the man's thick wrists, finally catching on the last tooth of the ratchet lock.

The Executioner grabbed Van der Kirk's arms while Woodsen took his legs. Together, they hoisted him off the wet carpet and out of the bathroom, finally dropping him on his back on the bed. Bolan returned to the bathroom, his eyes scanning the countertop for a water glass or some such similar object. When he found none, he dumped several tiny bars of seashell-shaped soap out of a shallow dish and filled it with water at the sink.

A few seconds later, the sudsy solution splashed into Dolph Van der Kirk's face. The man opened his eyes.

HIS EYES BURNED as they opened, and for a second Dolph Van der Kirk thought he was in the shower and had gotten careless with the shampoo. But when he felt his body automatically sit up, he realized he'd been reclining on the bed. His chin, lips and the inside of his mouth were all sore, and the coppery taste of blood was on his tongue. When his tongue rose to the roof of his mouth, he found one of his front teeth missing.

Van der Kirk tried to rub his eyes, but his hands wouldn't move from behind his back. Then, he remembered the attack that had come while he was in the bathroom. Gunfire from the hall, followed by the sounds of other shots just outside the window, and the arms reaching through the broken glass to grab him. There had been a struggle after that, but his brain wasn't clear on the rest. He supposed it would all come back to him eventually.

For the moment, it was enough to know that he seemed to have come out on the losing end of the fight. Otherwise, he wouldn't be sitting with his hands bound behind him.

As the stinging water dripped from his face and his vision began to clear, Van der Kirk saw the big man wearing the black one-piece jumpsuit. He'd never seen one quite like it before, but he could readily tell it was designed for battle. At the same time the South African recognized the purpose of the blacksuit, he realized who the man wearing it had to be. He had never seen him, but the guy had to be the one who had come to Lagos pretending to be a DEA desk jockey. The one he had twice sent men to kill. Men who had been killed themselves, instead. What had Wright told him the son of a bitch's name was? Clarke. Yeah, that was it. Kenneth Clarke.

Standing next to the big man was a younger one. And this man, Van der Kirk had seen before. He was one of Wright's DEA junior G-men. Van der Kirk couldn't remember the kid's name.

The South African let the soapy water continue to drain from his eyes as he looked back at the man in black. "You didn't do a very good job earlier," he said. "You didn't fool us into thinking you were the sissy-boy bureaucrat you wanted us to believe."

"Maybe I can make up for my shortcomings now," the big man said, as he pulled a straight-backed wooden chair from against the wall, flipped it around and sat facing Van der Kirk. "Regardless of how poor you think my earlier performance was, it looks to me like you're the one wearing the bracelets." He crossed his arms across the back of the chair and leaned forward, resting his chin on them.

Van der Kirk couldn't help but laugh. "Yeah," he said. "I

guess it does." He let the smile fade from his face before continuing. "So tell me. What is it you want? Or should I say *how much* do you want?"

The big man in the black combat suit shook his head. "No," he said. "You were right the first time. It's *what*. Not *how much*."

"Okay, *what* then?"

"Several things," the big man said. "First, I want to know what this deal you and Wright have going is. I want to know who it's with, and where it's going to take place." He continued to stare Van der Kirk in the eyes, and the intensity of that gaze made the South African vaguely uneasy. "Then I want you to take me there. I want Wright."

Silence fell over the room for a few seconds. The man in black prompted him further. "From what I've gathered, the deal doesn't have anything to do with your Ivory Coast cartel drug business."

Van der Kirk heard himself snicker through his bruised nose. "I love that name, Ivory Coast," he said. "Neither Wright nor I have ever even been there. But you're right about the deal having nothing to do with dope." He smiled what he knew would be an ugly, bloody, jack-o'-lantern smile with his missing tooth. "Beyond me telling you that, you can go fuck yourself."

The big man's eyes narrowed. "I could beat the rest of the information out of you," he said.

"I doubt it," the South African came back. "Maybe eventually you could." He glanced to the clock on the wall. "But you don't have time. It won't matter if I'm there for the deal or not. Wright will go without me. And I can outlast any beating you can give me until it's too late for you to stop it."

The big man's eyes narrowed even further, and Van der Kirk could tell he was trying to decide how much of what he'd just heard was true. The truth was, all of it was true. It was nearly 7:30 now. It wouldn't be that tough to get punched on for a few minutes. Particularly when he could tell that the man in black would have his limits in dishing out the pain. He was obviously one of those Goody two-shoes heroes who had some code of honor he stayed within. Good way to limit success, in Van der Kirk's opinion. In any case, he wasn't the kind of man who'd resort to any of the more creative, painful and abusive kinds of torture. And the South African had suffered bumps, bruises and broken bones enough times in the past to know he could get through them without talking.

The man in black continued to stare at him. "I'm afraid we're never going to know whether you could have held out while I beat you," he finally said. "Because there's an easier way out of this for both of us."

Van der Kirk stared back at him. "Okay," he said. "Just because I can take a beating doesn't mean I want one. Let's hear your idea."

"It's simple," the man in black said. "I want Norris Wright, and I want you to tell me about this deal, then take me to where it's going down. You do that, and I won't shoot you."

Van der Kirk shook his head. "No way," he said. "I stand to make a bundle tonight."

"Maybe so. But you won't be around to spend it."

The South African's eyes fell to the Applegate-Fairbairn combat dagger on the man's belt. "Okay, so you won't shoot me," he said. "The thought of getting my throat sliced doesn't do much for me, either."

"Let's cut to the chase," the big man said. "I won't kill you, period."

Van der Kirk laughed out loud. "You're a fucking idiot," he said. "You're going to turn me over to the cops? You know who'll have jurisdiction—Nigeria. And you can't be so stupid that you don't know I'll beat all this in court in an ass-backward country like this. Even if they don't rule this an illegal search and illegal entry—which it damn sure was—I can buy off a Nigerian judge for even less than you make a year. You've got to know that."

The man in black nodded. "I do," he said. "Which is why

I won't bother taking you to jail, either." His eyes narrowed. "Here's what you need to think about right now. I'm going to be leaving in just a few minutes. When I do, you're either going to be with me or sprawled across the bed there with your brains dripping off the wall." He indicated the wallpaper behind Van der Kirk with the big .44 Magnum Desert Eagle, which was in his fist.

The South African narrowed his eyes, studying those of the man in black. Earlier, he had sensed that the big fellow wouldn't resort to torture. He decided now, however, that the man wouldn't hesitate to kill him outright. That was a whole different ball game in the eyes of guys like him. No, he wouldn't torture him, but he'd shoot him, then go on with his business and never lose a wink of sleep over pulling the trigger.

"I want my cut of the cash tonight, too," Van der Kirk said. It was worth a try.

"You mean the money being transferred into the bank accounts I found on Wright's computer hard drive?" the big man asked. "I doubt the transfers can be stopped before they occur. So if you can get to the money before we do when this is over, more power to you. And if you can't, I'm sure you've got plenty of other funds squirreled away somewhere. You aren't going to starve."

Dolph Van der Kirk felt himself unconsciously nodding. The big man had a point. Even if he missed out on the billion he would be getting tonight, he already had almost five billion dollars scattered throughout the world's banks. What did he need with another billion?

Van der Kirk continued to weigh the situation in his mind. Okay, the fact was, he should never have gotten into this deal to begin with. He had enough money already and should have gotten out of the drug business long ago. He stared back at the man in black. "Let's make sure we've got all the ground rules straight here, shall we?" he said. "All I have to do is roll over on Wright, then I walk? I've got your word of honor that you won't kill me, arrest me or turn me over to anyone else who'll take me to jail?"

A look of impatience, like he was being forced to deal with an irritating child, crept over the big man's face. "How many ways do I have to tell you, Van der Kirk?" he asked. "I'm going to say it one more time. If you don't agree, I'm going to splatter your brains over the wall like I also promised. Here's where we stand. You take me to the deal, and Norris Wright, and I won't kill you, I won't arrest you, and I won't turn you over to the cops. Is that clear enough?"

Van der Kirk glanced at the young DEA agent next to the big man. The expression on the kid's face told the South African he didn't like the deal that was being offered, but he kept his mouth shut. The big guy obviously outranked him. A sudden thought suddenly hit him. "Oh, I see your game," he said. "*You* won't kill me. Your partner here will."

"No, he won't," he said. "And he won't arrest you, either. You have my word on it."

Out of most men, such a statement would have meant nothing to Van der Kirk. He could tell this guy wearing all black was honest. One of those fools who thought promises were meant to be kept, an idiot who actually believed a man's word was binding. With all the bases covered now, Van der Kirk's thoughts turned to Norris Wright. The man had been a good partner and, he supposed, a friend. But this was a dog-eat-dog world, and when it came down to ass-saving, he'd save his own first.

"Then consider it a done deal," the South African said. "Now, you suppose you could get me out of these cuffs and let me get some clothes on? Or do you want me to take you to Wright and Osama bin Laden's boys with my balls hanging out?"

The big man didn't flinch as Van der Kirk had thought he would when he heard the name Bin Laden. Without pause, he simply turned to the side and said, "Woodsen, go into the closet and get him some clothes. Then uncuff him and step back." His eyes turned back to Van der Kirk. "Do I have to tell you what'll happen it I don't like any of the moves you make while getting dressed?"

"I think I can guess," Van der Kirk answered. He smiled as the young agent left for the closet off the bathroom.

"First question," the man in black said. "What was in the drums you took off the plane after it crashed in the jungle? The ones you're about to sell to Bin Laden?"

Van der Kirk hesitated, then laughed out loud. "Nothing too special," he said. "I think you Yanks call it GB2. It's a derivation of sarin. The nerve gas. I understand it makes for a pretty horrible time before you finally kick off."

The big man in the blacksuit's eyes narrowed as he stared back at Van der Kirk. "Yes," he said quietly. "It does. You have any idea what Bin Laden's men were planning to do with it?"

"None of my concern."

The blue eyes set into the chiseled face narrowed even further. Van der Kirk felt the uneasy feeling creep deeper into his soul as he met the glare. The anger inside the big man seemed to be actually shooting out from within him, flowing across the empty space between them on his very gaze, and then penetrating his own body.

The temperature in the room suddenly seemed as if it had dropped thirty degrees, and the South African had to work hard to keep from shuddering. He didn't quite understand it. He had spent his entire life getting strong, both physically and financially. And he had done well at acquiring strength, especially since breaking out of the restraints imposed on him by the South African army. In any case he was strong, and had been for a long time. Strong enough that he thought he no longer needed to fear any man.

But that, Van der Kirk realized as the young DEA agent returned to the room carrying shoes, a shirt and pair of slacks, was exactly what he was feeling now.

Fear, in its rawest, purest form.

A NARROW SIDE ROAD led off of Ekos Bridge to a small rise on the coast of Iddo island. Bolan guided the Chevy along it, finally parking at a spot where he could look across Lagos Harbour to Apapa. His thoughts turned to Rupert Shelton for a moment. They had dropped the man off at a cheap hotel in Lagos where Shelton had once been a janitor. The Executioner didn't know what would become of the simpleminded man. He hoped he fell under better influences this time than he had the last.

Bolan reached across Woodsen and opened the glove compartment, removing a set of binoculars. "Where do I look?" he asked Van der Kirk.

The South African was wearing a short-sleeved white shirt that threatened to rip at the biceps, and a pair of loose-fitting cotton slacks. The Executioner had threaded the man's thick leather belt backward though his pants, buckling it at the rear at his spine. Then, he had looped the chain between the cuffs under the belt at the South African's navel before locking the steel restraints around his wrists. The belt would serve as a makeshift belly chain and keep Van der Kirk's hands at his waist. Simply locking the muscle man's thick wrists together without securing them further would have been like handing him a club.

Van der Kirk sat in the middle of the back seat. "You see the ferry terminal?" he asked.

Bolan adjusted the binoculars slightly. "Yeah," he said.

"Just behind it, there's a road."

The Executioner moved the field glasses once more. "I see it."

"Follow it along the shoreline, past the ferry terminal to the wharf."

Bolan moved the glasses along the road. Far in the distance, he saw several boats docked in what looked like a small private harbor. "Which one is it?" he asked.

"It's a hydrofoil," Van der Kirk growled. "It'll be flying colors of the Cameroons. You see it?"

The Executioner zeroed the lenses in on a large diesel craft. A gentle breeze was blowing in over the harbor—just enough to spread out the flag flying from a pole behind a life buoy aft of the boat. Under the lights mounted atop tall poles around the harbor, he could see the thick vertical green, red and yellow stripes of Nigeria's neighboring nation, the Cameroons. A yellow star set in the center of the middle red stripe.

Several men were busy at various tasks along the main deck. On the compass bridge, Bolan could see several more. "I've found it," he told Van der Kirk.

"You see the passenger cabin?" the South African asked.

Bolan shifted the binoculars again and nodded. "Along the side. The windows."

"Some of the seats have been removed," the South African said behind him. "Enough room for the drums to go on board."

The Executioner tried to look through the windows into the passenger area, but they were dark, and the harbor lights reflected off the glass. The binoculars' infrared feature would be impotent under such conditions as well, and he didn't bother trying it. "The men on board," he said. "Are they Bin Laden's?"

"Oh, yeah," Van der Kirk said. "But Wright is bringing some of ours, too." Bolan heard him chuckle in his low gravelly voice. "I'd say you'll have your work cut out for you."

"How many men?"

"Our men? Around twenty, I'd guess."

"How about Bin Laden's? On the boat?"

"No way to know," the South African said. "Couple dozen at least. Probably more. The main men—the big guys—flew in this morning. They'll be coming in with Wright. I'm supposed to meet them there."

"How about Nigerian customs?" Bolan asked. "They aren't paying any attention to all this?"

"They've been paid off," he said. "You won't find any Nigerian officials within ten miles of this place tonight."

"What time does it go down?" Bolan asked, dropping the binoculars into his lap. He turned to look into the back seat.

Dolph Van der Kirk bent to look at his thick handcuffed wrists. "I've got 8:50," he said. "The show should start in ten minutes."

Bolan turned to Woodsen. "You ready?" he asked the young DEA agent.

There was a certain amount of fear in the young agent's eyes. But there was a flicker of excitement, too. Like most young men who entered law enforcement, he had done so looking for adventure. Well, Bolan thought, he was about to get it.

The Executioner took one last look at the area across the water through the binoculars. Now, he could see a Land Rover moving along the road. Behind it, a two-ton transport truck followed. And behind the truck were four automobiles of various makes and models.

Bolan hit the binoculars' infrared switch and peered through the lenses. The cars were crowded with heads. It looked like there were two men in the front, and three in the back, of every vehicle. He could see long tubular-shaped objects pointing toward the roofs of the cars.

Rifle barrels.

The Executioner twisted the key and started the Chevy.

A few minutes later, they had crossed the bridge to Appa Island and were on the road leading to the wharf. Bolan glanced at the luminous numbers on his watch. They were roughly ten minutes behind the convey that Wright's Land Rover had led along the same path. A set of railroad tracks paralleled the road, and as soon as he spotted the wharf in the distance the Executioner pulled in behind several vacant boxcars.

"I'll have to go up there on my own," Van der Kirk said, before he could even kill the engine. "Wright knows both of you. There's no cover story we could dream up to get around that."

The Executioner turned to the man in the back seat. He didn't trust Van der Kirk as far as he could throw the hydrofoil boat that was about to take the drums of nerve agent to the most wanted terrorist in the world. But the South African was right. He and Woodsen would have to approach the site under the cover of darkness. And Van der Kirk needed to be there when they did. He was already late, and nobody in their right mind arrived late on a deal this important unless something was wrong. If the South African didn't show up soon, Wright and his men—as well as Bin Laden's terrorists— would double their watchfulness.

Reaching into a pocket of his blacksuit, Bolan pulled out a handcuff key and leaned over the back seat. A moment later, the cuffs were off the muscle man's wrists and he was turning his belt buckle back around to the front. His face had been doctored, and the bruises and missing tooth wouldn't show up in the darkness of the dock any more than they did in the back seat.

"You just keep one thing in mind," Bolan warned.

"What's that?"

"Your part of the bargain is to go down there and act as if nothing's wrong."

"To pull that off, I'll need the passports I was supposed to pick up at the office."

"No you won't," Bolan said. "Assure him you have them. Then stall him. And remember, Woodsen and I will be somewhere behind you. You won't know where, or how far. But we'll be watching." He reached out and grabbed the collar of Van der Kirk's shirt, tugging the man forward until their noses almost touched. "If I see one thing I even question out of you, our deal's off. I'll put my first round right through here." He dropped the South African's collar and tapped the man on the center of the forehead.

The snarl on Van der Kirk's face might have covered the man's fear had the Executioner not been close enough to see it in his eyes. "You're the one holding the cards," he said. "I'm not going to give you up. All I want at this point is out of here."

"If it turns out you've lied to me on any of this, Van der

Kirk," the Executioner said, "I'll hunt you down and kill you like a dog. There won't be any place on the planet to hide. You make sure you remember that. Is it clear?"

Van der Kirk nodded. "As crystal," he said. He was still scared—Bolan could practically smell it. He was trying to cover his fear with bravado. "Don't worry," he said. "After tonight, we'll never see each other again." He paused and forced the smile on his face even wider. "The type of places I plan to be, you couldn't afford."

NORRIS WRIGHT was only mildly irritated when he pulled the Land Rover up to the dock and saw no sign of Van der Kirk. He glanced into the side mirror and saw the truck carrying the GB2 nerve agent stop behind him. Behind the truck, the cars bringing his men pulled in and parked.

Wright glanced at his watch, then made himself relax. He was five minutes early. The South African would show up. And he would have the passports he had picked up at their covert office. In another hour, this whole deal would be over. He'd be a billion dollars richer than he already was, and he would be on his way to retirement in the Bahamas.

The DEA man got out of the Land Rover as the man calling himself Moe exited the passenger's side. Ali and Mohammed got out of the back seat. He had met the men up at the Excelsior only a few minutes earlier and driven straight to the boat. Wright glanced to the deck of the hydrofoil boat and saw that the dark-skinned men who made up the crew had lowered a gangplank from the boat to the dock. They were in the process of rolling several dollies across the deck. With the help of his men, it shouldn't take more than a few minutes to get the drums on board.

Looking at his watch again, Wright saw that it was now 9:02. It was time to get things rolling. They were all here but Van der Kirk, and he'd be along soon. He turned to Ali. "You have your test equipment with you?" he asked.

The man nodded and lifted his briefcase slightly.

"Why don't you go ahead and make your tests before we unload the truck?" Wright said. "No sense in doing it out in the open."

"Where is your partner?" Ali wanted to know.

Wright shrugged. "Don't know," he said. "But it's only a couple of minutes after nine. He'll be along soon."

Ali gave him a look that said he didn't like it. It also said that if it was his partner, and two billion dollars was at stake, he'd be royally pissed. Well, Wright wasn't going to let a couple of minutes ruin his mood. He was happy. It was almost over.

The DEA man led Osama bin Laden's three representatives around to the rear of the truck and pulled back the curtain that covered the rear. The drums hadn't been moved off the vehicle since it had been loaded in the jungle, and were still strapped to the floors and walls. Ali stepped up while the other two men waited at the tailgate. Wright waited with them. A few minutes passed, then Ali dropped back down to the ground and nodded to the other two. He looked at Wright. "It is good," he said. "Praise God. What you have done will further His work with the deaths of many infidels."

"Yeah, whatever," Wright said. "Don't you have a phone call to make?"

Ali pulled a cellular phone from the inside pocket of his jacket and tapped in a number. A moment later, he spoke in Arabic. When he finished, he returned the phone to his coat and looked again to Wright. "By the time we have loaded the boat," he said, "the transfers will have gone through. I suggest we begin."

"I suggest so, too," he said. "To save time. I also suggest you stay here on the docks with me until I make my own calls. Like we said earlier, we wouldn't want the banks making any mistakes now, would we?"

Ali shook his head in disgust. "Fine."

Wright motioned his men forward. They came, their rifles—a mixture of assault weapons stolen or purchased on the black market from the armed forces of several African nations—were slung over their shoulders. Several jumped up into the back of the truck and began rolling the drums toward the edge of the bed while others lowered the dollies from the walls.

Wright walked forward, looking down the road and wondering what could have caused Van der Kirk's tardiness. The DEA man was about to glance at his watch again when he saw the headlights round a curve and start toward him. He squinted into the oncoming light. Then, as the car drew closer, he saw it was a Chevrolet with a rental tag on the front bumper. He smiled when it pulled in next to him.

"Hope you didn't start the party without me," Van der Kirk said through the window.

Wright laughed. "I'm afraid we did," he said. "Come on. They're about to serve the cake. And half of it belongs to you."

BOLAN RAN ALONG the tracks, ducking in and out of the cover of the scattered boxcars as he neared the wharf. In addition to his standard Beretta and Desert Eagle, the Executioner had an M-16 A-1 slung over his shoulder in assault position. It had come from one of his equipment bags in the trunk of the Chevy. When he reached a spot directly across from where the boat flying the flag if the Cameroons was tied off to the dock, he stopped and glanced at his watch. He had estimated it would take him ninety seconds to cover the area to where Wright and Van der Kirk were. He had done it in eighty-seven. He peered out from behind the boxcar, back in the direction from which he had come.

Three seconds later, he saw the Chevy's lights come on. The car started forward.

Bolan waited. He had been forced to let Van der Kirk go on ahead alone because Wright knew both his and Woodsen's faces. And it would have looked incredibly strange had the South African arrived on foot. But simply giving the man the car keys would have been like buying him a first-class ticket to run. So the Executioner had gone on ahead on foot. Woodsen would follow the car the same way, carrying another M-16.

And Van der Kirk knew if he didn't keep the Chevy between them, or if he left the road and tried to dash off cross-country, the car would be saturated with so many .223-caliber rounds that his body might not even be able to be identified later.

The Chevy turned into the dock area and Bolan saw Wright walk out to meet it. Van der Kirk slowed to a halt, said something through the window, then left the vehicle where it was and got out. Together, he and Wright walked toward the boat where a mixture of Ivory Coast cartel men and Bin Laden's terrorists were already loading the drums aboard the boat.

Wright suddenly held up his hand and the loading stopped. Bolan watched him pull a cell phone from his pocket. He made several short calls, then waved to the men.

The loading resumed.

Woodsen came jogging up to meet him at the same time. The man was slightly winded, and his words came out short and choppy when he spoke. "Haven't had...a chance...to talk to you...alone," he said. "Since..." He nodded toward the wharf.

Bolan knew he meant since they'd captured Van der Kirk. "What is it you want to say?" he whispered in the darkness.

"That...letting him go...sucks." He took several deep breaths before saying, "You're not really...going to let him...go are you?"

The Executioner shrugged. "I gave my word that I wouldn't kill him or turn him over to the cops," he said. "And that you won't, either." He looked at the shadowy face in front of him and could see only the young man's silhouette. "Are you going to tell me you never cut deals with informants?"

"Not when they're like...him." Woodsen's breathing had almost returned to normal now.

Bolan knew the young agent didn't understand. "I'd relax

if I were you," he said. "Things have a way of working out for the best."

"It still sucks," Woodsen said. "It's wrong. If Brognola hadn't personally ordered me to work with you, I'd tell you to shove it."

"But he did order you," the Executioner said. "So you'll do what I tell you." He turned his attention back to the wharf. "They're about halfway finished loading. We've got to let them get the rest on board and out of the way before any shooting starts." He glanced across the harbor at the heavily populated Lagos Island, and felt the wind at his back. "One stray round into one of those drums is all it would take to kill thousands—maybe hundreds of thousands—of people. But in the meantime, I'm going to work my way around to the side. You stay here. When you hear my first shot, open up."

Woodsen might have been disgusted with him, but he was a good man. He nodded. "Okay," he whispered.

Bolan slipped away into the darkness. A boatyard, in which vessels in need of repair were left while being worked on, stood just across the pavement and separated him from the dock. Quickly, he made his way around the boxcars until he found a spot where he could cross the road without being seen from the water. Looking both ways, he sprinted across the pavement, then ducked behind a tall-masted schooner that was dry-docked at the outer edge of the yard. Weaving in and out of the other craft in various states of repair, he finally came to the bow of a large power trimaran. The trimaran stood on a trailer, a gaping hole in one of its hulls. By leaning around what appeared to be a loading door in the fore of the craft, Bolan could see both Wright and Van der Kirk standing next to the water with three men in dark business suits. The trio was obviously of Mideastern heritage. Bin Laden's men.

As he watched, the last of the drums containing the GB2 rolled across the plank linking the hydrofoil to the land. Bolan watched the men handling it roll it across the deck. It disappeared through a door somewhere inside the craft.

The Executioner's M-16 had been fitted with a night scope, and he threw the stock against his shoulder and flipped the selector switch to semiauto. He stared through the optical, the crosshairs falling on the back of Van der Kirk's head, at his nape. He hesitated. No, he thought. He had given his word. He shifted the rifle slightly and zeroed in on Wright's nose. Slowly, his finger began to draw back on the trigger.

Sometimes luck was with him, the Executioner had learned over the years. And sometimes, it simply wasn't.

Wright suddenly turned to look behind him just as Bolan finished the smooth trigger pull. The M-16 jumped lightly in his hands. The bullet sailed past the back of the DEA man's head, doing no damage.

Except to alert the entire wharf that trouble was afoot.

Excited voices screamed in both English and Arabic as Bolan heard more .223 rounds come from the boxcars across the road. Woodsen. The Executioner flipped the selector switch to burst mode and darted out from behind the trimaran, cutting between the bows of several more beached craft toward the docks. A hovercraft with Nigerian military markings was the last boat in the yard, and he dropped to his knees behind the blade lift fan when he reached it. Extending his rifle over the fan, he had a clear shot at the men in front of him, and he began mowing them down with the M-16.

A dark-skinned terrorist in the khakis of a seaman was the first to fall, his AK-47 flying from his hands to splash into the water behind him. An Ivory Coast cartel man took Bolan's second volley of fire, the soft-tipped lead inside the copper-jacketed slugs ripping through his chest. He fell to the wooden planks on his face, puddles of blood spreading out from under his body in both directions.

Both the Ivory Coast men and Islamic terrorists were

armed to the teeth, and they returned fire as soon as they'd pinpointed the Executioner's position. Bolan dropped below the side of the hovercraft and crawled along the sandy soil, coming up again behind the life raft. More men fell to his furious fire. He was careful not to direct his attack too close to the boat. The drums were on board, and he couldn't be sure where. The drilling, penetrating .223 rounds, even in soft-nose form, might go straight through the structure and then on to release the nerve agent. Such a mistake would spell death not just for the men on the dock. The breeze blowing in over the harbor would carry the gaseous death to the city beyond.

As he continued to fire, duck back, fire and duck back again, the Executioner searched the docks for Wright. He hadn't seen the man since his first shot missed by inches. The dirty DEA SAC, however, was nowhere to be seen. He seemed to have disappeared into thin air.

The trio of dark-skinned men in the business suits appeared in Bolan's sphere of vision, suddenly racing across the dock toward the plank that led to the hydrofoil boat. The Executioner cut loose with two bursts from his M-16. The first salvo took the lead man in the chest and lower belly just as his foot hit the plank. He fell forward in death, turning a complete somersault off the peer and landing in the water next to the boat. Bolan's second burst of fire entered the arm of the next man, passed through both bone and muscle and drilled through his heart. He dropped as if he'd run head-on into a brick wall.

The third man in the business suit leaped onto the loading plank and disappeared on the hydrofoil boat before Bolan could swing his rifle that way.

Turning back to the fight, Bolan triggered more rounds. More evil men—some cartel, others terrorists—fell. Magazine after magazine was loaded, the contents eaten by the M-16, then dropped and discarded. He was running low on ammo when the Executioner finally saw Woodsen come running across the road, his own M-16 chattering with every step. The young DEA agent took up position behind the same trimaran Bolan had used earlier.

The Executioner finished his second-to-last magazine on two more cartel men. He dropped the empty box, and the hot steel of the rifle barrel burned his fingers as they brushed it while inserting his final load. Bolan knew he was down to his last thirty rounds. After that it would be the Beretta, Desert Eagle and any weapons he could expropriate from the fallen men. He had no intention of backing off now. He wanted Wright, and he couldn't allow the GB2 to stay in the hands of Osama bin Laden's crazed murdering zealots. He would resort to the Applegate-Fairbairn if the dagger became his last option.

As he rammed the final magazine home and drew back the M-16's bolt to chamber the first round, Bolan scanned the area for Wright. He still saw no sign of the crooked DEA man. But he did see Dolph Van der Kirk sprinting toward the boat. The man ran past the crosshairs of Bolan's scope and the Executioner's finger started to tighten on the trigger. He relaxed his grip and turned the rifle toward another of the men in khaki as the South African leaped aboard the vessel.

The men already on the boat had taken cover when the shooting first broke out. Many had reappeared a moment later, bearing rifles and joining the battle. The fact that the drums containing the GB2 were somewhere to their flanks had limited the Executioner's return fire in that direction. From behind the Nigerian hovercraft he had chosen as cover, he had picked off several men who could be sighted in at angles of trajectory, which meant a missed shot would hit open water rather than the boat. For the most part, the men on the decks had been left unmolested. And as the battle had raged on, they'd figured out why.

A bearded terrorist in khaki pants and a brown T-shirt suddenly appeared and began loosening the lines that anchored the boat to the dock.

Bolan took aim. A trio of .223 rounds drilled through his

face, nearly beheading him. Another man took his place, and as the Executioner prepared to do the same to him, a volley of return fire drove him back down beneath the side of the hovercraft. Rounds continued to pepper the hull above the Executioner for a good fifteen seconds as he crawled back through the sand to the engine area. By the time he rose, the hydrofoil boat was slipping away from the dock.

The diesel engines were located near the center of the craft, right below the waterline. The Executioner took careful aim and started to squeeze the trigger. He stopped, glancing up, directly above the engine area into the cabin windows. A light had been turned on in the room, and the black fifty-five-gallon drums were visible through the window. He would have to shoot through the water if he attempted to disable the hydrofoil, and bullets could do strange and unpredictable things after they hit water. Sometimes they passed straight through it as if it were air. Other times they ricocheted off in directions impossible to foretell. And the GB2 nerve agent in the drums was simply too close for comfort.

Bolan raised his rifle as the fight along the docks began to die down. Many of the men lay dead or dying by the water. Others had fled for their lives. He searched again for Wright. Again, his search was futile.

As the Executioner turned back to watch the hydrofoil boat moving away, a familiar guttural laugh sounded across the water. He looked out to see a broad figure standing on the deck wearing a white shirt and slacks. He could see the massive chest heaving back and forth as the man continued to laugh at him, and then finally five words came drifting across the water.

"Thanks for the promise, asshole!" Van der Kirk shouted. A moment later, the South African's arm shot over his head, the middle finger extended.

An angry Dirk Woodsen sprinted up to the Executioner. "You blew it!" he accused. "They *both* got away! Van der Kirk and Wright! I saw Wright tear away in his Land Rover!"

Bolan turned to face the younger man. "Why didn't you stop him?"

Woodsen's face colored. "I missed the car," he said. "Then I got pinned down by return fire." His chin shot out in embarrassed defiance and he pointed out across the water. "But how about you? Bin Laden's men have enough GB2 to wipe out half of New York City. You and that stupid deal you cut with Van der Kirk."

Bolan lowered his M-16 as he turned back to the boat. "How many innings in a baseball game, kid?" he asked.

"What?" Woodsen shouted. "Are you crazy? What the hell—"

"You heard me," Bolan said. "How many innings in a baseball game?"

The young DEA agent looked at him. Then, with a disgusted snort, he said, "Nine."

"That's right," said the Executioner. "Just consider where we are now in the seventh inning stretch."

THE FIRST THING any law-enforcement officer who worked narcotics learned was that he or she always had a plan. The second thing they learned was that things never went according to that plan. Which prompted the third lesson: Always have a backup plan.

Mack Bolan knew that. And what was more important, he knew that Norris Wright knew it, too.

Bolan still had the envelope containing both Wright's and Van der Kirk's false passports. Which meant that Wright wasn't going anywhere as Alfred Blanchard. The Executioner, however, was betting that the man had indeed had a backup plan in case things went awry. Somewhere, he would have had a different passport that even Van der Kirk didn't know about. And unless the Executioner missed his guess, it was under yet a third name.

Bolan and a still-angry Woodsen had commandeered a

Ford LTD that had brought some of the cartel men to the docks. As he raced through the streets of Lagos toward the airport, Bolan pulled out his cell phone and dialed Stony Man Farm. As soon as he had Kurtzman on the line, he said, "Fast as you can, Bear. Check the passenger lists for any flights leaving Lagos in the next hour. Don't waste time on the name Wright. Check Blanchard just in case. My guess is he'll be under the name of one of the other men who were involved in the sandbar fight with Jim Bowie."

"Will do," Kurtzman said. "And I'll call you back as soon as I have anything. If I do."

"You will, Bear," Bolan said. "You've got to." He tapped the button, got another dial tone and called Jack Grimaldi. "I'm on my way to the airport right now, Jack," he said, "but I'm heading for the commercial terminal first."

"Sounds like you're in a rush," Grimaldi said. "Okay, I'll have the Lear warmed up by the time you get here."

"I've got another idea."

"What do you need?" the pilot asked.

Bolan told him. To his side, he saw Woodsen's mouth fall open at the order he'd just given. "You can do that?" the young DEA man asked. Bolan ignored him, listening to what Grimaldi had to say over the phone instead.

The pilot whistled into the instrument. "Okay, big guy," he said. "I'll get on the horn and try to dig one up. I don't know if that can be done as fast as you need it."

"Call Hal," Bolan said. "Tell him to pull in all his markers on this one if he has to. If we don't get this stopped, literally hundreds of thousand of innocent people somewhere are going to die horrible deaths with that nerve gas in their lungs."

"Hal's my next call, " Grimaldi said and hung up.

Bolan did the same, dropping the phone back into his pocket as he drove onto the airport grounds. He had thrown the shirt of one of the dead cartel gunners over the top of his blacksuit. His weapons were hidden. But a huge spot of blood had stained the front. He was going to draw attention—there was no way around it. So he would have to work fast.

The Executioner thought of the hydrofoil boat heading away to parts unknown with the GB2. He was going to have to work fast, anyway.

Bolan pulled up in front of the terminal and stopped in the zone reserved for taxis. There was no point in going inside and letting his blood-soaked shirt and the tight legs of his blacksuit draw unwanted attention until he heard back from Kurtzman. After that, he and Woodsen could make a direct beeline for his target. So he waited.

Next to him, Woodsen was silent for a moment. Then the young man cleared his throat. "Hey," he said. "Let me apologize. I didn't realize you—"

"Forget it," Bolan said. "Just follow my lead as soon as we get the call back. We won't have much time."

"Anything you say," the DEA man said grinning. "But for what it's worth, I'm sorry I doubted you. And I'm sorry—"

The Executioner held up a hand for silence as a uniformed Nigerian airport cop did a double take on the illegally parked Ford and started their way. When he reached Bolan's window, he leaned down to speak. Then he saw the blood on the front of Bolan's shirt, and he clawed for the pistol in the flap holster on his hip.

Bolan reached out, hooked his left arm around the man's neck and jerked his head inside the car. A right cross sent the cop to dreamland.

Woodsen was already out of the car and circling the bumper. He opened the back door and stuffed the unconscious man into the back seat. He had just returned to the front when the call from Kurtzman came.

"Alfred Blanchard was a no show on a flight to Nassau that left fifteen minutes ago," he said. "No Blanchard on any other flights tonight." He took a breath, then went on. "But there's a Colonel Robert Crain scheduled to depart in five minutes on a direct flight to Munich. And it was a Colonel Robert Crain who shot Bowie in the hip at the Vidalia sandbar fight."

"Give me the airline and flight number, Bear," Bolan said. He already had one hand on the door.

"I can do better than that, big guy," Kurtzman came back. "I can give you're the gate number. Twenty-three. Concourse D."

Bolan was out of the car and running a half second later. Woodsen was a step behind.

As he sprinted into the terminal with Woodsen on his heels, the Executioner saw a sign announcing Concourse B to his left. Farther down, an overhead arrow pointed toward the letter A. Turning the opposite way, Bolan darted through the busy airport, dodging surprised and frightened people. A few had time to note the blood on his shirt and reacted accordingly—either screaming or jumping far out of his way. Most noticed only a blur and wrote him off as just another rude traveler in a hurry to catch his plane.

But as he passed the entryway to Concourse C, another uniformed airport cop came strolling toward him. When he saw Bolan sprinting his way, his hand went to the wooden nightstick on the ring attached to his Sam Browne belt.

He never got it out.

Bolan sent a forearm smashing into the man's face as he passed, not even breaking stride. Behind him, he heard Woodsen sputter out, "Oh shit," as he ran. He raced on, toward the big overhead letter D he could see ahead, narrowly missing a young mother carrying an infant and sending a fat man in an expensive suit sprawling into a newsstand.

Just to the side of the sign over Concourse D, Bolan saw several rows of seats—a small waiting area just before the passengers passed through the metal detector at the security checkpoint. His eyes scanned the crowded area, guessing that it was where he would find the man he sought. Norris Wright—a.k.a. Colonel Robert Crain—wouldn't be able to "badge" a gun onto the plane under his new false ID. But considering everything that had happened, Bolan guessed he would want to stay armed as long as possible.

The overhead speaker called out, "Flight 4721 for Munich, now boarding at gate 23," as the Executioner drew nearer the waiting area. He slowed to a walk as several people stood, groping in pockets, purses and carryons for their boarding passes. Bolan's eyes flickered across them as they made their way toward the metal detector. He saw no one resembling Norris Wright.

The Executioner ground to a halt, staring at the passengers as they emptied their pockets of metallic objects and dropped their carryons onto the conveyor belt that would take them through the X-ray machine. He turned back from the security area to the waiting seats, again looking face to face. He still didn't see Wright.

"Maybe your man was wrong," Woodsen said, coming to a halt at Bolan's side. "Maybe he's flying under another name altogether. Maybe he's not even here."

The Executioner held up his hand for silence. Wright was here. He could feel him. The same way people could somehow sense evil the moment they walked into the wrong bar or accidentally found themselves in a bad neighborhood in the middle of the night.

Then, just beyond the seats, the Executioner saw a flicker of movement. He looked up to see an elderly man in a wheelchair. The man wore an off-white suit, and had hair and a beard that almost matched. He held a paper sack in his lap, and as Bolan's eyes met his the sack began to rise.

Bolan reached under the bloody shirt, and in one smooth motion the Desert Eagle leaped into his hand. He found the safety and thumbed it off at the same time his finger pulled back on the trigger. The Eagle screamed in his hand, the explosion echoing through the terminal and bringing screams and shrieks from people up and down the concourse.

A hole the size of a silver dollar appeared in the middle of the old man's forehead as the back of his head blew out. His chin fell forward against his chest and his hand, which had been hidden inside the sack, returned to his lap.

The Executioner walked forward and jerked the sack away to expose the 9 mm Glock 19 pistol. Then he jerked the false white hairpiece and beard away to expose the face of Norris Wright.

Epilogue

The Executioner didn't believe in going back on his word. But neither did he believe in leaving a job half done, or letting evil win out over good. And he certainly didn't plan to let the drums of nerve gas, currently in the hands of the world's most infamous terrorist, stay there. At least not as long as there was any breath left in his body.

Jack Grimaldi took off the runway and the plane entered the air, soaring quickly skyward. He turned in the cockpit to face the Executioner, speaking into the microphone in front of his face. "Not quite as smooth a ride as the Lear, huh, Striker?"

Bolan heard the man's words over the earphones wrapped around his head. "No, Jack," he said. "It isn't. And it's going to be harder to sleep on the way home."

"Well, you better give it a shot," the pilot said. "Because we aren't going home."

Bolan frowned.

Grimaldi grinned. "When I called Hal to have him find this baby," he said, patting the plane's seat beneath him, "he said something about Peru."

"What?" Bolan asked.

Grimaldi shrugged. "Danged if I know, big guy," he said. "And we were both too busy trying to run this thing down to get into the details." He patted the seat again. "You don't just pick them up at the local convenience store, you know."

Bolan nodded. He relaxed, letting the vibrations of the plane work on him like a massage chair. He closed his eyes, then opened them again. Not yet, he told himself. He would sleep on the way to Peru. There was one more thing that needed doing first. Turning back to Grimaldi, he said, "What were the last coordinates you got?"

The pilot glanced at the chart hanging from a clipboard on the plane's control panel. "I have 6.38 degrees west, and almost to the equator," he said. "They've passed Principe and are heading toward Sao Tome."

The Executioner nodded again. "How long until we get there?"

"Well, these old birds are still fairly fast. In fact, if I was you, I'd start looking down about now." He leaned forward on the control and the plane began to drop through the air over the blue waves of the Gulf of Guinea. A few minutes later, a tiny spot appeared bobbing across the sea below.

"That it?" he asked Grimaldi.

"Probably," the pilot said. "I'll buzz them for a closer look." He glanced across the plane to Bolan. "You might want to double-check, too. In case it isn't, I'm sure whoever it is below would appreciate it."

"I expect so," he said. Reaching inside his jacket, he pulled out his cellular phone. He had found the number to a similar phone under the initial DVdK in the address book on Norris Wright's body, and he was hoping the South African had the phone with him. He tapped in the number now, and waited.

He wasn't to be disappointed.

"Hello?" the gravelly voice said, sounding somewhat surprised.

"How are things on the water, Dolph?" Bolan asked.

There was a long pause, then Van der Kirk growled. "Not bad. Be a lot happier when I get where I'm going, though."

"I doubt it," the Executioner said. "I understand it's awfully hot."

"Don't play that process-of-elimination game with me," the South African said. "You'll never see me again. Besides, you made me a promise. And you're just the kind of good goody asshole who goes for that man of honor shit."

"I'm afraid you've got me pegged," the Executioner said.

"So why did you call?" Van der Kirk demanded. "And where the hell are you that you could reach me?"

"I called just to tell you that I intend to keep my promise," Bolan said. "And if you'll look up in the sky, you'll see where I am. We're just about to pass over you."

Bolan handed the phone to Jack Grimaldi. "Hey, Dolph?" the pilot said.

"Who's this?"

"Just a friend of Kenneth Clarke's. And I only wanted to say one thing to you."

"Huh?"

Grimaldi reached forward to the control panel and flipped a switch. "This is my doing," he said into the phone.

Bolan heard the rumble at the rear of the big aircraft as the bowels of the B-52H bomber opened to release its cargo. By the time the explosion took place on the sea below, they were a half mile past it in the air. But the Executioner heard it. And when he looked back over his shoulder, he could see the flames leaping into the air from what had once been the hydrofoil boat.

Grimaldi dipped a wing to the west. "Peru's that way, isn't it?" he asked jokingly.

Bolan didn't answer. He settled back into the seat and closed his eyes.

Don't miss the action and adventure of Mack Bolan on these titles!

DON PENDLETON's
MACK BOLAN®

#61472-1	CONFLAGRATION	$5.99 U.S.☐	$6.99 CAN.☐
#61471-3	KILLSPORT	$5.99 U.S.☐	$6.99 CAN.☐
#61470-5	EXECUTIVE ACTION	$5.99 U.S.☐	$6.99 CAN.☐
#61469-1	VENGEANCE	$5.99 U.S.☐	$6.99 CAN.☐

(limited quantities available on certain titles)

TOTAL AMOUNT	$
POSTAGE & HANDLING	$
($1.00 for one book, 50¢ for each additional)	
APPLICABLE TAXES*	$ _____
TOTAL PAYABLE	$ _____

(check or money order—please do not send cash)

To order, complete this form and send it, along with a check or money order for the total above, payable to Gold Eagle Books, to: **In the U.S.:** 3010 Walden Avenue, P.O. Box 9077, Buffalo, NY 14269-9077; **In Canada:** P.O. Box 636, Fort Erie, Ontario, L2A 5X3.

Name: _____

Address: _____ City: _____

State/Prov.: _____ Zip/Postal Code: _____

*New York residents remit applicable sales taxes.
Canadian residents remit applicable GST and provincial taxes.

GSBBACK2

James Axler
OUTLANDERS®

PRODIGAL CHALICE

The warriors, who dare to expose the deadly truth of mankind's destiny, discover a new gateway in Central America—one that could lead them deeper into the conspiracy that has doomed Earth. Here they encounter a most unusual baron struggling to control the vast oil resources of the region. Uncertain if this charismatic leader is friend or foe, Kane is lured into a search for an ancient relic of mythic proportions that may promise a better future…or plunge humanity back into the dark ages.

In the Outlands,
the shocking truth is humanity's last hope.

GOUT20

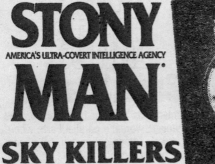